David Brown served in the British army for almost forty years and between 1969 and 1976 spent a good deal of time in Northern Ireland serving with a top infantry regiment as both a platoon sergeant and later as a platoon commander. He eventually left the infantry for the elite Army Physical Training Corp and received a commission, eventually reaching the rank of Major.

For Carole.
In memory of Lt Col HBJ Phillips, MBE Soldier, mentor
and true gentleman.

David Brown

HARD RAIN

AUSTIN MACAULEY PUBLISHERS™

LONDON • CAMBRIDGE • NEW YORK • SHARJAH

A CIP catalogue record for this title is available from the British Library.

ISBN 9781528900560 (Paperback)
ISBN 9781528902281 (ePub e-book)

www.austinmacauley.com

First Published 2022
Austin Macauley Publishers Ltd®
1 Canada Square
Canary Wharf
London
E14 5AA

My thanks to Jane White for all her help and support and Lynda Sweet for her help with the final proof reading.

Prologue

Bomber's story is based on the conflict in Northern Ireland, which, for the British Army, started in 1969 when the Royal Ulster Constabulary lost control of the civil unrest and the violence between the Protestant and Catholic communities became a terrorist war.

The government of the time called in the army to restore control and for a few precious weeks, both communities calmed down and welcomed the army as protectors. This was the politicians' chance to establish an answer to the troubles and the genuine grievances of the Catholics and the fears of the Protestant community. This they failed to do but to be fair they were not going to dispel over two hundred years of bias and bigotry in such a short time.

The Irish border between the north and south is over three hundred miles long which does not include the coastline where boats could and still do move with ease. The option of placing a Cordon Sanitaire was so distasteful to everyone that in the end it was just left alone, allowing easy movement from both sides of the border for any terrorist group or just plain old smugglers. Interestingly, the Rhodesians did place a cordon along their somewhat longer border during the period of UDI. They were not afraid of world opinion.

Bomber's story is based on the events in Northern Ireland between the years 1969 to 1972. I continued with tours of duty after this until the middle of 1976. Not a continuous seven years, but as with many other soldiers, short and long tours as the situation demanded. The events related in this book are fictionalised events, based on my experiences as a soldier, stories heard and my imagination, not necessarily government or army facts.

During this period, I grew to admire the people of Northern Ireland, both Catholic and Protestant, for their courage and resilience in the face of the most appalling destruction and death. In the middle was the British soldier soaking it all up and who can blame him if at times when he suffered being stoned, petrol bombed and nail bombed, along with road side bombings and shootings, he became a little angry and used what force he had at his disposal to control the situation. I never saw any of the politicians on the streets, politicians who have since given immunity to prosecution to known murderers, but who are now happy to allow witch hunts of the security forces. If they had been required to stand up to a rioting crowd, a bomber or a gunman, perhaps they would think differently and hold the security forces in higher regard. If what I have written stirs the resolve not to let this happen again, then I will be a happy man.

For peace.
David Brown

Chapter 1
Hard Rain

The rain had finally found its way through the flak vest and the fabric of his combat jacket. As the dampness chilled his body, he resisted the temptation to move and generate some body heat. Instead, he cradled his rifle closer to his chest, drawing comfort from its weight. This was his insurance against the hate-filled street he found himself standing on.

He had been in the shadows for over two hours waiting. Waiting was part of the game, staying still in the shadows, hoping to get lucky. The army had left alone the illegal drinking den on the Ardoyne near Flax Street Mill. They could have gone in mob handed and demolished it. However, it was considered better to have the so-called targets drinking in the place that the Int (intelligence) boys knew rather than having to waste time tracking them down to some other godforsaken den.

Suddenly, a shaft of light flooded the pavement, like a beacon in the otherwise dark street. Voices, loud voices, fuelled by cheap booze could be heard, then a figure stepped out of the doorway into the light before slamming the door shut.

The figure stood still for a few minutes, allowing eyes to adjust to the darkness, unaware that seven pairs of eyes were watching him from the shadows—eyes that could unleash death should the figure make any hostile movement. Then the figure moved, purposely striding to the end of the road. He was a big man in his thirties but running to fat. His right arm was held loosely by his side, something heavy held in his hand.

At the end of the street, he stopped. On the opposite side of the road, a single street lamp shone, bathing a small radius of pavement in light. How this had remained intact after the last riot was a mystery. Its pale light shimmered in the rain, marking the dividing line between the two communities. The man stood facing the houses on the opposite side of the road and he too waited and watched, seemingly oblivious to the heavy rain.

Bomber eased the safety catch off his rifle. He knew he could bring it into his shoulder, fire, killing the man opposite in less than a blink of an eye but that was not his job tonight. He shivered, not because of what he knew was about to unfold but because the rain was coming down even harder than before. It was almost as if it was trying to wash them and the hate from the street.

The man fidgeted as if he was not sure about standing in the rain any longer. Then a door on the opposite side of the street opened and the man raised his arm pointing towards the door. In his hand was a heavy .44 semi-automatic pistol.

Bomber shouted the routine chant, "Army, drop the weapon or I fire."

The man spun round in the direction of Bomber's voice and fired blindly. Bomber heard the rounds hit the wall to the left of him but didn't move. The lighter *"crack, crack"* of the pistol was echoed by the heavy deadly crack of a 7.62 high velocity round. The sniper on top of Flax Street Mill hit the man squarely in the chest. He crumpled to the ground, almost in slow motion, ending facedown in the gutter, his pistol falling from his hand.

Bomber shouted, "Go," and he and five others charged from the shadows. Four of them grabbed a limb each and dragged the body towards the Land Rover that had raced out from the mill.

Bomber scooped up the pistol and ran after the Land Rover that was already half way back to the mill. The ops officer had emphasised speed for the recovery of the body and the weapon. 'Rent a Crowd' could be there in minutes, making recovery of the body and weapon impossible.

Bomber looked over his shoulder, people were already spilling out of the drinking den and shouting. Several doors had opened and heads peered out. Bomber felt safe enough knowing the sniper was still in position, covering their withdrawal.

Back inside the mill, the ops officer was jubilant that finally they had got 'Paddy the Pistol', a nickname given to him by the lads.

Paddy would turn up at riots, take a couple of shots at the police or security forces, then disappear back behind the rioters. His favourite pastime though was waiting on the Catholic side of the Ardoyne and shooting at Protestants leaving their houses at night.

This reign of Paddy the Pistol had been going on for months and the company commander had been ordered to put a stop to it when the company took over the mill three weeks ago.

Now it was done.

Chapter 2
Containment

Bomber could hear the sound of a riot gearing up in the street. The shooting of 'Paddy the Pistol' was bound to spark a well-orchestrated response. He could hear the shouting, the crump of nail bombs exploding and from behind the high walls of the mill, Bomber could see the flicker of flames from petrol bombs.

He was shivering now, he had not had a chance to change into dry clothes but had just enough time to down a mug of hot tea.

TC, the platoon commander called him, "Sgt Brown, get the platoon together; we are going out to help the ready platoon."

"The men are ready, sir, we have four pigs (old armoured personnel carriers) and full riot gear loaded."

"Good, we have the four-street junction to the left of the ready platoon. I will take the first, Cpl Jones the second, Mills the third, you and Cpl Bush will be the last to link up with the unit next to you."

Bomber climbed into the last pig armoured personnel carrier and shivered. The driver, a chain smoker, called Blackman, looked at Bomber and said, "You look a little bit wet, Sarge."

"So will you in a little while because when we get in position, I want you out with that SMG of yours, covering our backs."

Blackman shrugged, took a deep drag on his cigarette, then let the clutch out and the pig lurched forward out through the open gates and onto the rain swept street.

It only took a few minutes to get in position. Using the pig to block the end of the street, they kept the rioters at bay with a few well-aimed rubber bullets. The rubber bullets had only just been issued and were actually rubber. Fired from a baton gun, they were designed to help subdue rioters without killing them or inflicting permanent damage. Trouble was, some good padding or a makeshift shield and they didn't have any real effect.

After an hour of nothing more than a few well-aimed rocks, things suddenly got lively. Young teenagers gathered in large numbers. Then using the sides of the streets, they advanced on Bomber and his boys. Volleys of rocks, then petrol bombs soared towards them. Several landed against the side of the pig; flames shot under the chassis and two of the lads staggered backwards, their legs on fire. Jinks was manning the fire extinguisher and smothered the flames on their legs.

"Fuck it, fuck it," yelled Peters as he sat down on the rain-soaked road holding his right thigh.

The flames had burned through the top part of his combat trousers and in the light of his torch, Bomber could see the flesh was burnt and starting to blister.

Using the radio, Bomber called for Starlight, the call sign for the medics who arrived in less time than it took them to get Peters into the back of the pig.

"Here they come again, Sarge," shouted Cpl Bush, who had his rifle in his shoulder, aiming down the street.

The orders had been that no live rounds were to be fired unless lives were in danger. Rocks and petrol bombs weren't considered a danger to life but nail bombs were a different matter.

The first one exploded short of the pig but the second skidded under the pig. When it exploded, the armoured chassis deflected the blast out at ankle height. A nail bomb was just a small amount of plastic explosives with six-inch nails embedded around the outside. A short fuse was attached and when fired up could be thrown with about a four to five-second delay before it exploded.

Nails flew out in all directions, many finding a home in the heavy-duty tyres of the pig. Cries of pain came from Smith and Palmer as nails ripped into their legs, tearing through muscle and bone.

The medics, in their armoured ambulance, treating Peters, jumped out and rushed to the downed pair. Bomber rallied the rest, giving orders that the next nail bombers should be shot.

Hardly had the words left his mouth when Cpl Bush fired two shots. Peering over the pig's snout, Bomber could see two men, probably no more than eighteen years old, lying still on the wet tarmac. Two nail bombs could be seen fizzing close by. Now several rioters had run out to drag the shot men away, not realising that the nail bombs were live. Bomber found himself counting four, five and before six, the bombs exploded, scything down the rescuers. The screams and howls of pain rent the air.

"That's a very nice own goal," came from Blackman.

The MO (Medical Officer) interrupted Bomber, sending a contact report on the radio.

"We have to go to them as well, can you protect us?"

Bomber stifled the urge to say, "Let the bastards die!"

Instead, he looked at Cpl Bush and his four unwounded men and said, "Blackman, stay and guard the pig. Cpl Bush and everyone else, on my "Go", we run out, grab all of them and drag them back, no staying in the street."

"Okay, Sarge, we're ready."

Bomber nodded and shouted, "Go."

They raced out. To Bomber's surprise, the MO and one of the medics followed on his heels. Lying on the tarmac were the two shot bodies and two more wounded by the nail bombs. Two others were dragging themselves away and round a corner.

"Okay, get them back, fast, Cpl Bush, and I will cover."

Moving a few paces forward, Bomber and Bush knelt in the shadows, covering the street. Grunts and groans could be heard as the four lads and the MO and his medic half-dragged and carried the dead and wounded back to the pig.

"We've got trouble, Sarge." Bush had lifted his rifle back into his shoulder, squinting along the barrel.

Bomber did not need telling as he could hear the rabble coming, except this time there seemed to be hundreds of the buggers.

Looking over his shoulder, he could see that the rest only had a couple of yards to go.

"Okay, let's move slowly now, no running." Bush grunted a reply and they started to withdraw. Halfway back, the first rocks crashed down around them; one smashed into Bomber's right shin. It would have broken his leg if he had not been wearing the padded aluminium shin guards under his combat trousers. These had been made for them by the Belfast Bus Company workshop. Still it hurt and he cursed, wishing he was allowed to shoot the bastard who had thrown it. Five yards to go and a volley of petrol bombs landed too close for comfort. Then they were back behind the relative safety of the pig, where Bomber found re-enforcements had arrived. TC, the platoon commander, was there with four others to bolster the now depleted section. Cpl Bush and Chalky White now sent several volleys of rubber bullets at the advancing rioters, causing them to halt on the edge of the rubber bullets' effective range.

Suddenly from behind Bomber, a voice demanded, "Who authorised live rounds to be used?" The voice belonged to the 2i/c (Company Second in Command).

The 2i/c was a very tall, thin captain, who, because of his height, always stooped when he spoke to anyone. It had been clear to Bomber on his arrival in the unit that the 2i/c did not like outsiders and especially did not like Bomber.

After having to deal with rent a crowd, petrol and nail bombers, Bomber did not feel like playing silly buggers. Stretching himself up, Bomber looked him straight in the chest saying, "The brigade commander, sir."

"What?" the 2i/c said in a startled voice, looking round the street. "Has he been here then?"

TC butted in, "I think the Sergeant means it's authorised under the yellow card, which is as per the brigade commander's orders."

"I do not think that overrides my orders here on the ground."

"Well, you could try explaining that to Peters, Smith and Palmer at the hospital, but I think Sgt Brown acted correctly and within the law." TC had a trace of irritation in his voice and as he had to raise his voice to be heard over the mob, which was kicking off again; the 2i/c took a step back as if to reconsider what he was about to say.

"All right, but let's not get carried away. We just want to keep them contained in their own area." With that, he strode off in the direction of the company HQ (Headquarters) vehicle.

Bomber watched as the ambulance started to drive away and he realised he had not had a chance to check on the injured lads.

Cpl Bush gave a shout of, "They are on the move again, Sarge". TC and Bomber moved to see over the snout of the pig. Sure enough, a large group was advancing down the street. This time, they were more organised with a group on each side of the road with two men in front, holding what looked like wooden doors as shields against the rubber bullets. As they advanced, teenagers would dodge out and hurl rocks and half bricks towards the pig, where they clanged against the side armour.

Then the first petrol bombs flew through the air, two landing just short, but one hit the top of the pig, sending flames in all directions.

Bomber felt his helmet getting hot but before he could remove it, Jinks had sprayed him with the fire extinguisher. From the corner of his eye, he could see TC had flames coming from the back of his flak jacket and was struggling to get it off. Before he could help, Jinks had quenched the blaze with his fire extinguisher. Blackburn was already up on top of the pig with another extinguisher, completely oblivious to the rocks aimed at him.

"Get down here, you prat, before someone shoots you," yelled Bomber at Blackburn.

Having put out the flames, he jumped onto the snout and then down behind the pig. "You nutter, you could have let it burn out, it would have just blistered the paint on the armour," Bomber said, patting Blackburn on the back, admiring his foolhardy bravery.

"No one burns Gerty and gets away with it on my fucking watch, Sarge." With that, he turned to White and snatched the baton gun from him along with the satchel of rubber bullets. Moving to the right-hand side, he fired at the nearest makeshift shield only to see the round bounce harmlessly into the air.

"Getting a bit hot here," said TC rather too calmly for Bomber's liking. "Another few yards and they could rush us and get through." TC had shrugged off his flak jacket and was peering over the snout of the pig.

"Blackburn, Jacobs, aim under the doors at the legs. Skid the rounds along the ground." Bomber knew this was the only way the rubber bullets would have any effect.

They both blasted away three rounds in quick succession. Howls of pain could be heard and both doors were dropped. Two more rounds and the mob fled, dragging the limping shield holders with them.

"Got the bastards," yelled Blackburn, reloading the baton gun just in case they returned.

TC pulled Bomber to one side. "I think it's going to be a long night. They have a habit of organising rent a crowd into two groups, one resting and one performing."

"With three of the lads in hospital, we are a bit pushed here so any chance of leaving two of your HQ section with me, sir?" asked Bomber. "That way I can rest three while three are on watch."

"Okay, I'll leave Parker and your namesake. I know the 2i/c said to be careful using live rounds but I don't want any more of our boys in hospital or worse. So do what you have to do."

"Will do sir," Bomber replied, only half convinced he had been given the okay to use live rounds.

Bomber's namesake, Pte Brown, was not called Bomber as per anyone else called Brown but Armalite. This was because his initials were AR, which stood for Armalite Rifle. A tall, well-built lad, who was a good soldier but would not accept promotion even though he was worth it. Some people just did not want the responsibility of giving orders. Orders that might get a mate killed.

Pte Parker, known as Parky, was a no-nonsense Mancunian. Short, stocky and hard as nails, he didn't take crap from anyone. Bomber had witnessed him throw down his shield and baton in a riot when the rioters were at arm's length. Then he waded in with his fists, putting three rioters flat on their backs before the lads dragged him back in line.

Bomber moved next to Cpl Bush and looked over the snout of the pig at the empty street. The rain had now turned to sleet and he felt drained. Cpl Bush, known as Thorny to the lads, spoke quietly to Bomber, "With a bit of luck, this shit will keep them in doors." When Bomber didn't answer, Bush looked at him and said, "You okay, Sarge, you don't look so good?"

Bomber felt chilled to the bone. He was soaked to the skin and kept shivering and he knew he had the early symptoms of hypothermia.

"Nothing that a hot cup of tea and some dry clothes wouldn't put right and a let up on this fucking weather."

"Well, we can do something about the cuppa and here it comes."

Several doors on the opposite side of the main road had opened. The Protestant side of the green line housed the normal working-class people and old and young ladies now appeared with mugs of tea. One girl of about sixteen, wearing a long coat with a hood up, approached Bomber, pushing a mug of tea at him, saying, "There's more where that came from and Ma said bacon butties will be out in a few minutes."

The girl was tall, thin and spoke with the hard Belfast accent but used her voice in a way that caressed the tongue, giving an almost musical quality.

Bomber gratefully took the offered mug of tea. It was piping hot, sweet and as it went down, Bomber could actually feel the heat flooding through his body.

As he finished his tea, Millar (Dusty), the platoon radio operator, turned up. Under one arm was a plastic bag which he offered to Bomber. "Here, Sarge, the boss sent me to the mill to raid your bunk for some dry clothes for you. Full outfit in there except socks, couldn't find them."

"Thanks, Dusty, appreciate you doing that. Please thank the boss for me."

"Will do. Guess we have a little break from the other lot. As soon as the tea stops coming and they close the doors, we know that the other mob are on the way back. Not with tea and butties though."

Bomber nodded in agreement as he stepped into the back of the pig to get changed. Thinking it wasn't that long ago that both sides brought them tea and butties.

As he changed, he could hear Dusty though one of the air vents talking to Parky. "The Sarge's bunk is immaculate, all his kit is on the shelves folded and pressed regimental style. No photos though, nothing personal."

"That sounds like him, once a boy soldier always a boy soldier. Can't help himself."

With that, Dusty moved off back to platoon HQ.

As Bomber stepped out of the pig, for the first time that night, he felt warm. The dry clothes and the tea had done the trick.

"Would ya like a buttie and some more tea?"

It was the girl again with a tray piled with bacon sandwiches and mugs of tea. Bomber noticed the rain had stopped. The girl had the hood of her coat down, revealing long brown hair and a strong face with high cheekbones. She smiled at Bomber and said her name was Kirsty. Then she spoiled the magic of the moment by saying, "When those fucking wee bastards come back, you promise me you'll shoot the shits."

Bomber nodded, avoiding replying by stuffing the bacon sandwich in his mouth. The girl moved away and Bomber watched her as she handed out sandwiches and tea.

Fuck me, thought Bomber. *Not many months ago, the two communities were fine. Men from both sides were walking to work together, having a drink after work, talking about football and the cost of a pint. Now they were trying to kill or drive each other out.*

As much as he tried, he could not understand the deep-seated hatred fed by a fear of religious dominance between Catholics and Protestants, which dated back to even before the Battle of the Boyne in 1690, when William of Orange, Protestant, defeated James the second, Catholic. As much as Bomber tried, he could not understand the religious division that set friend against friend. *How the hell can it happen in a so-called modern society?* Bomber's thoughts were interrupted by Thorny calling him.

Looking over the snout of the pig, Thorny pointed out that a group of lads was crossing over the street junction, roughly a hundred yards away, heading towards the street manned by Cpl Jones. Bomber radioed the information to TC who acknowledged.

The explosion shook the ground they stood on. The sound of breaking glass could be heard as the shock wave receded.

"Fucking Nora, where the hell was that?" Blackman shouted.

"Came from the direction of the city centre," Thorny replied.

"Can't have been that far away; we felt it here," Blackman countered.

"Must have been massive," L/Cpl Jacobs replied in a subdued voice.

"The shock wave gets channelled by the buildings along the roads, so it must be in a straight line to us," Bomber suggested.

Their speculation was interrupted by cheering from the Ardoyne. The mob had obviously got the message it was one of their bombers who had planted and exploded the bomb.

Then the rain started again!

Chapter 3
Haunted

Bomber raised the Browning semi-automatic pistol and fired twice, the man went down and Bomber went to him. As Bomber looked down, he could see the man's eyes staring back at him, wide and unblinking as he mouthed silent words. Bomber kept shooting but the man wouldn't die. He just stared at Bomber, mouthing silent words.

Bomber woke with a start and stared in the dim light at the wooden walled cubicle that was his bunk in the Flax Street Mill. He was drenched in sweat and shaking. His heart was thumping and he could clearly hear it. He realised he had been having the old dream again. One that took him back five years and, had, on occasions, haunted him. Strangely, it was a dream he had shared with one of his old Irish pals from his previous regiment. They had talked about it once after having a few beers. The next day, they both avoided the subject as if it had never been mentioned.

During his time in Germany, operating in an armoured infantry unit, he had subdued it by hard exercise and alcohol. His body exhausted and his mind numbed by the alcohol had worked for a while but became less effective as time went on.

Bomber decided to deal with it in the same way as everything that was out of his control by saying, "Fuck it! You can try as much as you like, but you won't break me!" But even this approach had its limitations.

When he had been on exercise in Libya, the dream had not bothered him. The desert suited him. The lack of people, having to rely on his skills and ingenuity to get himself and his section across the empty land, filled his entire being.

Then in Catterick Garrison, time was filled by course after course. Close quarter combat, counter surveillance and the make or break course, the senior NCOs (non-commissioned officers) tactics course at Brecon in South Wales during one particularly cold winter. Then, large helicopter deployment exercises in the wild but beautiful Northumbrian countryside had also been new and exciting.

Catterick also allowed him to reaffirm his love of rock climbing and mountaineering in the Yorkshire Dales and the Lake District. He attended several courses at the army school for mountaineering. Situated in North Wales, this centre had started to mould him into a competent mountaineer.

He had been promoted to Sgt early on his twenty-first birthday. Some thought too early, as his only world was the army. To remedy this, he was sent to an army youth team in Norwich for a year, working with youth clubs and schools.

At the time, Bomber thought it the biggest waste of time and resources going. On reflection, he found that it had rubbed some of the rough edges off him and removed that regimented thinking that everything was black or white.

At the end of that year, he received his orders to return to the life of an infantryman. However, it was not to his original regiment that had just been posted to Londonderry for a two-year tour but to another of the division's units that had also started a three-year tour in Northern Ireland in the barracks at

Ballykinler, south of Belfast, at the foot of the Mourne Mountains.

His new regiment was short of SNCOs (Senior Non-Commissioned Officers) and junior officers. As with most regiments, they were a close-knit unit and outsiders found it difficult to break down the barriers to be embraced by the regiment.

Bomber had not tried to do or say anything special. Since Aden, he had never felt the need for close friends. Losing a comrade in action was bad enough but a close friend as well was too much. It made you resentful with hate and revenge that could eat away your very soul. Then there was never any peace. Where had he read that? Wherever, it was true, you had to stay detached to give orders when all hell was let loose.

After his dream and thoughts of the past, Bomber threw back the blankets as it was clear he was not going to get back to sleep. Despite only having slept for four hours, his mind was restless and he knew he would feel worse if he lay in bed. Having shaved and showered, he put on clean combats, carefully folding everything back into its rightful place in his bunk. He could put his hand on exactly what he wanted in the dark without having to search for it. He walked quietly along the corridor in the semi-darkness to the combined officers' and Sgts' mess.

In the mess, he found TC sitting in one of the old broken-down armchairs, drinking tea. He was of average height with the physique of a field athlete. He was called TC but not to his face, after the cartoon cat, Top Cat. Bomber had no idea why this was so but it suited him.

"Can't sleep," TC said, without looking up from the two-day old newspaper on his lap. "Kettle's just boiled if you are after a cuppa."

Bomber nodded and fixed himself a brew, then sat in the only other armchair in the room.

"Well, how's it going with the lads in the platoon, David?" Bomber must have looked a little surprised at the use of his first name. TC must have noticed, for he said, "When we are on our own, you don't mind me calling you David? Can't call you Bomber, now you are a sergeant."

Before Bomber could reply, TC went on. "I know everyone calls me TC but it is Tom to you, never Thomas, only my mother calls me that when I'm in the dog house."

It was not unusual for senior officers to address junior officers by first names but it never normally applied the other way round.

"It's going okay for me sir, sorry, Tom. I've worked with each section on several hairy jobs now and we have some good lads. Some lack experience but they are learning fast, but I would like to get everyone on the range when we get back to Ballykinler. We all need to sharpen up on our close quarter combat shooting for working the streets in Belfast." TC nodded. Bomber went on, "Cpl Bush is a good man, Mills runs a tight section and his men respect him, but…" Bomber paused.

"But…?" prompted TC.

"Cpl Jones worries me. He does just enough and always holds back. Lazy? I'm not sure but he never checks his lads have done what they should have done. Perhaps he just has complete confidence in them."

"You're right about him. Came to us from C Company stores. Not my choice, I wanted Wells but the Recce Platoon got him."

"I'll keep my eye on him and gee him up a bit, remind him of his duties."

Just then, the door opened and in came the company commander, followed by the C/Sgt and a chef carrying a large tray with plates of eggs, bacon and beans.

"Ha, there you both are. Well done, C/Sgt, you were right of course! They are both here plotting the new day, ha!" Without waiting for a response, he sat down at the long table as the food was plonked down in front of him.

"Well, come on then, tuck in and I will tell you what's a foot. Going to be a fun day, ha!"

Bomber glanced at TC who just raised his eyebrows and then set to on the food. Bomber saw the company commander smile and knew he was enjoying keeping them in suspense.

When they had finished, the company commander pushed his plate to one side and looked at Bomber.

"I've not had a good chance to talk to you properly, Sgt, since you arrived. I know we have been very busy but I should have made an effort to get to know you again."

"Again sir?" Bomber was sure they had never met before.

"Yes, Oh I know all about you. I was on the brigade commander's staff when you were in Aden and the Radfan. Had to prepare your file along with the rest of that Irish mob of yours after that little incident with the military police."

He paused, smiling to himself, then went on.

"Got up to a lot of good stuff, a bit close to the edge but good never the less, liked the covert stuff didn't you."

Bomber felt TC staring at him as if to say 'We can talk about this later'.

"Now the 2i/c thinks you are sailing too close to the wind after shooting the two bombers but it was clear you were within the law. However, be careful, there are two camps here. One wants a tough, no-holds-barred approach and another camp who want a softly, softly approach to the troubles."

"Where are we in this, sir?" interrupted TC.

"Oh, we are what the brigade commander wants. Today it's tough, tough, tough. Tomorrow it could be softly, softly, softly."

The company commander paused, sipped some tea and seemed to go into a trance.

Bomber looked into his empty cup and toyed with going to put the kettle on but decided to sit still. Finally, TC coughed and the company commander looked up. "Ha, yes today you will go back to Ballykinler. Before dawn tomorrow, you will deploy to the Mourne Mountains. This is where your mountaineering skills and covert experience will be useful." He stared at Bomber and smiled. Bomber wondered what else he knew about him.

The commander pulled a map from his pocket and spread it out on the table. Their camp at Ballykinler, right on the seashore, was marked in red. On the west side of the Mourne, a valley was also marked.

"Now you, Sgt, with say three others, will get into the mountains and set up an OP (observation point) where you can watch this valley. The platoon commander, with the rest of the platoon, will be here and here." He marked two points on the map. "This one is an old TA (Territorial Army) centre and this is a police station. From these two points, you should be able to respond and cut off anyone trying to leave the valley. Questions?"

"How long do we stay in position for, sir and what intel (intelligence) do we have on who we are looking for?" asked Bomber.

"Three days at least and the intel is thin. It's believed the IRA are using the valley for some small arms training or testing detonators for IEDs (improvised explosive devices) and it will be happening over the next few days."

Standing up, the company commander handed the map to TC and said, "Once you have made your plan, liaise with the 2i/c, he has the radio frequencies for you."

Chapter 4
The Mountains of Mourne

Bomber checked the compass bearing again. It was still dark and the low cloud swirled around them in the wind. He would stay on this bearing until he reached the massive stone wall that ran along the top of the ridge, then he would head for the summit of Slieve Donard. From there, he would follow a different bearing to the head of the valley, where they would establish an OP.

Bomber had checked the weather forecast with the RAF met office, and the cloud was due to lift later in the morning, but rain was expected that evening and to last for twenty-four hours.

They stumbled on the deep heather, making progress difficult and painful. He had selected Cpl Bush, L/Cpl Jacobs and Chalky White to go with him. He had abandoned the issued webbing to carry all their needs and instead had taken mountaineering rucksacks from the AT (Adventure Training) store. He had picked the olive-green-coloured ones with a sixty-litre capacity, which were big enough to contain all their needs for at least four days.

They had kept the webbing belt with the ammunition pouches and water bottles attached. Field dressings were taped to the belts and onto the shoulder straps of the rucksacks.

Chalky carried the radio and spare batteries. Communications was a worry as the 'A41' radio did not have a great range, unless it was line of sight and mountains always made communications difficult. To solve this, TC had put another OP hidden in the Tollymore Forest on the other side of the road that passed the entrance to the valley. They would have a radio and act as a relay station for Bomber, passing messages to TC at the TA Centre.

Bomber almost walked into the wall. It was taller than a man and several feet thick. In fact, it was the biggest natural hand-built dry stonewall he had ever seen. At intervals, stone steps had been set into the wall so that people could climb over.

Being able to follow the side of the wall uphill would make the going much easier, as all the heather and rocks had been cleared away by countless feet passing that way over many years.

Arriving at the summit, the wind speed increased. At an altitude of two thousand eight hundred feet, with the summit directly facing the Irish Sea, it was exposed to all the violent weather going. To speak to the others, he had to cup his hands around one of their ears and speak. After passing the huge pile of stones that marked the summit, Bomber changed the compass bearing to head directly to the valley head. He was getting concerned now since it had taken longer than planned in the darkness but now the wind had cleared the low cloud, he could see the sky getting lighter in the east.

He could also see the faint twinkle of lights in Newcastle on the coast. Newcastle was the nearest town to Ballykinler and he imagined the other half of the platoon warm and dry in the police station and TA centre. He hoped that Cpl Jones, as the senior person in the police station, would be alert and ready if they needed him.

It was light now and from their position part way up the side of the valley, they could clearly see the valley stretching out before them. They dug out a shallow trench, stretched a waterproof nylon sheet over it and pegged it down tight. On top of this, they had placed the heather they had carefully put to one side.

Before Bomber had wriggled into the hide, he had carefully looked at it from all directions. From fifty feet away, it was undetectable.

It was cramped but snug in the hide. Lying flat, they could see the sweep of the valley flowing northwest. As the sky lightened, the beauty and majesty of the view became apparent to all of them.

Thorny summed it up, "Fucking wonderful, worth the slog just to see this!"

They quickly established a routine for the OP. Two watching while the other two rested or ate cold rations. If they needed a pee, they used a bottle; as for anything else, it had to wait until nightfall.

Bomber soaked up the view. He loved the mountains and as the clouds scudded across the sky, the colours on the mountainside and valley changed with them.

At about mid-afternoon, the promised rain started. A light steady drizzle, not heavy enough to restrict their view of the valley, but enough to make it unlikely for anyone to come into the valley to test weapons or IED triggers.

Now that darkness had descended, they took turns to crawl out of the hide. A chance to stretch limbs and to do their business into a plastic bag. The QM did not have any heavy-duty zip lock bags so they had to make do with what the NAAFI manager could find. They were big enough and strong but had to be tied to secure them. Everyone took extra care securing them as they had to be carried out when they left.

The QM had promised to source the heavy-duty zip lock bags before any more covert Ops were deployed. *Some hope*, thought Bomber. *He hates my guts and likes to make things difficult.*

Bomber had a restless night and was wide-awake two hours before dawn. An hour later, they all stood-to and watched the dawn break. They took turns estimating ranges to different boulders and bushes. Not that they expected to have a firefight, but it was best to be prepared and knowing the ranges in advance was always a good thing. Speaking quietly, Bomber gave each an arc to cover, both for observing and in case they had to use their weapons.

After eating a cold breakfast of cheese and hardtack biscuits washed down by cold water, Bomber settled down to sleep.

In his dream, he was sleeping on the floor of Shipton's cave on the slope of Kilimanjaro, thinking about the climb-up to the high hut the next day. Hands were shaking him, a voice whispering in his ear. Bomber came awake, looking into a face which he expected to be Ben, his Kikuyu mentor on the mountain. Instead of a smiling black face, he saw the pale cam cream face of Thorny. Thorny whispered, "We've got company." Pulling himself back to reality, Bomber looked through the binos that Thorny pushed into his hands.

There were four people walking together. They appeared to be young, late teens or early twenties. Dressed in walking gear, they strode up the valley, slowly gaining height. Bomber instructed Chalky to send a contact report and gave him a grid reference.

Chalky gave a thumbs up that it had been acknowledged.

"They seem like normal walkers to me, heading up to the summit." Thorny had his own binos to his eyes as he spoke.

Bomber watched. *If they were going to the summit, then why are they in the valley instead of on the ridge, where there is a good path?*

The walkers were now less than five hundred yards away and appeared much clearer in the lenses of the binos. Bomber could see two were girls. Both had long black hair and appeared to be about five foot four inches in height. The others were lads, one tall and skinny looking with a number one haircut, the other shorter, stockier and older than the others. He wore a ski hat and had his jacket open.

Jacobs was working the SLR camera, taking photo after photo for the Int boys to study later.

The stockier one suddenly stopped and looked around, scanning the area, distance, middle distance and finally the ground around himself.

He's done this before, thought Bomber.

As if reading his mind, Jacobs whispered, "That's not the first time he's done that, now is it?"

"I know that fucker," hissed Thorny. "You know him too, Chalky. It's that shit from the Drums Platoon, used to play football for the HQ Company. Left the regiment last year, wife was a good looker from Londonderry. She dumped him and went off with some guy from the Signals Unit."

Chalky took the offered binos from Thorny and studying the figure, now talking to the girls, he confirmed the ID by saying, "Yes, it's him; we used to call him O'Hooligan because of his animal behaviour on the pitch but it's really O'Halligan."

"Call it in," instructed Bomber.

The four now split, O'Halligan sat on his rucksack while the other three walked off. The two girls stayed together and went up the west side of the valley to an outcrop of boulders. There they stopped and sat back-to-back, one looking up the valley, the other down the way they had come.

"Where's the other guy?" Bomber demanded, cursing himself for staying too focused on the couple of girls.

"Up on the east side behind us." Jacobs had wriggled his way to the back of the hide and had gently lifted the cover to poke the binos through.

"What's he doing?" demanded Bomber. concerned he could be standing there with a pistol pointing at their backs.

"He's still going up," whispered Jacobs. "No, wait, he's stopped and looking round, he's now sitting down and lighting a ciggy."

"Okay, call it in, Chalky, here's the grid references for each." Bomber thought for a moment, then whispered to Thorny, "O'Halligan, what sort of soldier was he?"

"A real rough neck, always picking fights, got kicked out of the Recce Platoon for stealing, so they say, and ended up in the Drums for a few months before he left the army."

So if he was Recce, he would know a lot like how to read an area for any signs of intruders. And how to be patient and wait before he gave an all clear.

"Did he have anything to do with explosives while he was in the Recce?"

Chalky answered, "All of the Recce lads did the normal stuff at Warminster and the surveillance course at Chatham. O'Halligan was one of them."

Bomber's mind was working overtime, putting himself in O'Halligan's shoes, checking out an area. *I'd put people up high looking for signs of any new paths being forced through heather or long grass. Any vegetation that had been cut for camouflage but was now dying off. The glint of light off a weapon or binos.*

"He's using a scope to scan the area," Chalky whispered.

"Okay every one, still, binos down. Thorny what's the range to where he is?"

"About three fifty, I can take him if you want but it's a risky shot at this range."

"No, but it's an option so be ready. Jacobs, what's matey doing?"

"He's looking through a small pair of binos, mostly down the valley. What do you think they are up to, Sarge?"

Before he could answer, Chalky spoke, "He's put the scope away and is talking into something."

Bomber raised his binos and studied the target, for that's what he was now. In his hand was something black, possibly a radio similar to the type the RUC used.

Before he could tell Chalky to call it in, the OP in the forest came on air reporting a dark-blue Ford car, with three men in it, parked near the pathway that would be the starting point for the valley.

Could this be who O'Halligan was scouting for? Bomber wondered.

A shrill whistle sounded from the direction of the two girls.

Bomber heard the voices and laughter before he saw the group walking down the valley from the direction of the ridge. There were seven of them, a tall man leading, followed by six young lads probably about thirteen to fifteen years of age. They stopped at a junction of two small streams. They all took off their rucksacks and the man produced a compass and map.

"Christ, he's giving them a bloody map-reading lesson," Thorny hissed.

"What's our target doing, Chalky?"

"Still sitting there and talking into his radio by the looks of it."

"Okay let's call it in."

Things are getting complicated, thought Bomber.

"Target's on the move, Sarge, looks like they are heading back the way they came." Chalky kept the binos jammed to his eyes as he spoke.

"Thorny, keep watching the others, let me know if they head towards us. Chalky, call this in and, Jacobs, you keep watching the target; let me know if they deviate off route."

Bomber was trying to work out what was going on. Had the target called off the testing? Were they moving to a different location? Had O'Halligan spotted something suspicious before the boys arrived or did he think it was just a tiny bit busy?

Chalky interrupted his thoughts, "Message from Sunray; we are to pull out at plus three for pickup at this grid reference." He held his field notebook for Bomber to see the six-figure grid reference. Finding it on the map, he quickly estimated the time and distance factor for moving in the dark.

Plus, three was three hours after dark, which was 18:30 hours. Bomber estimated that it would take two hours to get to the spot for pick up on the road to Newcastle.

He would allow an hour to clear up the hide site and so, as soon as the light was fading, they would fill in the scrape, re-lay the heather, which they had cut out, still attached to a square of peat. When they had finished, it would take a close inspection by an experienced eye to recognise there had been a hide there.

The map-reading group spent an hour by the stream and then walked down the valley, the boys talking and laughing in their innocence of what could have happened in the beautiful valley of the Mourne Mountains.

Later in the debriefing room, the heat was making Bomber drowsy. Looking around, he could see heads drooping then jerking upright, desperately trying to stay awake.

The door opened and in came the op's officer, followed by TC and a Sgt who Bomber did not know but assumed he was Int.

The regiment's ops officer was a no-nonsense captain, a very tough white Kenyan called Bass. His normal job was as the Recce Platoon commander, but the day-to-day running of that was left to his number two, an equally tough rugby playing giant, a C/Sgt called Pillar, while Bass doubled up as the regiment's ops officer.

"Well done, a good deal of useful information has been gathered due to your efforts," he said in an educated accent. Very little trace of his place of birth could be detected.

"The car was traced and followed to Anderson Town, the occupants are all known to the RUC and the Int boys. As for the others, they are new players except O'Halligan. After he left the army, he slipped off the radar somewhat."

Bomber raised his hand.

"Yes?"

"Pte White made an interesting observation, which we have only just discussed; tell them, White."

"Well, sir," Chalky spoke slowly as if not sure of what he was saying. "I noticed he looked a bit lean and fit. O'Halligan was always a lazy, fat bastard in the regiment, sir. The other thing, he had a really good deep tan. Not the sort you get from a week in Blackpool." Chalky dried up and looked at Bomber.

"Could have spent his time at some training camp, sir, it's possible."

The Int Sgt was scribbling furiously into a notebook.

Bass looked thoughtful. "He was lazy in the platoon, except when it came to football. Could be he has been up to no good or perhaps he has been on a football course in the sun."

They all noticed he smiled when he said that.

With that, the meeting broke up and they went for some rest as they were off back to Belfast at sparrows fart the next morning.

Chapter 5
Man Down

In the basement of Flax Street Mill, the twice-weekly disco was in full swing. The flashing lights were painting a picture that Bomber felt he would rather not see. The teenage girls flocked there looking for some relief from the reality of life outside by meeting the squaddies and having a good time, dancing the night away.

Bomber pushed his way through the dancers and tugged on the DJ's arm. He was one of the company chefs, a L/Cpl by the name of Chipps, who doubled up as the DJ. He was sifting through records but he bent down to hear what Bomber had to say. Shouting in his ear, he told him to announce that all One Platoon were to gear up and be ready to move in fifteen minutes.

There were groans from the lads as they all believed they were on a promise with the girls up until then. Bomber smiled to himself. The girls at the disco were from the local area, that is the Protestant area and seemed to love the twice-a-week rave-up. Many showed their appreciation in the garage area of the mill before chucking out time.

Bomber studied the street and didn't like it. They had been called out to assist an RUC officer to deliver a summons to a house in the Water Works area. The area was mostly Catholic with about twenty-five percent Protestant, who lived on the fringes of the area.

Normally, Bomber would have expected to have seen some interest from 'rent a crowd' or worse 'rent a mob'. There were groups of teenage boys, jeering and geeing each other up to throw stones but nothing was occurring.

TC obviously did not like it either, deploying the lads to cover every side street and alley.

"What do you think is going on, Sergeant?" TC spoke quietly.

"It's not normal. By now, we should be seeing some aggro. It's almost as if we've been set up for something other than a stoning."

"I agree and they know we cannot cover every doorway, window and alleyway. When we leave, we will do it a section at a time, keeping each other covered."

"Okay sir." Bomber watched the door open after the RUC officer had pummelled it for at least five minutes.

The man in the doorway did not even stop to argue with the RUC, he just snatched the papers and slammed the door closed.

Bomber started to shout "stay sharp everyone" but by the time he had said it, a volley of shots rang out. He glimpsed the flashes from a bedroom window less than a hundred yards away.

"You two with me," and without thinking, he ran full pelt at the house. He felt, rather than heard, more bullets pass his head. Perhaps it was the shock wave of the rounds passing through the air at supersonic speed, he didn't know or care. Only smashing through the door and killing the gunman mattered.

He hit the door at full speed with his left shoulder and it caved in. Rifle ready, he speed-scanned the room before running into the next room. Cowering on the floor was an older man with a small child hugged to his chest. A woman of middle years was behind him crying.

Bomber felt no sympathy, killing had taken over his mind. He heard someone, a stranger snarl, "Where's the fucking gunman!" The man and woman said nothing but the child pointed towards the door leading to the kitchen. Now Parky and Armalite where there.

Bomber nodded to Parky, who opened the door, revealing an empty kitchen but an outside door just swinging closed. They raced through into a neat but small garden at the end of which was a high wooden fence in which was a gate. A man was struggling with the catch that seemed to have jammed. Bomber heard himself shout, "Army, drop the weapon or I fire." Bomber half hoped the man would try and fight and that would be when Bomber could legally kill him.

The man dropped the rifle and put his hands in the air, Bomber felt cheated. Armalite stepped forward, kicked the man in the back of the legs and as he went down on his knees, he smashed him in the back of the head with his rifle butt, laying him out cold.

Sensing more was to follow from Armalite, Bomber shouted, "That's enough, pick up his weapon." As he said it, he felt the force that had driven him headlong at the gunman drain away.

Armalite was having none of it and Bomber had to pull him off the unconscious figure. "Christ's sake, I said enough man." Armalite slumped, his anger spent.

He looked at Bomber and said with anger in his voice, "He killed the boss, Sarge."

By now, Cpl Bush had arrived and they dragged the gunman away. As Bomber walked through the house, he could hear the RUC officer questioning the man and woman.

Outside was the armoured ambulance and the MO. TC was being loaded into the vehicle and Bomber could see he was still alive but red froth kept appearing on his lips. Bomber stepped forward and gripped TC's hand. He responded and winked. As he did so, he mouthed silently, "Did you get him?" For a split second, Bomber saw the man in his nightmare mouthing words and had to shake himself back to reality.

"We got him sir." Bomber felt himself being pushed roughly away by the MO. The doors closed and the vehicle sped away.

"Sarge, we've got trouble," it was Cpl Jones calling him. Bomber looked around and felt for once Jones had taken a lot of trouble deploying his section to cover the mob that was advancing towards them. He called Cpl Mills over and told him to move his baton gunman over to Jones. Then he was to cover the rear.

"Where the fuck is Dusty?"

"I'm right here, Sarge." Bomber jumped at the sound of the radio operator's voice so close to him. Looking down, he could see Dusty kneeling in the shadow of a parked car not two feet away. Bomber realised he was keyed up and had to take a deep breath to enable himself to think clearly.

Kneeling down next to Dusty, he asked for an update on what had been sent to HQ and what had come back. Dusty duly responded missing nothing out. *Basically,* Bomber thought, *we have to sit tight and secure the area until support arrives.*

Fortunately, the mob seemed to be keeping its distance. Bomber wondered if that was because another sniper was lurking waiting his chance.

Bomber went back to the house where he found the RUC man busily writing in a report book. He looked up as Bomber entered. He was a big man, heavily built, and Bomber knew he played rugby for the RUC and was a member of their mountaineering club.

"Just finishing up the statements from the family, grandpa, daughter and granddaughter. I'm convinced they were victims. There were three men one with the rifle." He nodded to the weapon lying on the chair. "The other, much younger, had a pistol with which he forced them to stay in the back room on the floor. He ran for it as soon as the firing started, scared as a rabbit according to the old man. The third who was in charge had set the rifleman up in the room upstairs but he left before the shooting started. Professional too, window not open, just a pane removed to fire through, table to rest on set back from the window and so on."

"Tell me more about the third man."

"Well, from his accent he was a Londonderry man and he had a very good sun tan and that's about it."

Bomber stopped looking at the rifle which he had already identified as an American M1 .30 semi-automatic rifle, issued to officers and others during World War Two. This lifted his attention away from the rifle and thought, *So O'Halligan, it seems you are more than just a scout. What next, you fucker?* Bomber's thoughts were interrupted by shouting and the sounds of a scuffle.

Outside, a man in his thirties, was being restrained by Cpl Bush and Chalky White. Thorny came over to Bomber and said, "Says it's his family in there, Sarge. I've searched him and he's clean."

"Okay, let him through." Bomber turned to the RUC man and asked him to keep an eye on the man, and if possible, listen to what was said without the family knowing.

He nodded and went back into the house. Bomber followed and went upstairs to the front bedroom. Looking from the doorway, he could see care had been taken. The window had an old-fashioned wood frame with nine-inch panes of single glass. The bottom left pane had been removed from the window. A small table had been placed in front of the window and two small pocket-sized bags of sand had been placed just where a gunman needs to steady his aim.

Kneeling down behind the table, he aimed his rifle down the street. He had a perfect line of sight through the hole without his rifle barrel having to be poked through the hole. *Nice one, you bastards,* mused Bomber.

"Sarge, you're wanted on the radio!" a voice yelled up the stairs. Bomber went down two steps at a time. It was Dusty Miller, the radio operator.

"What is it?"

"It's zero, Sunray wants you," Dusty said in a hushed tone as if someone might be listening in.

Sunray was the name for the company commander and Bomber half guessed that it would be about TC and what they were to do next.

Twenty minutes later, they were pushing 'rent a mob' back into a decreasing circle. The company commander had the whole company deployed, surrounding the area and was tightening the noose.

He had informed Bomber that TC was in the operating theatre and everything looked good. His plan now was to squeeze the mob in tight, then there were three target houses to be searched.

Rent a mob was under-performing Bomber noticed, as the circle got smaller the numbers in the mob decreased. Boys were slipping off into the houses not wanting to be lifted. Rocks and bottles were the only missiles coming towards the platoon but each section had two men covering windows and doorways ready to shoot at any sign of a gunman.

The street they were on bordered onto the New Lodge area. The house they wanted was Number Twenty-two, which was near the end of the street. They would not go into the house until given the okay from the company commander, as he wanted all three of the houses hit at the same time.

Putting Cpl Bush and his section at the end of the street facing the mob, Bomber told Cpl Jones to cover the rear and Cpl Mills, in the middle, to react either way should it be needed. When it came to the search, he would use the men from the HQ section, less Miller, who would stay listening to the radio in case any change in orders came from HQ.

Bomber stood behind Thorny, watching the mob.

"I think they have realised we are not pushing them anymore, Sarge."

"Yes, any time now, they will come closer and start up with more than just rocks. I'll send Cpl Mills baton gun up to you." With that, Bomber moved back to Dusty, who was waving at him.

"Go in five minutes, Sarge."

"Okay, let's get ready." Having told Cpl Mills to send his baton gun to Cpl Bush, he briefed the HQ section.

They would do a hard entry as they could not get to the back of the house to secure the rear entrance beforehand.

Miller would stay in the doorway with the radio. Brown (Armalite) and Parker were to go straight through the house and secure the back entrance. Taylor (also known as Tinker) with Spencer would go upstairs and clear that floor. Bomber would be back up as they went in. Once rooms were cleared of any threat, they would start the search.

Dusty said, "Wilco," into the radio mic and Bomber said. "Go." Armalite and Parky hit the door together. It was a solid wood door, but with only a Yale type lock, it burst open with a mighty crash. The two charged straight through, shouting as they went, "Army, don't move."

Taylor and Spencer dashed up the stairs also shouting. Bomber followed into the lounge where a woman in her thirties sat looking shocked. Standing and starting to shout in protest was a man of similar age but unlike the woman, he was fat and had the face of a drinker. On the coffee table were several empty beer cans.

The man stepped towards Bomber but Bomber pushed him hard in the chest and the man sat down heavily on the sofa directly behind him.

"Stay still and be quiet. This will be over the quicker if you do."

Shouts were coming from the rear of the house and Bomber looked through the window. Armalite was cuffing a tall youth around the head, driving him back into the house. Parky had an arm-lock on another shorter lad who was protesting with his best Belfast swear words.

Pushing them into the lounge and onto the sofa, Armalite declared, "Caught them in the shed, Sarge, making up some petrol bombs. Must be thirty at least plus bags of nails. Okay to go back and look some more?"

Before Bomber could answer, Spencer came down holding onto a girl of about sixteen by the arm. She was calling him an English bastard and a fucking shit head.

Spencer was smiling as if he was enjoying the insults. He pushed the girl down hard onto a chair. He stepped over to Bomber and whispered in his ear. Bomber nodded and told him to stay and cover them. Then, taking his notebook out, he handed it to the woman whom he had been watching.

"I want you to write down the names of everyone here and if they live at this address. It's nothing to worry about. I just have to confirm with my boss that you are who you say you are. If someone here is not a resident, then write down their name, then I will get them to put in their address, okay?"

The woman nodded; taking the notepad, she removed the pencil from its holder. Bomber noticed her hands were shaking. Her face looked haggard, as if she had been ill but she had nice hair, well cared for, and manicured fingernails painted pink, matching her blouse. *Must have been a really good looker when she was younger,* he thought. *What the hell is she doing with that fat beer-swilling knacker?*

While she was doing this, Bomber went to Dusty and gave him some instructions. Then he called Cpl Jones over and told him to send in two of his section to help with the search downstairs.

As he went back in, Dusty spoke up, "The mob's getting bolder, Sarge, rocks are reaching Thorny, sorry, Cpl Bush now."

"Let me know if it gets any worse."

"Will do, Sarge."

The woman had finished writing and Bomber looked at the names. "Thank you, but I want you to know if any of this is incorrect with what we have at HQ, those named will be arrested and taken in for questioning."

The woman started to cry, softly at first, then louder. The two lads looked uncomfortable and the man stood up and started shouting, calling Bomber a fucking fascist shit. Armalite stepped behind the sofa, reached over and jerked him down by the collar of his shirt.

The girl spoke up and asked for the notebook. Taking it and the pencil, she wrote boldly across the page, 'Fuck off!'

Bomber took the book back, smiled at the girl and said, "Thank you."

The girl stuck a finger up and sat down. The woman carried on crying; the man put his arm around her but she shook him off.

"They're here, Sarge," Dusty called from the doorway.

In walked the company commander with two RUC officers, one a female. The CSM was also there with the Provo Sgt. Bomber nodded at the two boys and without fuss, the CSM and Provo Sgt marched them out holding them firmly by one arm, both boys protesting loudly but they were helpless in the arm-locks they were held in.

The girl had jumped up to intervene but the RUC officer held her. The female officer spoke. "We can do this the easy way or hard way; you can give me what you have stuffed in your knickers or I will do it for you now."

The girl reluctantly lifted her skirt with a look of pure hatred on her face and pulled a semi-automatic pistol from her knickers. The RUC girl snatched it expertly, ejecting the magazine as she did so. Then she cocked the weapon, ejecting a live round from the chamber.

With the three of them taken into custody, Bomber had the man removed to the kitchen.

"Do you want to tell me what's going on?" Bomber said gently to the woman.

The woman shook her head, sobbing and holding a tissue to her eyes.

"Pity it might help get them released. The two boys don't live here, do they?"

Again the woman shook her head but this time she spoke quietly. "The tall one, Shaun O'Corran, he started it, got Mary involved. Thinks he is a big shot with the IRA. He's just a stupid tool they are using to organise the local kids for riots, makes petrol and nail bombs to hand out."

"Who's the other lad?"

"Patrick Gilley, lives at Number Eighteen. Follows Mary like a puppy, will do anything for her."

Bomber was interrupted by the company commander putting his hand on his shoulder and indicating they should step outside. Bomber was a little taken by surprise; he had not been aware that he had re-entered the house after the other three had been taken away.

"Nicely done, Sergeant, I will have Number Eighteen searched. Oh, the good news is Lt Mickleson is out of theatre and is stable, doing well. Tell the lads, ah."

"Yes sir, thank you, sir, that is good news."

"Good, well carry on then."

Bomber felt a great sense of relief at the news that TC was going to be okay and passed the word to Dusty to spread to the rest.

The woman had dried her eyes and Bomber asked her if she would like some tea.

"No, but I want to tell you I have said too much, no one must know I have said anything."

"They won't hear anything from me or my lads, you have my word."

In the kitchen, the man was sitting on a hardback chair, overflowing the seat by about five stone but saying nothing. He had a red welt on the side of his face, which he kept rubbing. Looking at Bomber, he said, "I want to make a complaint; that bastard hit me."

"Well, if you call him a bastard, he may well hit you again. Now come with me."

The man followed him to the shed. It was about twelve-by-twelve foot and made of wood on a concrete base. It took up about a third of the rear space that doubled as a yard and garden.

A few plants struggled for life on a neglected border. A spilt black plastic bag displayed a large quantity of empty Premium Lager cans.

Parky was methodically emptying the shed. Old garden tools, a bike, some paint tins. Next to them were two seventy-litre bags of fertiliser. Bomber stared at them, then at the man. The man shifted uncomfortably.

"Planning on starting an allotment, are we?"

"Just looking after it for a friend who has an allotment."

"Name of this friend?" Bomber paused then nodded to Armalite who was behind the man.

Armalite smacked the man on the back of his head with an open hand. The man yelped and went down on his knees.

The man was trembling now, his rolls of fat moving like waves on the sea.

Bomber changed tack saying, "Bloody hell, why did you hit him, can't you see he is upset? Help him up and take him to the kitchen." Between them, they lifted the tub of lard up and sat him back on the chair. "Put the kettle on; we all need a cup of tea." Armalite filled the kettle and put it on the gas stove.

"Now I know it's not you and your wife up to no good. Yes?" Bomber had his hand on the man's shoulder and spoke gently.

The man nodded and looked at Bomber. His eyes were watery and Bomber knew this was a man who badly needed a drink. Nodding to Armalite, he said, "See if there is a beer in that fridge for me, will you?" Armalite looked surprised but complied and handed over a can of lager.

Bomber rolled the can against his face then popped the tab. The can fizzed and Bomber sniffed the opening. "Argh great, damn shame I'm on duty, guess I'll have to throw it."

"No, no give it to me."

"But you're having tea. Much better for you; there, the kettle's boiling."

"Fuck the tea, give me the can," his tone was now one of pleading and Bomber made his move.

"You can have the beer if you tell me where the explosive for the nail bombs is hidden."

"I don't know."

"All right take him and hand him over to the RUC outside." As he said it, he started to tip the lager into the sink.

"No, I know nothing about explosives but Mary and the lads were messing about by the drain cover in the corner of the yard." The man was now holding out his hands pleadingly towards the can of lager.

"Go check it," Bomber said to Armalite, who went outside calling Parky to him.

Still holding the can, Bomber said, "You can have it if they come back with something."

In didn't take long; both came back in grinning and dumped a package on the kitchen table. It was the size of a two-hundred carton of cigarettes. Parky opened it, inside was a slab of PE (plastic explosive) complete with ten detonators and a coil of fuse cord.

Bomber held out the beer. The man grabbed it, drinking greedily, draining it in a single go.

"What else have you found in the shed?"

"Nothing, Sarge. Only odd thing is a bin which has about twenty pounds of sugar in it."

"Okay bring that, the fertiliser, nails and the P.E. and we will get out of here."

"Why that stuff, Sarge?" fired back Parky.

"Sugar, fertiliser mixed together, give it a primer such as a small amount of PE and you have a bomb, a big bomb in our case."

"How do you know that, Sarge?" Armalite was looking closely at Bomber.

"Must have read it in an Int report."

Armalite gave him a look that said, 'Pull the other one.'

Outside, the mob had faded away. Thorny said there had been about ten minutes of intense stoning, then it all went quiet after some shooting was heard from the other side of the New Lodge.

Chapter 6
Promotion

Back in barracks at Ballykinler, Bomber was heading for the platoon lines to check that the lads were getting some much needed rest when a voice called out from the doorway of the Company HQ.

"Ah, there you are C/Sgt (Colour Sergeant), need to talk to you, ha."

C/Sgt what's he talking about? Bomber looked at the company commander as if he had gone a little daft.

"Don't look at me like that, I've not gone batty, ha." He turned and went into his office and Bomber followed.

"Sit down. Firstly, your promotion has come through thanks in no little part to some very strong recommendations. Many people think you are too young to be even a Sgt, but we know different don't we, ha?" He finished the sentence with a smile as if he was sharing some secret.

Bomber was a little stunned by the news but had a dread of what his next job would be. C/Sgts normally looked after the company stores and, in the old days, protected the regimental colours in battle, hence the title 'Colour Sgt'.

"Now the Quartermaster, who I know you do not get on with heard the story. He wants you to take over A Company stores. How does that grab you, ha?"

Bomber paused and said, "Can I speak frankly, sir."

"Yes, would expect nothing less."

"I would rather refuse the promotion than do that, sir."

"Jolly good, that's a bottle of whisky the CO owes me, ha."

Bomber was now getting tired of the game but before he could say anything, the commander went on.

"The CO agrees with me you would be wasted in the stores. The regiment is desperately short of experienced young officers and SNCOs. Lt Mickleson, although he is making good progress, will be out of the game for some time to come. So you are now the acting platoon commander in his place. How do you feel about that then, ha?" The commander sat back looking at Bomber, a grin a mile wide on his face.

Bomber shifted in the chair uncomfortable with the look the commander was giving him.

"I like it very much, sir, but I will need a good Sgt."

"All fixed, Bush will be made up to Sgt next month but he can put his third stripe up next week. Jacobs gets the section, sadly not on promotion until December, but he will be made acting Cpl until then. Also you will get three new recruits that won't bring you up to full strength but for now, that's the best we can do. Peters and Smith will be fit for duty in a few days but Palmer is being sent to Chessington for rehabilitation. God, I feel like Father Christmas, ha."

"Thank you, sir, that is good news, except for Palmer."

"Indeed, now I want you to use your special skills and experience to turn a good platoon into the very best in the regiment. A word of caution, there are those who would love to see you fail. The CO and I are not in that group so avoid any confrontations with anyone senior to you; instead, bring it straight to me, yes?" He looked intently at Bomber who nodded. Finally finishing with, "No letting that temper of yours get the better of you, ha?"

"No sir." *Time for a change of tack,* thought Bomber. "Did you see my training programme for the next three days, sir?"

"Yes, all approved, the 2i/c has booked your range time. Anything else, no, let's get on then shall we, ha?"

As it was now lunchtime, Bomber walked to the warrant officers' and sergeants' mess in something of a daze.

He had been promoted, given command of a platoon and told the CO expected a lot from him. He had been warned that he had enemies, one or two he knew of but who else? He was pleased for Bush being promoted to platoon Sgt and grateful that they had some new boys to bolster the depleted sections.

Entering the mess, he put his beret on a spare hook by the cloakroom. The mess Sgt was standing by the dining room door, blocking Bomber's path.

"You're wanted by the RSM, Bomber, he's in the bar, having a drink."

Bomber shrugged, walked the short distance to the bar and pushed the door open. Shouts of "congratulations" and "get the beers in" hit him like a blast.

People were slapping him on the back and congratulating him. Some, he thought, were genuine, others seemed to speak through clenched teeth or not at all.

Later, when the bar was almost empty, Bomber found himself in a corner with Steve Pillar, the number two of the Recce Platoon, Mike Dale, the chief clerk and Mad Mac Reagan, the Provo Sgt.

Steve leaned forward and spoke in a conspiratorial tone; Bomber, along with the other two, found himself leaning forward, head down to catch the words.

"Something big coming up! Everyone, and I mean everyone, will be deployed and the shit will hit the fan big time, mark my words." Bomber noticed that despite the large amounts of beer Steve had consumed, his words were clear and concise.

Mike, the chief clerk, who knew everything that happened in the HQ, nodded. "He's right, something is up; the old man, ops officer and the company commanders are up there now in a huddle."

"Let's hope it's a cross border push to sort out the hide outs of the fucking IRA. Sick and tired of them slipping over there after a job and we can't do a hot pursuit. Fucking Garda just turn a blind eye as usual." Mad Mac didn't raise his voice but the venom in his tone was obvious.

"Don't think that will happen but it will be something heavy." Mike sat back and downed the rest of his pint. "That's me done, better go and find out what cockups my clerks have made in my absence."

Bomber watched him walk in a dead straight line out of the bar. Bomber had only had about half as much to drink and wasn't sure if he could get up out of the chair.

"I better get back to the guard house; they are bringing in a couple of likely lads in an hour for us to hold until the RUC can pick them up. Always like to give them a welcome."

Bomber felt sorry for the prisoners. Mad Mac was a fearsome looking man and could be very intimidating when in the mood.

"Never been the same since he did that interrogation course with the SAS boys a year ago." Steve was smiling when he said it. "Gets results, I think he has a sadistic side to him if you know what I mean."

Bomber didn't but nodded anyway.

"Right, I'm off," said Steve. "We are reorganising the Recce Platoon into sections of an armoured Land Rover and a Mark Two Ferret armoured car. Complete new role for us but no one's telling what it is yet. Need to see how the driver training is coming on."

He stood up and left saying, "Keep up the good work."

Thank God, I have the rest of the day off and can go and sleep this off, thought Bomber. As he made his way out of the bar, a cheerful voice hailed him.

"There you are, heard you had the afternoon off so thought we could play our squash league game. See you in the court in fifteen minutes, yes?"

It was the Signal Platoon's warrant officer. *Shit*, thought Bomber, *but drunk or sober, I can beat him.*

Later, standing under a hot shower, he wondered how he lost without scoring a point. *That will teach me to be cocky; oh well, another day tomorrow and there's always time for a re-match.*

Bomber stood on the range which backed on to the large, grass topped sand dunes and smelt the sea air. At the one-hundred-yard firing point, he had organised pop-up targets to come up at different ranges from twenty-five yards, forty and so on. No one knew what order they would come up in. He and the platoon NCOs had gone first and Bomber was pleased to see they all scored more than eighty percent hits. All that was except Cpl Jones number two, who had a Greek sounding name, L/Cpl Zika, he never missed anything. At the end of the session, Bomber phoned range control on the field telephone and spoke to them for a couple of minutes.

They all moved back to four hundred yards. Bomber explained that targets would pop up for four seconds during which they would engage. This would happen five times.

At the end of the five exposures, Sgt Bush phoned the butts and spoke to the controller who told him who had hit the target and where the hits were on the target.

Zika had hit each time with one shot and it was in the same spot each time, the head. Moving back to five hundred, then six hundred, Bomber repeated the exercise. While others got the odd hit, Zika never missed. Changing his point of aim from the head to the centre of the body, he was spot on. *Amazing,* thought Bomber, *I think I have found my sniper. Hitting a man size target at five and six hundred yards with an SLR just using the fixed iron sight was top stuff.*

Weapons cleaned and returned to the armoury, they changed into shorts and vest, then headed to the gym for a workout organised by the army physical training corps instructor named Patterson. He was as hard as nails, fitter than a racing greyhound and an army-level boxer. So when he said fifty press-ups, everyone kept their mouths shut and did them.

Firstly, he took them for a run through the sand dunes by the beach. The soft sand soon had their leg muscles screaming. Back in the gym, he had organised circuit training, upper body, abdominals and leg exercises. The instructor was merciless, pushing them to the limit. At the end, as they crawled out of the gym, Bomber thought they had done well, considering they spent so much time just walking the streets of Belfast.

Chapter 7
Orange, the Colour of Hate, 1970

Flax Street Mill had become a second home for the regiment and Bomber, its red brick wall towering up four floors. On one side was a large court yard with an equally imposing wall that gave it an air of solid menace. The mill had been built in the Victorian era by a Michael Andrews to weave flax that was grown in the local area.

Bomber sat with the other platoon commanders in the mill's briefing room, listening to the company commander giving his orders for the coming Orange Day Parade, which would take place tomorrow, the 31st of March. The Orange Day parades were a fixture of unmovable proportions in the minds of the Protestant Orange Order to celebrate the victory over James the second by William of Orange.

The platoon had to line one part of the parade route to ensure that firstly the parade, made up totally of Protestants, kept to the agreed route. Secondly, that the Catholic areas they passed were unviolated by the parade. Finally, that the parade was not disrupted by any Catholic protests of any sort.

This is like a red rag, orange in this case, to a bull, thought Bomber. *The Prods are trying to rub the Caths' noses in the shit and they sure as hell will respond.*

As if reading Bomber's thoughts, the company commander went on in his normal up beat way.

"Now I don't have to tell you we will be lucky if this goes off without any trouble. I expect there will be an armed presence by the so called UVF (Ulster Volunteer Force) with the parade. If spotted, they are to be identified and then we will pick them up after the parade. Any gangs of youths not in the parade but looking to start trouble as they pass the Catholic areas are to be thinned out as they pass you. In other words, nab them and hold them."

They had been standing for hours blocking the side streets leading to the Catholic Ardoyne area. They could hear the bands approaching. On the opposite side of the street, Prods were already waiting to cheer the parade as it passed. The Ardoyne was strangely quiet, there was no sign of any groups of youths gathering. Bomber wished he had some eyes that could see into the heart of the Ardoyne, ears that could hear what was being said and a sniper in a position that could target any gunman on the prowl.

He had none of this but still had to be able to watch and react to trouble from both sides, not an easy task, as they would be reacting and not proactive in stopping any trouble.

"Here they come, C/Sgt," said Dusty, the radio operator. Bomber looked, the lead band was approaching. Baton-twirling boys were leading, the pipes and drums were bashing out the 'The Sash My Father Wore'. Some of the crowd were singing, "It was orange it was beautiful the sash my father wore."

"Fucking morons," muttered Sgt Bush (Thorny).

"You're right there, Sarge, but you have to remember it was only two hundred years ago. That's like yesterday here." With that, Dusty let out a loud laugh but Bomber didn't join in. He thought it was a sad indictment of how everyone had failed to move on.

"Stay here, Sgt, I am going to check the sections."

"Okay boss."

Bomber was slightly amused how they had started calling him boss. As he moved away, Armalite shadowed him, keeping a few paces behind covering his back. Bomber had not asked him to do this but found out that Thorny had suggested it and Armalite had volunteered.

It was comforting to have the six-foot two Armalite watch his back. He moved easily and was quick to react to any situation. With prematurely grey hair, he had been in the regiment for five years; his only down side was his love of getting as pissed as a brewery rat every chance he got.

At the first street leading into the Ardoyne, Bomber had placed Cpl Jacobs and his section. Jacobs was watching some movement further down the street, leading into the heart of the Ardoyne.

"What's happening?"

Jacobs looked round, "Something going on boss. There's dickers (look outs) at the end of the street and every now and again, lads are crossing over going in Jones' direction."

"Okay, pass it to Dusty and tell him I said to relay it to HQ."

Making his way to Cpl Jones just ahead of the leading band, he wondered if this was where everything would kick off.

Cpl Jones was agitated. Bomber thought he was looking uptight.

"Everything all right here, Cpl Jones?"

"No boss, end of the street, house with the tatty blue door. Window directly above reminds me of the night TC was shot."

"What have you done about it?"

"Got L/Cpl Zika covering it and sent a radio report to you a few minutes ago."

Bomber nodded and said, "Well done."

Fiddling in his combat jacket pocket, he pulled out his Zeiss monocular that he had purchased in the American PX store in Germany three years ago. Sighting on the window, he noticed that one of the panes was not reflecting anything. Moving to Zika, who was lying on the road under the pig, Bomber handed him the monocular and said, "Look at the bottom right-hand pane of the window, what do you see?"

Zika studied the window. "It's a sniper set up, boss, bet my wages on it."

"Okay, keep watching; any shot from there, take it out, don't wait for orders."

"Right boss."

Bomber got in the pig and used the radio to talk to the company commander.

Bomber knew that if they tried to storm the house, the dickers would sound the alarm and the gunman would be off. What was needed was to block the gunman's line of sight to the parade, assuming it was his target.

That assistance arrived as if cued to do so. It was the CQMS (Company Quarter Master Sergeant) four-ton truck which was a lot taller than the pig. The CQMS was delivering tea and sandwiches. Parking at an angle, it completely blocked the view of the parade, which was only yards away.

The CQMS climbed out of the cab. He was a big Belfast man who had eighteen years' service under his belt. As he started to climb out of the cab, a shot rang out and he hit the ground. Zika fired with hardly a split second between.

Bomber shouted orders, "Cpl Jones, send in a contact and call for Starlight. You three, with me!" Running down, the street he noticed the dickers had disappeared. Bomber was aware that Armalite was on the other side of the street, running level with him. He could hear the others behind him. The door was another hundred yards and Bomber hoped that Zika was still sighted on the window in case the gunman was alive and waiting to take them out.

Armalite hit the door, it shuddered but held firm. *Shit,* thought Bomber, *they have barricaded it.* Before he could say anything, Armalite jumped at the window to the right of the door. There was a crashing of glass and wood. Bomber stepped through the hole. followed by the other three. Armalite sat on the floor looking dazed. His helmet was off to one side the protective visor split in the middle.

"Upstairs, go." The three charged through the house and up the stairs while Bomber dragged Armalite to his feet.

"You crazy twat, you could have broken your neck."

"Seemed like a good idea at the time, boss, not so sure now."

Shouts of "clear" came down to Bomber. Telling Armalite to watch the ground floor, he took the stairs two at a time. Entering the room, he saw the same set up as before, missing pane of glass, a table with two small sand bags. One thing was different this time, blood and lots of it.

"Look here, boss," it was one of the new boys, a stocky lad of nineteen called Harris, who the lads called 'Arry'. Bomber looked at where he was pointing. On the wall was blood and bits of bone. On the floor were drag marks in the blood as if someone had pulled a body from the room. Bomber had seen marks like that before.

Well done, Zika, thought Bomber.

"Boss, we need to get out of here!" shouted Armalite. Bomber could now hear the baying mob. *Time to go and fast,* thought Bomber as they sprinted down the road like racing greyhounds.

Back at the pig was the company commander, the MO and several others all gathered round the figure of the CQMS who was sitting with his back against the wheel of the truck.

A tickle of blood was being wiped away by the MO. "You are okay, very lucky, half an inch more, you would be dead." The MO was smiling, looking at the CQMS beret and cap badge. His finger poked through a hole in the beret where the cap badge dangled, cut in two.

Apart from the cut caused by the impact of the bullet passing through the cap badge, he was un-hurt. Meanwhile, another band went by playing 'It was Orange'. "Better make that your lucky song CQMS," the MO said, laughing.

Jones called out, "Trouble coming, big mob." As he said it, the first rocks clanged against the pig.

"Rubber bullets and plenty of them, Cpl Jones, they must not get through," ordered the company commander.

The bullets went down and the mob drew back and after a half hour, disappeared completely.

Bomber and everyone in the platoon were exhausted. They were into the second day without relief on the street. The rioting had been going on more or less without a break since the shooting. Their job was containment, keep them in the Ardoyne at all costs.

The CQMS had become a celebrity overnight. Someone must have thought it good public relations to let the press know. For several hours, they had newspaper reporters and the local TV people all over them. When it started to get dark, Bomber told them to turn off the camera lights as it was a target for another gunman. The TV people just laughed and carried on but they stopped and legged it fast when several shots were heard close by. Bomber knew the shots were at least two streets away towards the unit on their left, but it got the TV crew out of their way so they could concentrate on the job in hand.

The mob had left the streets, leaving the platoon alone. *Perhaps they considered us a bit too trigger happy*, Bomber thought as he spent his time walking between the four pigs of his platoon. He talked to everyone, ensuring they took turns resting and eating when the CQMS came by with his container meals. Bomber noted that he was now wearing a steel helmet the same as everyone else. *We all learn the hard way*, he thought, *if we survive that is.*

Bomber took the chance to have some rest. Sitting in the back of the platoon HQ pig, he closed his eyes and drifted into a light sleep.

He was woken by the noise; it hit him like a fist in the chest. The pig rocked gently on its suspension and he heard the radio squawking and Dusty answering. Looking at his watch, Bomber was surprised to see that he had been asleep for almost two hours.

"Boss, we are to be on the alert for two vehicles, a red ford escort with two men in and a white transit van," Dusty was shouting so that the others would hear.

"Okay, where was the bomb?"

"It was a car bomb near the Crumlin Road RUC Station, the red ford was the get-away vehicle. The white van was hijacked twenty minutes ago."

Bomber redeployed the lads so that both the Ardoyne and the road at their back could be covered in case the car was spotted. While he was doing it, the company commander arrived, accompanied by the CSM, his radio operator and a bodyguard.

"Good morning, C/Sgt." Bomber glanced at his watch; it was ten past twelve.

"Well, that was some bang, probably the biggest we have had yet. It will not be the last though the Int boys say PIRA are about to start a massive bombing campaign."

He stopped talking and looked over the snout of the pig and said something to Sgt Bush who chuckled. Turning back to Bomber, he spoke in a no-nonsense tone.

"The rioting's losing momentum, the rioters are exhausted; they cannot break out of their areas and we are determined to keep them penned in. Now they want to regroup and listen to whoever is controlling them. Whether it's IRA, PIRA or on the Prods side, the UVF." Pausing to let his words be digested, he then carried on in the same tone.

"PIRA, it would appear, are concentrating on bombings and shootings. Only using the youngsters to stage riots when they wanted the security forces distracted." He paused and looked round at the lads. "I know you boys are tired and we will be withdrawing soon for some rest and then back on the streets again, lots of patrols, ha."

Bomber wondered if the finishing of his sentence with 'ha' was there for effect, or was it a trait that officers developed with promotion. He'd known another that always said 'eh' at the end of sentences.

Chapter 8
Working the Streets, Belfast, 1970

Despite it being the middle of June, Bomber felt cold as he passed the burnt-out houses on Kashmir Street. Cupar Street, Bombay Street and others had all been attacked and burned out during the start of the trouble last year. These attacks caused many of the Catholic occupants to flee to other enclaves or even out of Belfast completely.

The night was dark and still; he paused and looked round at the two sections of his platoon patrolling with him. His drills of moving at night from shadow to shadow were paying off. Even from where he was standing, he found it difficult to see them. He had endured the criticism of the 2i/c for making the boys use cam cream on their faces and for using new drills to leave and enter the gateway of Flax Street Mill. The 2i/c had openly accused Bomber of escalating the situation by doing this.

After some discussion, the company commander had sided with Bomber. Another notch in the 2i/c stick to remember when the chance came to beat Bomber with it. Bomber sighed at the thought then said to himself, *What the hell?* The smell of the burnt-out houses made him grimace.

The shells of the houses made good cover for gunmen but were also providing a new playground for youngsters on the street so care in reacting to anyone there was needed.

They moved quietly along the street moving in pairs; near the end of the street, Cpl Jacobs signalled a halt and Bomber went forward.

"What's happening?" Bomber asked quietly.

"Listen, boss."

Bomber cocked his head opened his mouth and waited. Then he heard it, a groaning sound followed by weeping and someone saying, "Oh God, oh God".

Cpl Jacobs pointed towards an alleyway between the last two houses. Bomber and Jacobs moved forward, stopping and listening for any sign of an ambush. Bomber stared into the shadows, huddled against the wall was a figure gently rocking from side to side.

Positioning men either side of the alleyway, Bomber turned on his torch. The figure just carried on rocking in the light. Bomber reached down and touched his shoulder; it was a young man. His scream made Bomber jump back and some of the boys cocked their weapons expecting an attack. In the light of his torch, Bomber could see the man's trousers were soaked in blood. Shining his torch onto his face, he could see that he was about seventeen to nineteen years of age. His eyes were wide and staring, and now he was pleading, "No, no please."

Bomber told Dusty to call for back up and an ambulance. Placing his rifle on the floor, he sat next to the man and put his arm round his shoulder; he could smell the mix of blood and urine on the man's clothing. The man rested his head on Bomber's flax vest and sobbed.

"It's okay, we won't let anyone hurt you now. There's an ambulance coming and people to protect you." Bomber wanted to make the man feel safe and talk to him. Not that he expected someone who had just had both kneecaps drilled through with an electric drill would feel like having a chat.

"Who did this to you? I can find the bastards and kill them for you." Bomber immediately regretted the last part of the sentence. The man had stiffened at his words and Bomber thought he had lost any trust he might have gained.

"They did it because I play football with my cousin." Bomber was taken by surprise but gathered his thoughts.

"Why would they do that?"

"He's in the RUC, one of the few Catholics. They think I am telling him what's going on and who is doing it."

Bomber thought he would try again. "Did you recognise those that did this?"

He shook his head, "They put a hood over my head, but…" his voice trailed off and his body shook.

Shit, he is already in shock hope we are not in danger of losing him due to loss of blood and shock.

Bomber pressed him. "But what? What did you think?"

The shuddering stopped, "I recognised the voice of one of them, he used the drill on me. Before they hooded me, I saw the ring on his left middle finger, a silver skull." He stopped talking and cried softly.

"What's his name; you know it, just tell me?"

Bomber had to put his ear close to the man's mouth to hear. "Denny, Denny Murphy."

The backup squad arrived in a pig with an armoured ambulance driven by the regiment's medical Sgt, a tall, calm man by the name of Mike Smith. He quickly loaded the boy in and drove away at high speed.

Back in the mill, Bomber and Cpl Jacobs sat in the debriefing room but it was not the ops officer doing the debriefing but a six-foot tough-looking guy in civvies. He had long hair and a slightly superior air about him. Sitting in the corner was an older man also in civvies. He looked like the boss, dressed in a charcoal grey pinstriped suit that had cigarette ash down the front, more of which kept falling from the cigarette in his mouth. He never said a word but just stared at Bomber, squinting through the smoke. *Keep this up,* thought Bomber, *and I'm going to ask what the fuck's going on.* The company commander was sitting next to 'Fag Ash' as Bomber had named him in his mind.

Long Hair had been repeating questions to them but not listening to the answers. "So you say you found him in the alleyway, did you?" For the tenth time, the tone was sarcastic.

"Yes," Bomber replied wearily.

"Well, it may surprise you that we know he was in another part of town when he was snatched, how do you explain that?"

What the fuck is this clown on about? thought Bomber. *Something's going on here, stay cool.*

Jacobs was shifting uncomfortably next to Bomber and suddenly blurted out, "We found him where we found him; anyway, who the fuck are you?"

Long Hair stopped in surprise, then stepped towards Jacobs and snarled, "You will fucking well answer my questions and you won't be leaving this room until you do." Before he could take another step towards Jacobs, Bomber stood up and stepped between them, his hand, out of habit, gripping the six-inch length of cold steel he kept hidden in the right leg pocket of his combat trousers, half sliding it out with practiced ease. Long Hair stopped dead.

Bomber had felt the anger rising and now he didn't give a shit. He wasn't going to let someone from outside of the regiment treat them like dirt as if they were the guilty party.

In a steady but menacing voice, Bomber spoke, "I don't know who you are as you have not introduced yourself, but one thing you don't do and that's threaten my Cpl for doing his job. I've already guessed your agenda and you take one more step towards me, sunshine, and I will show you something they didn't teach you in Ashford." Bomber now had the blade almost out at his side, out of sight of the company commander and Fag Ash. Long Hair could see the knife and his eyes were wide.

"You wouldn't dare," he hissed, but his eyes told a different story and Bomber knew he had him.

Before Bomber could do or say anything, the company commander stood up and said, "That's enough." His voice was stern and held a threat that Long Hair noted. He dropped his gaze from Bomber and walked out of the room.

Bomber carefully slide the blade back into the sheath concealed in the trouser map pocket without the commander seeing it, then stepped back and sat down.

"Cpl Jacobs, that will be all, go and get something to eat in the cookhouse," ordered the Commander.

Jacobs stood up saluted, glanced at Bomber and left.

"What the hell do you think you are playing at C/Sgt?" The company commander was angry and Bomber knew it but he was also angry and realised he would have used the knife on Long Hair had he pushed it.

"That temper of yours will be the death of you."

Sitting behind the commander, Fag Ash was smiling. This annoyed Bomber even more.

"Well, sir, I resent being accused of something by some jumped-up Int prat, who is trying to protect a source no matter how bad he is or who he hurts and if I can see through it, then so can everyone else."

Before the commander could speak, Fag Ash laughed, then he spoke. His voice was gravelly from too much smoking. "You said he was good, Christopher, and you did advise me against this method."

Bomber felt angry now but spoke out quickly to the commander, "Sir, with respect I think we should put our own men on guard at the hospital to look after the man we brought in."

"Why?"

"Yes, why, C/Sgt?" Fag Ash had stopped smiling.

"Because I think you would be happier if he was dead." The commander turned and looked at Fag Ash.

"No, as much as my young colleague thinks that is the best option to protect someone, I, sorry, the government, will not allow murder for any reason."

Bomber could not help himself and snorted.

"It's true, you have my word on it." Fag Ash stared directly at Bomber.

Bomber felt the anger subsiding in him slightly. Keeping his gaze, he replied, "If he dies, I will make trouble, sir."

"So will I," the commander joined in.

Fag Ash nodded saying, "Quite right too," stood and left the room.

The company commander waited until the door closed, then turned to Bomber.

"Don't ever do anything like that again, C/Sgt, or it will be me busting you down the ranks."

Bomber nodded and said, "Yes, sir, I'm sorry but—"

"No buts, this is serious, now tell me what you didn't tell them." Bomber gave him the description and the name.

"Sit down." Bomber sat and listened.

"Well, we can't have IRA torturers going round doing that sort of thing protected by so-called Int necessity. Not on my patch anyway. So this is what we will do, I will get the address of this Murphy character without going through the normal sources. Then you and your rough necks will create an incident there and nab him. How's that, ha."

"Good, sir, I like it. However, won't they release him once they get wind we have arrested him?"

"Leave that to me, ha, now the games afoot, come on, C/Sgt, cheer up; they can only court martial us, ha." The commander was smiling as if it was some great prank.

Shit, I thought it was me that was crazy, now I know the company commander is totally bonkers as well.

Bomber left the briefing room and went out into the courtyard, where the vehicles were parked, to get some fresh air to clear his head. He smelt the cigarette smoke and turned to the source. Fag Ash was standing in the shadows, puffing away.

"C/Sgt, there you are!" As he spoke, he pushed something into Bomber's hand and spoke quietly into his ear. Bomber could smell the stale tobacco breath as the words were spoken, "If you ever want something more rewarding to do, give me a call any time."

Then he was gone sliding into the backseat of a powerful-looking black car that had the interior lights turned off.

As it pulled away, he saw Long Hair looking at him from the front passenger seat. It was one of pure hate.

In the privacy of his bunk, Bomber looked at the crumpled card in his hand. It simply said in small black print 'Brigadier (Retd) J. A. Rogers CBE' and a phone number, nothing else.

Now what the hell is a retired brigadier doing here in Northern Ireland? Bloody sneaky beakies never straight forward, always using people and never giving a shit.

Bomber was met in the platoon room by Sgt Bush, Cpl Jacobs and Armalite. Thorny spoke quietly, "Jacobs has briefed us, what do you want doing?"

Bomber looked round the room. Most of the lads were sitting on their beds, cleaning weapons. Some reading, others had their eyes closed as if asleep but Bomber could tell they were waiting to hear more.

"Let's go outside." They followed Bomber to the door where Armalite took over, opening the door and checking the yard was clear before they went out.

Armalite stood in one of the corners where he could see all three entrances to the yard. *He's taking things very seriously*, thought Bomber. Then he understood when Jacobs told him that when he left the room, he had loitered in the shadows and listened to Long Hair speaking to Fag Ash in the yard.

"I quote," said Jacobs, "I'm going to have that cocky bastard's balls."

"What did Fag Ash say?"

"He laughed, then said, he (Long Hair) had fucked up and was to get in the car."

Bomber stood silent for a moment. "We need to lift this bastard, Murphy, but we need an excuse to make it look like it's unrelated to this incident."

"Do we know where he hangs out?"

"No, but the company commander is looking into it. Once he tells me where and when, we will do it. Now I don't want stories going around and word leaking out, so make sure everyone keeps stum."

Chapter 9
The Lift, June 1970

It had not taken the commander long to find out where Murphy spent his time. A dingy drinking den in the Ardoyne was his favourite hangout, but it was decided to hit him at his house two streets away when he wasn't surrounded by a bunch of drunken IRA have-agos.

Bomber had split the platoon into two groups. Thorny would take one half to the rear of the house and secure all the exits. Once he was in position, Bomber would lead the others up the street.

"It's Brown Dog from the sarge, boss," said Dusty quietly to Bomber who nodded a response to the code word that they were in position.

Bomber was watching the street for anything out of the ordinary. Two kids stood a short distance from the target house, dickers keeping watch for Murphy. *So he must be in,* thought Bomber, *the commander was right.*

"Okay, Dusty, call it in."

"Zero, this is one zero, contact, Herbert Street shots fired in pursuit."

"Go," said Bomber and the lad took off down the street eager for action. The two dickers took off, one shouting the other blowing a whistle. Two of the platoon crashed the front door of Murphy's house. Jacobs was leading the house-clearing group, shouts of "room clear" came back to Bomber.

Entering the house, he noticed it was typical of most in the Ardoyne. A sitting room at the front, another room at the back with a kitchen set at a right angle to that. The kitchen opened onto a small yard that had seen better days.

As Bomber entered the rear room, he could see through the window. Thorny and his lads were marching three men back into the house at the point of their rifles.

Armalite grabbed each one as they came in, pushing them face first against the wall. "They have been searched, nothing on them, going for the back alley when we nabbed them." Thorny looked pleased.

"Okay, make sure the perimeter is secured, rent a crowd will be along soon." Thorny nodded and went back out.

Bomber picked out Murphy from the photograph supplied by the ops officer. He was about five foot six and very stocky. Long, dirty brown hair hung almost to his shoulders and Bomber thought he needed a good bath and some fresh clothes. Up close, he could smell the body odour of someone who had not bathed or changed his clothes for days.

The silence must have got to Murphy as he opened his mouth, "What the fuck?"

That was as far as he got; Armalite pushed him hard between the shoulder blades so that his chest and face slammed into the wall. "No talking!" Armalite screamed into his ear.

The other two flinched and faced front. Bomber quietly leafed through his book of known IRA and PIRA members or associates. There! He poked the book with his finger; he had them side-by-side, brothers Sean and Patrick Kelly. "I bet they were the two with Murphy when he drilled the lad's kneecaps," he muttered to himself.

The HQ section was calmly and methodically searching the kitchen. Miller called, "Boss, come look at this."

Bomber went into the kitchen and looked at the floor where Miller was pointing. Two faint grooves could just be seen in the lino. "Looks as if the fridge gets pulled out now and again, boss."

Bomber nodded. "Okay, let's pull it out and see what's there."

It came out easy enough. The lino it was standing on had been cut so it could be lifted back like a flap. Miller peeled it back revealing a twelve-by-twelve-inch square of concrete that had a small metal bar set in the middle but flush so that a hook was needed to lift it. Dusty was checking the cutlery drawer and found a butcher's S hook. Fitting it in, he lifted the concrete square up. Beneath was a neatly cut hole about nine inches deep. In the hole were two small bundles. Lifting them out and opening the bundle, Miller found two semi-automatic pistols, each with a fully loaded magazine.

Bomber put his gloves on and picked up one of the pistols. Going outside into the scruffy garden, he walked to the rain butt standing against the wall. Pushing the lid off, he could see it was three quarters full. Cocking the pistol, Bomber put the barrel into the water and fired twice. The sound was muffled completely by the water. Turning to Miller, he instructed him to retrieve the empty cases and spent bullets.

Returning to the room, he unloaded the pistol, then he pulled Murphy's right hand behind his back and wrapped his fingers around the gun butt.

"What the fuck are you doing, you English cunt?" He shut up when Armalite slammed him back into the wall.

"No talking!" It was clear to the three men that Armalite was not to be messed with.

Thorny came in and beckoned Bomber. "Rent a crowd are closing in and the pigs are here, boss."

Jacobs came down from upstairs. "Nothing up there, boss."

"Okay, let's cuff these three and get out of here."

They drove out through a volley of rocks and curses back into the mill.

The rest of the company spent the night containing a mini riot centred on Herbert Street.

In the mill, the RUC Special Branch was waiting and quickly took charge of the prisoners who looked sullen and pathetic now that they were stripped of the protection of the mob.

Bomber handed over the two pistols and the spent cartridge cases. The bullet heads he kept in his pocket. He gave a statement to a uniformed RUC man, sticking to the part that was true and leaving out anything planned before the lift.

The RUC man smiled as he went saying, "We've been after these three for some time; we think they were responsible for several shootings, including an off-duty colleague of ours."

That cheered Bomber a little but not enough to make him feel better about the subterfuge they had to use to get the murdering scum off the street.

Later, the company commander sent for him. "Good job, well done, the pistols were an excellent addition to the three wanted men, ha."

"Yes sir, any come back from the man yet?"

"The man, as you call him, phoned me about two minutes after you hit the house to congratulate me. Took me back a bit I can say, the old bugger is sharp, misses nothing and has a lot of influence."

"So he guessed we would follow up, strange he's not pissed off that we got his inside man." said Bomber.

"It's my opinion that Murphy had become a liability and was double dealing. So we were just a convenient tool to get rid of him. said the commander." He continued, "Now I'm standing your platoon down so get some rest but be ready in case we need you back out on the street."

Bomber lay on his bed exhausted but sleep eluded him. A little voice in the back of his head kept saying, *You'll be sorry you didn't kill him.*

Bomber began wishing the banging would stop but it didn't. Slowly, he came to and realised it was someone knocking on his door. "Okay, okay I'm awake, what is it?"

"Company commander's O group in fifteen minutes, boss, and I got a mug of tea here for you."

It was Dusty. Bomber took the tea from him, "What time is it?"

"O five fifteen, boss, drivers are getting all the pigs sorted and Sgt Bush has the platoon getting ready."

"Thanks for the tea." Bomber closed the door and quickly pulled on his trousers and boots. A quick swill and shave, fresh shirt and combat jacket and he was at the briefing room still drinking his now cold tea with a minute to spare.

The company commander strode into the room, followed by the 2i/c and ops officer. He looked over his assembled platoon commanders and Sgts. Then he started, "Yesterday, the Nationalist MP Bernadette Devlin was arrested for her part in inciting riots. This has sparked heavy rioting in Londonderry and it's now spread to Belfast. A short while ago, loyalist and republican gunmen had a shootout. So far the death toll is seven. We are to get out on the streets and put a stop to it spreading to our area. The earlier riot in the Falls (Catholic area) has petered out but it's more likely to be replaced with gunmen. Then later, I expect the rioters to start again so load the pigs with full riot gear. Now we will deploy as follows."

Thirty minutes later, Bomber had his sections spread out from the junction of the Crumlin Road, Brompton Park Junction to the Ardoyne Road, Estoril Park Junction. It was a long perimeter for his thirty men to police.

Bomber stood with Thorny, discussing what other precaution they could take to improve the platoon position. Each section had the ability to put a road block on as well as block the side streets leading into the Ardoyne. To the south of them, it was all Prods and this extended to the east and part of the west of the Ardoyne but the north side was mostly Caths. So unless the north was blocked off by the security force, it was easy for rent a mob to be reinforced by outsiders.

Bomber looked at his watch; it was just coming up to eight o'clock and people were beginning to go to work. He knew that this was a good time to start a riot so that the routine of life was disrupted to the maximum.

That was when it happened, a huge explosion came from the direction of the town centre. The sound had hardly died when a second ripped the air. Bomber turned as the cheering started in the Ardoyne. People were banging pots and pans and shouting; the noise increased when shots rang out.

Bomber looked in the back of the pig at Dusty, who was fielding the incoming calls from each section. Thorny took over the other radio that linked them to company HQ, who were asking for a report. Cpl Jones had reported shots fired at them but no casualties and no fire returned. Cpl Jacobs was under attack from rent a mob, who were throwing stones and petrol bombs. Cpl Mills was getting the same treatment.

Thorny turned to Bomber and said, "From HQ, it's lockdown, no one in or out."

Great, thought Bomber, *sit and take it again, time we were more proactive.*

Bomber stood with Cpl Jones, looking first down Brompton Park and then along Balholm Drive. It was clear that Jones had a difficult junction to control and needed more manpower. Using the radio, he had one man from each of the other sections, including the platoon HQ, sent to reinforce him.

"I can see why you are a target for the shooters. We need to get our own man in a position to counter the gunmen."

Jones agreed, saying, "If we could get L/Cpl Zika in that burnt-out house," jerking his head in the direction of a terraced house slightly behind and to the right of them, "he could cover both streets."

It was an ideal sniper position. The roof had partly collapsed and Bomber liked the idea.

"Okay, let's do it but I don't want anyone seeing him go in and I will send Parker to you. He will go in with Zika and cover his back in case anyone gets wind of Zika being there and decides to sneak in the back way to take him out."

Watching Jones organise the deployment of Zika into the house, Bomber was beginning to change his opinion of Cpl Jones.

Jones had put Zika and Parker in the back of the pig, then backed it up to the house. When it was against the open doorway, the two slipped into the building. Jones continued to make a show of re-positioning the pig, pretending to admonish the driver for getting it wrong, just in case they were being closely watched.

Before Parker had got into the pig, he had told Bomber that Thorny was a bit concerned that with sending two men to assist Cpl Jones, with Bomber and Armalite away, he was down to just himself, Spencer and the driver to cover their street.

Bomber and Armalite made their way back to Thorny who looked relieved to see them.

"Getting a bit worried here, boss, just three against 'Rent a Mob'." He indicated to the end of the street.

Bomber looked at where Thorny was pointing. About twenty youths were making a show of taunting the soldiers and throwing rocks in their direction but were hopelessly out of range.

Bomber wondered if the mob had realised that they were under-manned here or were they trying to distract them from something else?

Pity I have not got a burnt-out house and another Zika to use, thought Bomber. Looking at the houses behind him, he wondered. "I won't be a minute, Sgt." With that, Bomber walked across the green line to one of the Prod houses and knocked on the door.

After a few moments, the door opened and Bomber found himself looking at a man with a shock of white hair, who was as wide as he was tall but none of it was fat.

"Yes, son, what can I do for yer?" He spoke slowly and deliberately, then listened intently to what Bomber said.

A few minutes later, Bomber and Armalite stood in the front bedroom which looked straight in to the Ardoyne. They could see over the top of their pig and a long way down the street.

"Now you may wish to use this, lads," said the man, who explained that he had served in the Royal Engineers for six years before being medically discharged with a bad back. The man knelt down to where an air vent was in the bedroom wall. With a deft movement, he removed the grill and the bricks to one side.

Lying down, Bomber could see clearly in to the street and much more. "Okay, Armalite, this is your position. I'll have Dusty bring you an A40 radio and you will be able to report directly to me anything you see, no matter how mundane it might seem. Also I know you are a good shot. Any gunmen are yours to engage."

Armalite looked pleased with the opportunity to be proactive and stretched out his long frame behind the hole.

"I prepared that when the troubles first started," the man said. "Got me a .22 hunting rifle all licensed. Not letting any bastard burn me out, that's for sure," he told Bomber as they descended the stairs.

Bomber thanked him and he replied, "No problem, L/Cpl Paddy McNee Royal Engineers retired is at your service." As he closed the front door, Bomber could hear him shouting up the stairs, "I'll bring you a cuppa and some biscuits in a minute lad."

Seems like Armalite is going to be spoilt, better not tell the lads or they will give him some stick later.

Back at the pig, 'Rent a Mob' had become a little bolder and the rocks were now bouncing off the road and clanging against the armoured sides of the vehicle. Having sent Dusty to give the radio to Armalite, with strict instructions not to stop for a cuppa, Thorny had to man both radios.

That just left Blackman, the driver, Taylor (Tinker) and himself to try and give the impression of eight men behind the pig.

Thorny called Bomber, "Armalite reports that the mob are getting petrol bombs handed out by two guys with ski masks on."

Bomber acknowledged and reached for the spare baton gun, of which they had two. They now had the new baton rounds to fire which replaced the soft rubber ones. These were much more effective, being make of some sort of hard plastic but restrictions on their use had been ordered. They were to be fired into the ground in front of the rioters so the round skidded into the legs and not the body.

A breathless Dusty re-joined them, telling Bomber that others were now joining the mob at the end of the street, before jumping in the pig to take over the radios from Thorny.

Now the rocks were landing all around them making it difficult to poke a head around the pig to fire the baton gun, which was the mob's aim to allow the petrol bombers to get close enough to throw.

Taylor had the other baton gun and Bomber told him on the count of three, they would expose themselves and fire. "Ready, one, two, three," they swivelled round opposite sides of the pig and fired. Shouts of pain reached their ears while they reloaded and fired again this time the rounds did more damage. Skidding off the hard road surface they ricocheted into the legs of the rioters hitting several and doing some real damage.

Having reloaded again, Bomber risked taking a long look. Most of the rioters were withdrawing, some helping those that were limping. Two fires were burning in the street where petrol bombs had been dropped. Near one of the fires, a figure lay still and Bomber thought he could see blood spreading on the pavement.

It was fifty yards to the figure and Bomber knew they had just one chance to recover the body before Rent a Mob regrouped. Dusty had already sent a report and asked for an ambulance. Bomber called Thorny, "Tell Armalite to cover us, then you cover us from here as well. Myself, Taylor and Blackman will go and recover the body."

Once they were ready, Bomber called "Go!" and they dashed out sprinting the fifty yards to the figure. The fire had reached the figure's hand which was beginning to burn. Grabbing an arm each, Bomber and Taylor dragged the dead weight back to the pig, Blackman following with his SMG (sub-machine gun) pointing towards the mob that was reforming.

Now they had a chance to see who they had dragged in. The boy looked about fifteen years old. Dressed in jeans, trainers, T-shirt and a zip jacket, he had a fist-sized hole in his chest from which blood leaked in large quantities. "No pulse, boss," said Taylor who had his fingers on the boy's neck.

Turning the boy over, Bomber found the hole in the back of the jacket and in the back of the body. "Thorny, check Armalite didn't fire any shots." He knew no one at the pig had, so who shot the boy and why?

The ambulance arrived with Sgt Mike Smith driving. He pulled up with a screech and the armoured ambulance back doors swung open. Two medics jumped out with a stretcher. The medics quickly placed the body on the stretcher and back into the ambulance without any ceremony. Bomber spoke to Mike. "Christ almighty, you didn't even check to confirm he was dead. What's the hurry?"

"Firstly, you said he was dead and secondly it's kicking off everywhere, we have two more casualties to pick up and one of them is one of our boys." Then with a tyre burning turn, the ambulance disappeared the way it had come.

Dusty stuck his head out of the pig's rear doors, "Armalite reports he has not fired any shots, boss."

Now, thought Bomber, *let's try and find out how this kid came to be shot and left on the street.*

Bomber sat in the bedroom with Armalite and Paddy looking down the street. Bomber asked Armalite what he saw.

Armalite paused for a moment then spoke in a clear voice, "I was concentrating on the two men at the far end of the street wearing ski masks. Two other guys were at the corner talking and pointing. Paddy here was watching as well and taking photographs."

"Photographs?"

"With this, son," and Paddy lifted up an old Olympus SLR camera with the biggest telephoto lens Bomber had ever seen.

"I use it for my bird watching but since the troubles, I take photographs of any riots and pass them to my brother in the RUC."

"Would you let me have the film to get it developed?" Bomber asked hopefully.

"I can do better than that, son, I have my own dark room under the stairs. I'll go and develop them now."

"Give me a call on the radio when he has done them and I'll come back." Armalite acknowledged and Bomber went back to the pig.

Thorny updated Bomber on the radio traffic.

"It's kicking off big time in the Falls, gunfights everywhere. IRA, PIRA and the UVF with the army in the middle. There are three cars we are to watch for, believed to be carrying gunmen." Thorny passed a page from a field note book with the car descriptions and numbers.

"Boss, Armalite says they are up to something. He thinks they have corrugated iron shields."

Bomber peered over the snout of the pig; the mob had split into two groups and were edging their way along both sides of the street. At the front of each group, they held two corrugated iron sheets.

"They must have bolted on handles to hold them as shields, see the way they are keeping them only an inch or two off the ground so we can't skid the baton rounds under them." Bomber nodded his agreement to Tinker's observation.

"Sgt, tell Cpl Miller and Jacobs to send one man with a baton gun to us on the double."

"Okay, when the others get here, this is what we will do and you will brief whoever arrives with the extra baton guns."

Fucking hell hope this works or we will end up having to use live rounds, thought Bomber.

Now the mob's rock throwers were in range and the missiles clanged against the pig like giant hailstones. Jinks from Cpl Jacobs and Green from Cpl Miller's section turned up and Bomber put one each side with Tinker and Thorny, who had decided he wanted in on the fight.

With no response from the soldiers, the mob started to push forward more boldly and a couple of petrol bombs flew towards them landing just short of the pig.

"Now's the time, 'Fire!'" shouted Bomber. Four baton rounds roared out and hit the corrugated iron shields smack in the middle where Bomber guessed the handles would be.

Without being told, they kept up pumping baton rounds into the shields. The force of the impact of the rounds on the handle area of the shields would be finger and arm breaking. Suddenly, the shields were dropped and the baton guns now fired into the exposed flanks of the mob, the hard plastic rounds bouncing off the tarmac and hitting legs with a force great enough to break them.

Screams of pain were now coming from the mob instead of the jeering and shouts of "Kill the bastards". Several petrol bombs had been dropped, the glass shattered and the fuel ran into the gutter and ignited. It reminded Bomber of a painting he had once seen but at that moment could not remember what it was called or where he had seen it.

Just as the last of the mob disappeared out of sight, a figure stepped out from a doorway. He had obviously been watching too many westerns. He wore a ski mask and stood with his legs apart in clear sight of all. At his hip, he had some sort of sub-machine gun. After what seemed an age but could not have been more than a second or two, he fired. A long burst, rounds pinged against the armour of the pig. Then he died a pointless and needless death as a 7.62 round tore through his chest, ripping muscle, shattering bone and blowing his heart apart. Armalite had done his job as the dealer of death perfectly.

After a quick discussion with Thorny, they decided the body and weapon was too far away to risk retrieving with the few men they had available. Getting cut off too far into the Ardoyne was not an option, especially as there were not any spare troops to get them out.

After a few moments, a priest appeared from a doorway on the opposite side of the street, waving a handkerchief. He walked uncertainly at first towards the pig, still waving the white cloth. As no one fired at him, he stepped out firmly. When he got within ten yards of the pig, Bomber stepped out from the side and said, "What do you want, Father?"

"I'm Father Dooley and I would like to collect the body there with some help if you promise not to shoot."

Bomber thought quickly, *The body no problem. They would bury him and then we will find out who he was but the weapon, that's another thing.*

"I agree on one condition, Father, and that is you go and get the weapon and bring it to me, then you can recover that poor soul."

The priest looked at Bomber for a second then nodded an agreement, saying, "I have your word?"

"You have my solemn word as God is my witness, Father."

The priest nodded and turned, walking quickly back to the body.

Suddenly, Bomber had a mental panic and shouted at Dusty, "Quick tell Armalite not to shoot, he's a priest."

Dusty relayed the message and called back, "It's okay, boss."

Bomber watched the priest pick up the weapon; he held it by its metal butt with the muzzle pointing to the ground. As he started to walk back, shouts rang out. When Father Dooley ignored the shouts, several rocks were thrown at him, luckily none connecting. The door that he had originally came out of suddenly opened and several women came out looking in the direction of the rock throwers. They waved their arms and shouted what sounded like, "You fucking wee bastards, throw any more stones at Father Dooley and we'll give you hell."

Father Dooley arrived looking a little ashen and shaky. Bomber realised then he was much older than he first thought. He held out the gun to Bomber who took it. "I'm sorry, Father, I seem to have got you in trouble. Please be careful when you go back."

"I'll be all right; most are too scared of their mothers to do me any harm but there is an element that have no respect for the church or its servants."

"Rather him than me," muttered Thorny to Bomber as Father Dooley strode back to where the women and two men were now rolling the body into a blanket.

"Braver than your average Bible thumper, now let's look at this little toy."

It turned out to be an American made SMG, sometimes called a grease gun because of its similarity to an actual tool for greasing heavy vehicles. A Second World War weapon but it was still very useful for street fighting.

Dusty stuck his head out of the vehicle saying, "Armalite says the photographs are ready."

Thorny gave Bomber a look of 'holiday snaps?' Then Bomber realised that he had not told him what was going on.

Paddy opened the door and ushered Bomber into the kitchen. Spread on the kitchen table were a dozen large black and white photographs. Nine were put to one side and Paddy had three in the centre of the table. He was excited and jigging from one leg to the other, pulling Bomber closer to the table. "We got the murdering bastard, there's no doubt, there's no doubt."

Bomber looked at the photographs and he felt his body go cold. He could see the dead boy being held by the arms and forced along by two older boys. Right behind him was another figure that he could not see the face of on the first photo. The next one showed the boy pitching forward as if falling face first. Behind him, gun in hand, was the murderer. Bomber was beginning to hate this man more than he had ever hated anyone in his life.

The third photo showed the two who had been holding the boy and O'Halligan standing there with a half a smile on his face.

Bomber must have been grinding his teeth or something because the next thing he knew Paddy was shaking him by the arm and asking, "You all right, son."

Bomber force himself to concentrate, "Yes, can I have this set now and could you run me off another set?"

"Already done, plus I'm doing another set for my brother in the RUC. Now I think you should have a word with your boy upstairs."

Armalite was lying stretched out staring though the sniper hole. An empty mug and half a packet of custard creams sat to one side on the carpet.

Bomber lay down next to him and looked at the empty street. No rioters, no gunmen and no bodies.

"Good shot that, must have been two hundred yards in poor light, well done."

Armalite nodded but said nothing.

"First time?" Bomber asked gently.

"Yes, boss, and it was so easy. Killing him I mean."

"Yes, killing is easy; it's living with it that's hard. Sometimes we have to do it because it's our duty to protect others and ourselves, but we don't have to enjoy it."

"No boss."

"Okay, keep watching I'm going to get someone to relieve you soon; you did the right thing and you did it well."

As he walked back to the pig, the little voice in the back of his head kept repeating, *It's so easy to kill.*

Bomber sat in the pig, studying the face of O'Halligan with the half smile and the gun in his hand. This bastard enjoyed killing the boy while the other two held him. Why do it on the street though? Was it a statement of some sort? Was the boy an informer? Was he trying to make it look like the army shot the lad?

Thorny stuck his head into the pig, "Commanders coming this way with the 2i/c and CSM. There are others with him, don't recognise them."

Bomber got out of the vehicle and met the company commander with a salute. "What the hell is going on, C/Sgt? Everyone's screaming blue murder that you are opening fire at young, unarmed boys?"

"Not us, sir, he was murdered by O'Halligan right on the street there. Shot in the back while being held by two others."

"You expect us to believe that. Well, I don't," it was the 2i/c who had stepped out from behind the commander.

"I think he should be arrested now and got off the streets," said a familiar voice. At first Bomber did not recognise Long Hair. He was in combat dress and his hair was stuffed up under a steel helmet. He had lieutenant pips on his shoulder. Bomber could see both the 2i/c and Long Hair exchange a look that indicated they were in this together.

"I have proof he did it."

"Oh, yes, all your lads going to swear it was not you, are they?" Long Hair was beginning to enjoy himself.

"Well, no, sir" Bomber made the 'sir' sound almost like an insult. "I have photographs of the lad being held and O'Halligan shooting him."

Long Hair gaped for a second, "Give them to me now; they are Int property and I want to know who took them?" Long Hair's voice had gone up a few octaves and he looked shocked and then a little scared at the sound of the panic in his own voice.

The 2i/c had stepped back as if trying to distance himself from Long Hair.

"No, I don't think I will give you the photographs or tell you who took them as I will need them for my defence at the court martial."

"No one is being arrested and no one is being court martialled. Please show me the photographs, C/Sgt." The company commander turned to Long Hair and the 2i/c and said, "Stay here," in a tone that indicated he was not very pleased with them.

Bomber went to the back of the pig and the commander followed him.

"These are the ones of the rioters, which I have not had a chance to study yet, but these three show clearly what happened." Bomber handed them to the commander who studied them intently.

"You're right, it's clear it's O'Halligan shooting the boy, but why like this?"

"There could be a number of reasons, sir. Firstly, the boy could have been one of our informers. Secondly, they could use it to stir up the world press and locals and thirdly, as unlikely as it may sound, it could be something to do with Long Hair trying to get me screwed. It's clear he hates my guts and I think he has too many of the wrong sort of contacts in the Ardoyne."

"I concur to the first two notions but the third is a little far-fetched for me. However, I wouldn't put anything past that weasel." The commander suddenly realised what he said. "You didn't hear me say that. Now have you got a copy of these photographs?"

Bomber nodded.

"Good, keep them hidden, I will take these and get the ops officer to study them with the RUC liaison officer and don't tell anyone who took them. I need to report this to the commanding officer immediately to stop brigade calling for your head."

The commander strode off, and the 2i/c and Long Hair, who had been talking together, fell in behind him. The CSM and an RMP warrant officer lingered and then the RMP spoke to Bomber.

"I thought I was here to arrest you but thankfully not. Watch out for that sneaky beaky; my lads say he is trying to make a big name for himself and doesn't give a shit who he destroys to do it."

"Thanks for the warning."

The CSM put his hand on Bomber's shoulder and said, "Be careful, the 2i/c hates your guts as well." Bomber nodded. He didn't need telling and watched the two double after the company commander.

"Not nice, thank Christ you have the photographs," Thorny spoke quietly as if someone who shouldn't be was listening.

"Do the lads know what was said?"

"More or less, question is what are we, sorry, you going to do about it?"

"Make a phone call," said Bomber. "Send someone to relieve Armalite, will you, and find out when we will get to eat as soon as you can."

Later, back in the mill, Bomber did two things: he got a bottle of single malt whisky from the mess honesty bar and then phoned Fag Ash.

That night in the mill's darkened car park, Fag Ash's car pulled up and out stepped the brigadier.

Bomber could just hear Armalite and Thorny move in the darkest of shadows so they could cover the other two occupants of the car who had now got out.

"Well, C/Sgt, what's so urgent?"

Bomber outlined what had happened and asked directly, "Is this your doing?"

The brigadier took his time, lighting yet another cigarette. "Hood does not work for me anymore. He now belongs to a new intelligence unit, something called MRF (Military Reaction Force), which plays things very close to its chest, and is, it appears, answerable to no one." He paused and sucked deeply on the cancer stick.

"However, I do keep tabs on him and he is playing a very dangerous game for high stakes. The lad who was killed was one of mine. His father was shot by the IRA for standing up to them in early '69. The boy gave us a lot of useful information and Hood knew of him. I do believe he would try to frame you and now he has failed, he may well try a more direct approach through his PIRA contacts. Just petty revenge but then what can you expect from an egotistic megalomaniac?"

"So you are telling me that he will try and top me because of what? The standoff in the debriefing room?" asked Bomber.

"What you have to understand is that to people like Hood, this terrorist war is just a chance for rapid advancement. The people on either side are just tools. Dead or alive, man, woman or child makes no difference to him. Anyone who gets in his way is a threat."

"What about the good people who stand for law and order, can't they stop men like him?"

"Maybe, but the political will is not there at the moment. The politicians think this will be all over in a few months. I believe it will drag on for years, possibly decades, thanks to ignorance and centuries of bias education by schools and the church."

The brigadier paused and discarded the butt of his cigarette and lit a fresh one, inhaling deeply. As the smoke trickled out of his mouth he said, "I will find out what I can and let you know but this is strictly between us and I want a copy of the photographs." Bomber pulled a set from the inside of his jacket and handed them over.

The brigadier looked hard at Bomber and even in the darkness, he could feel the eyes searching, trying to reach into his mind. Finally, the brigadier spoke, "I want you to seriously consider coming to work for me, think about it."

Bomber nodded, his mind working overtime. He had a thousand questions but the brigadier was already heading back to his car. Suddenly, he stopped and turned saying to Bomber, "First chance you get, kill O'Halligan before he kills you." Then he was in the car and away.

Chapter 10
Paddy Bashing

Bomber had tucked the bottle of malt whisky into a spare ammunition pouch he had attached to his web belt. He intended to go via the back alley to Paddy McNee's house and give it to him as a thank you for his help.

The alley was dark, apart from the light coming from one or two kitchen windows. Using the shadows, they crept along. At the back of Paddy's house, Bomber found the gate unlocked and open. Bomber signalled Armalite to take the lead with Harris, the new boy. Bomber was pleased with Harris' progress, he never needed telling twice and moved fast when required.

Bomber followed, then stopped. Armalite was crouched down by the kitchen window where the curtains were drawn but he could see the light was on. Moving next to Armalite, Bomber could hear the noise of someone getting a beating.

Waving Harris forward, he gave the signal. Armalite hit the door, smashing it open and raced in, Bomber followed close on his heels with Harris at his shoulder. The scene that met them made Bomber's blood boil. He was ready to kill.

Paddy was tied to a kitchen chair, his face was bloody and he looked unconscious. Three men in their early twenties were in the room. One, standing in front of Paddy, had leather gloves on and his chest was heaving from the beating he had been dishing out. The other two stood with cans of beer in their hands and their mouths open in amazement.

Armalite smashed the beater to the ground with one swipe of his rifle butt. The other two dropped their cans and went to run for the lounge but Harris blocked them and they stopped and raised their hands, to little avail. Harris delivered a left and right with his rifle butt that was so fast, Bomber was not even sure that it had happened. Both men dropped to the floor, one tried to get up but Harris stamped hard on his right kneecap, bringing a scream of agony from him, which Harris silenced with another smack from his rifle butt.

Armalite was tending Paddy, talking to him while untying him. Bomber picked up a tea towel and soaked it in cold water at the sink and then wiped Paddy's face. Paddy opened his eyes and smiled. "I knew you would come, pretended I was out for the count to gain some time."

Paddy refused to allow an ambulance to be called but asked Bomber to call his brother in the RUC. Bomber agreed but wanted a bit of time to question the three men before he did so and Paddy agreed.

Bomber had Armalite and Harris pick up the beater, then tie him to the same chair. He was coming round and Bomber splashed water into his face to help him.

Bomber pulled up a chair and sat facing the beater, who had to tilt his head sideways to see Bomber as his left eye was swelling and closing fast from the smack Armalite had given him.

"You're a fucking dead man, soldier."

"Maybe," responded Bomber. "We all have to die some time, it's just the way we die that's important."

"What yer mean by that, you fucking cunt?" He spat as he finished the sentence and the spit ran down Bomber's combat jacket.

Bomber looked again at Paddy's smashed face and felt all the emotion and sense of fairness slip away to be replaced with a cold anger.

"It means that you can answer my questions honestly or I can inflict pain on you like you would not believe possible."

"Fuck off, you wouldn't dare; they would lock you up and throw away the key."

"No, I don't think anyone will care because when I have finished with you, I'll kill you and dump your bodies. Yes, I'll kill the other two monkeys, and no one will be the wiser."

"Shit," Harris said and lifted his foot away from a puddle of urine coming from the one he had stamped on. Both had their hands secured behind them and were sitting on the floor, eyes wide with fear.

"You should know," said Bomber, keeping his voice low but with menace in every word, "I was in the Middle East for a couple of years fighting rebel tribesmen. The federal troops who we worked with had a really good way of torturing captured rebels. They would heat up a knife and then insert it into the poor bloody prisoners in various places. Arm pits, soles of the feet, eyes and the penis. The heat as well as the cut caused incredible pain but stopped the bleeding at the same time."

Bomber stood up and turned a gas ring on and picked up one of Paddy's nasty-looking kitchen knives, placing it in the heat. "Of course they always finished by castrating the poor buggers."

The beater had gone pale and shook his head in disbelief. Turning his head first to Armalite, then Harris, he said, "You can't let him do this."

Armalite grabbed him by the hair and yanked his head back and snarling, said, "If he won't, I will, shithead."

Bomber was impressed, not sure if Armalite was either a very good actor or that he really meant what he was saying.

Bomber sat down again, holding the knife with the handle wrapped in a tea towel. Bomber held the knife close to the man's face and he struggled to wriggle back on the chair as he felt the searing heat of the red-hot blade.

"Okay, what the fuck do you want to know?" the words came out half strangled as he could feel the heat of the blade.

Bomber drew the knife back a little and nodded to Harris and said, "Take notes." Bomber looked the man in the eyes and the man looked down. Bomber grabbed his chin forcing his head up. "Don't look away, you shit, and if you lie, I'll know. Now let's start with your names."

Forty minutes later, Paddy's brother had arrived with three other RUC officers, one was an inspector. The commander, the CSM and Mike Smith, the medical Sgt were also there in response to Bomber's radio call so the little house was crowded.

Bomber briefed them all, leaving out the intimidation and threat of mutilation. The three toughs were already shouting that they had been tortured but the RUC inspector, having checked them over for injuries, was having none of it and had them dragged away to the waiting van.

Finally, everyone left and Mike and Armalite started fussing over Paddy like a mother hen with an injured chick, while Harris made the tea. Paddy protested, saying he was fine but it was clear he wasn't and Armalite was having none of his protests.

They sat and sipped the tea Harris had made and it was laced with a good slug of whisky.

Harris broke the silence. "Would you have done it, boss?" Bomber looked at Harris who dropped his gaze.

"No, and before you ask, I also draw the line at murder." *Such a bloody hypocrite,* the little voice in his head chanted.

Speaking through swollen and split lips, Paddy said, "That's good, son, because that's what separates us from the likes of them." The effort making him cough. "Need some more medicine." Armalite poured more whisky into his cup and Paddy nodded his thanks.

"The secret to good interrogation is actually not having to do anything more than make someone believe you will do what you say. Half the job was done for me because the three of them knew that their own side will do things like knee-capping and much worse. So the fear is there already."

"Did the federal troops really castrate the prisoners?" Armalite asked casually.

Shrugging his shoulders, Bomber said, "I have no idea, never actually worked with the useless buggers." This raised a chuckle all round.

They sat in silence and sipped the whisky-laced tea, then after a few moments, Bomber said, "Paddy, I am leaving Armalite, Harris and one other with you; are you happy to let them use the bedroom with the sniper hole?"

Paddy nodded and mumbled through his mashed lips, "Be glad of the company."

Back at the mill, Bomber sat in his bunk with the light off. He had to see the commander in half an hour and he needed to get his thoughts together. He knew he had gone beyond the limits of what was permissible but those toughs only respected one thing. Someone tougher and more ruthless than them. The bastards had been after any copies of the photographs and the negatives and wanted to know who knew about them. Paddy, bless him, gave them nothing but if they had had longer, Bomber knew they would have killed the old soldier.

So the questions were, who told them it was Paddy who took the photographs? Who sent them and why would they be so worried about them? True O'Halligan was shown as the killer of the boy but then he was already wanted for plenty of other terrorist activities. Someone had tipped them off about Paddy and Bomber had a prime suspect in mind.

There was a gentle knock on his door and the company clerk responded to his grunt that the company commander would see him now.

Bomber made his way to the briefing room. Inside, he was surprised to see Fag Ash, puffing away. The commander and CSM were all looking at the photographs.

"Ah, there you are, C/Sgt, come here to the table and tell me what you see." Two photographs were separated from the rest, a large magnifying glass lay beside them.

Picking up the glass, Bomber studied each one. They were similar, catching the group of rioters collecting petrol bombs from two men in ski masks. However, it was two figures by the corner talking that held his interest. One was clearly O'Halligan, the other in civilian clothes was familiar, the profile, something, then it clicked. *My God,* thought Bomber, *the bastard the absolute bastard!*

Bomber dropped the glass back on the table and looked first at Fag Ash who was studying him intensely. He gave nothing away; the commander tapped the table and said quietly, "Well, what do you think, ah?"

"I now know why the photographs are so important to someone, what I don't know is who tipped him off that Paddy took them, but I'm willing to give it a good guess, especially as he is not here."

"Quite, quite," the commander said a little irritably. "The 2i/c has been sent on leave; the CSM has taken over his duties. The main problem is Lt Hood and his involvement with O'Halligan?" He paused and looked at Fag Ash, who squinted back through the haze of smoke.

"Hood is out of my field of influence but I have done some checking and I can tell you that Hood and O'Halligan joined the army at the same time, attending the same training depot together. Hood got picked up and sent for officer training, O'Halligan came to your regiment. Hood, and I am sure it's him in the photograph, will claim he is infiltrating the PIRA but I think he is in deeper than that. He is half Irish on his mother's side, Dublin, so when he wants, he can put on a very good accent." said the brigadier.

He continued, "I can also confirm that O'Halligan and Hood took a holiday in Morocco not so long ago, travelling separately. It's believed they both travelled on from there to Libya to Gaddafi's new Islamic socialism. That's about all we know at the moment."

"Interesting but what are we going to do about Hood?" the commander sounded angry.

"Absolutely nothing. I have been told to lay off in no uncertain terms. Someone raided my office while I was out and took the photographs. It could be that he is playing a very deep game but if he is sacrificing our informants and even our soldiers to do this, then I will intervene."

"Yes, that's all very well but if he endangers my men…" The commander let the words hang, then went on, "They tried to take our photographs as well but I was having none of it. The captain in charge, if that's what he actually was, said he had the authority of the brigade commander. When I phoned brigade, they said they knew nothing about it. They beat a retreat then at high speed. I've given orders that they are not to be allowed into the mill again, ah."

The brigadier lit another cigarette, blew out a long stream of smoke and spoke quietly. "I think the best course of action is to stay under the radar. First job is you have to get O'Halligan but hand him over to the RUC Special Branch. Superintendent O'Neil is the man to call. I don't think Hood's nasty little organisation will prise him loose from O'Neil. Of course, that's if he is alive when you take him. Strikes me he will not want to be taken alive."

He didn't emphasise the words but the meaning was clear and he stared at Bomber as he said it. Bomber shifted uncomfortably as all three of them looked at him.

"Right, I have to be off; the brigade commander wants a chat, can't think what about." It was the first time Bomber had heard Fag Ash come anywhere near a joke.

When he had left, the CSM called the clerk to get some tea and biscuits sent in. The commander collected up the photographs and tucked them behind the large map of Belfast pinned to the wall.

The tea and chocolate biscuits arrived and the three of them sat at the table. Finally, the commander spoke, "I've discussed what you gleaned from the thugs you caught at Paddy's house and your idea for tracking down O'Halligan and indeed others. The CO has forbidden you setting yourself up as bait no matter how much faith you have in your lads keeping you safe. The covert ops, on the other hand, he likes very much."

He paused munching another biscuit and sipping his tea. "Now the covert ops will go in here, here and here," he said, pointing at the map. "Plus we will have two on top of the mill. Do you think your friend Paddy will continue to allow us to use his house?"

"Yes, I think he will, sir, but I will check."

"Good, that way we have covered lots of options and will be able to monitor those moving in and out. Still some gaps, but we will plug these with normal foot patrols. All coverts are to go in and out at night by back entrances to avoid detection. Except the ones on top of the mill which will carry on as normal."

"Who has cleared the other properties we are using, sir?"

"Why, our own local hero the CQMS! He knows most of the Prods in the area as he was born not a stone's throw from here and he can move around easily in civvies to do this." The commander studied the map for a moment as if he was looking for inspiration, then stood and said, "Right go and get some sleep; it's going to be a busy few days starting from tomorrow."

As Bomber left the briefing, the clerk called him, "Excuse me, C/Sgt, but the one in civvies that's always smoking asked me to give you this." Bomber took the package and nodded his thanks.

In his bunk, he pulled off the brown paper and opened the shoebox. Inside, wrapped in a cloth, was a semiautomatic pistol. Two mags and a box of ammunition containing fifty 9mm Corto rounds. There was a typed note which said, 'A little extra insurance. It's untraceable'.

Bomber handled the pistol and could see all numbers and marks had been erased. The pistol felt light and comfortable; he guessed the weight to be no more than one and a half pounds. It would be easy to conceal. Opening his first-aid kit, he took out the medical gloves and put them on. Taking the gun, he stripped it down, cleaned it then did the same to the two mags, which he then loaded each with seven bullets. They seemed small compared to those for the issue Browning pistol. Later, Bomber discovered that they equated to the British .38 rounds.

Taking the spare ammunition, he climbed up to where a steel roof support beam met the wall. Here, he removed a brick and slipped the ammunition in with the spare photographs, which Paddy had made for him. Going to his locker, he took out one of the three books in there, entitled 'Small Arms of the World'. He left the Bible and 'Battles of World War Two' neatly positioned so that they lay flat with the Bible on top.

Leafing through the book, he found what he was looking for, a match to his new pistol. It was an Italian Beretta 1934 issue. More than a million made for the Italian forces and copied by several other countries. It was considered a good and reliable hand gun.

The pistol he would keep close. Suddenly, a thought struck him. Was Fag Ash setting him up with the pistol? He already knew that Fag Ash would like him to kill O'Halligan but was it a set up? He would make sure that at no time would his finger prints be on the Beretta. Dismissing the idea of a setup, he lay fully clothed on his bunk and surrendered to sleep, a sleep that spun up the old dream that would not leave him alone.

Bomber awoke to the sounds of an explosion; it took him a minute or two to realise it came from the direction of the city centre. By the time he had showered and changed, he had counted three more. This wasn't a good start to the day for the people of Belfast.

The day was spent organising the details for the covert ops. On top of the one at Paddy's house, Bomber's platoon would be responsible for one other, two streets north of Paddy's house. The CQMS was to take them in and introduce them to the house owners. Bomber read the slim file on them. They had lived there since getting married thirty years ago. A middle-aged couple whose three children were grown up and working away from home. All were staunch Protestant's and were considered reliable.

The secret to a good covert op was to recognise anything out of the ordinary and to do this you needed continuity. So the teams were organised in groups of six but with only four in location. After three days, two of the team would be changed, ensuring that there were always two observers who knew the routine of those they were observing. The two off duty observers would go back and relieve the other two. This meant that the first on would do six days in location, a long time to remain alert and interested in what was going on.

It also required good notetaking and photographs. All of which needed to be analysed by the CSM with the platoon commanders and then sent up the line to HQ.

It was eleven o'clock at night when Bomber, the CQMS and the four for the op slipped into the house. Cpl Jacobs waited outside with three of his section.

The couple welcomed the CQMS like a long-lost brother and after hugs were exchanged, John led everyone upstairs. On the landing, a pulldown ladder led into a loft conversion, which was now a small bedroom complete with a toilet and sink. On a table sat all the makings for a brew.

Moving to the far end of the room, a skylight window gave a fantastic view into the Ardoyne perfect for the op. Acting L/Cpl Chalky White was in charge and Bomber helped him use a couple of army blankets they had brought with them to make an alcove around the sky light.

This done, Bomber and the CQMS took their leave. They were to meet another op group from two platoon and hand over the CQMS who would take them to their house. Handing over the CQMS, Bomber was surprised when he turned and grasped Bomber's hand, shaking it firmly before turning away.

Bomber stood for a moment, watching him walking away with the other patrol. Bomber was wondering what the handshake was about.

As Bomber led his lads back towards the mill, Dusty suddenly hissed, "Wait, boss." Bomber looked at Dusty who was kneeling and scribbling in his notebook. Finally, he gave a 'wilco' and then said, "We are to put on a road block right here and stop and search a dark-blue Ford, no registration number, involved in a shooting, possibly three men in the car."

Bomber looked around. With only five of them and no equipment; they could not effectively stop a speeding car but they would try. Bomber sent Peters fifty yards up the road and Jinks the other way to act as cut offs. Cpl Jacobs and Dusty with the radio, he put behind a parked van for protection. He would do the waving down of any vehicle, not that he thought any car full of gunmen would stop.

Bomber just had time to position himself facing towards the mill's direction when he heard the roar of an engine being revved and driven too fast. He could not see what car it was because the headlights blinded him. Standing his ground, he waved the car down and could hear the engine note dropping as the car slowed. Bomber began to sigh with relief, believing the vehicle was stopping. Suddenly, the car accelerated and he knew it was aiming at him. He could hear Cpl Jacobs shouting at him and he threw himself towards the parked van shoulder rolling and hitting the kerb with a bone jarring crunch. The car side swiped the van and as it careered away a burst of gunfire raked the van.

Bomber sat up feeling battered but otherwise unhurt. Then he heard the "*crack, crack, crack*" of an SLR. It was Peters firing at the car which Bomber could now see was driving erratically away at high speed.

Bomber got to his feet and looked at the van. He could see half a dozen bullet holes in the side of the van. Some owner was going to be very unhappy in the morning. Dusty was confirming the contact report with HQ when they all heard multiple shots further up the road followed by a crash.

Dusty listened in on the radio, then said "The patrol we handed the CQMS over to, got them." Dusty carried on listening, then started to repeat the messages word for word.

"The car crashed after they opened fire. Three occupants, two men, one woman. Driver dead, other two wounded."

Then he paused and Bomber had to prompt him. Dusty looked up at them and quietly said, "The car hit the CQMS, he is being taken to hospital, sounds bad, boss."

Back at the mill, nursing a bruised shoulder, Bomber reflected on the handshake. Did the CQMS have some sort of premonition that something was going to happen or what?

In the briefing room, Bomber spent an hour helping the CSM and the clerk go through the information coming in from the ops. They knew it would take some days before they discovered a regular pattern, but the car registration numbers they could check straight off. Seeing who was from out of area and who they visited could lead to a good intelligence.

They got an update from the hospital, the CQMS was in intensive care but stable and expected to pull through.

It had been four days since the ops had been established and now things were coming together. Three different cars from the Falls area had been identified as regular visitors to certain houses. The registered owners had no blood relationship either by birth or marriage. The drivers and other occupants had all been finally identified as having connections to either the IRA or PIRA. One other car registered to a high-ranking IRA man from Anderson Town was also identified turning up at a house occupied by, according to the electoral register, a man and wife, both pensioners. The man was considered to be an IRA old gun and not active in any way, so why was he being visited?

It was two evenings later when a break came; the OP watching the pensioner's house reported the Anderson Town man arriving. He had parked a street away and walked there. Dickers were at each end of the street. Twenty minutes later, three local men turned up at the house, the only one they could identify was O'Halligan. The alarm bells went off and the commander ordered an immediate raid.

Bomber and his platoon were on standby, so they were tasked. To prevent the targets having time to escape once the dickers raised the alarm, it was decided to go in at full speed. As they were preparing, a voice in the back of Bomber's head kept saying, *Why is O'Halligan there? He is PIRA and the others, well two are IRA the other two no one knows.*

The pig armoured personnel carrier was an absolute bastard to drive. It handled like a three wheeled brick. Arms of iron were needed to steer the monster and sometimes the brakes could be a little dodgy but it was great for scaring the hell out of bad people, including scaring those inside it.

The plan was to drive up the Crumlin Road, then once level with the relevant street, to go hard right and straight to the house. One pig would make for the back alley and that section would race for the back of the house. Two others would block each end of the street and Bomber's pig would stop at the house.

Bomber clung grimly to the handle inside the door as Blackman swung the pig into the street at full speed, threatening to tip it over. Bomber could hear the rear section led by Cpl Jones on the radio saying "In position."

Blackman slammed on the brakes, bringing curses from the lads in the back as they cannoned into each other. Bomber pushed the heavy side door open and jumped out, only to be jostled aside by Armalite, who prepared to swing a door ram at the lock on the door.

The dickers had fled, blowing whistles as they went, and Bomber knew they had just minutes before 'rent a mob' appeared.

Armalite drew back the ram but before he could smash it at the door, it opened. A little old lady neatly dressed in a frock more related to the '50s than 1970 stood there. She smiled and said, "Come in, dear."

They went in, some splitting to clear the rooms upstairs. In the kitchen, Bomber found four men sitting at a pine table. Jones and two of his section were already at the back door and Jones confirmed no one had got out the back way.

As calls of "room cleared" came in, Bomber wondered where the hell O'Halligan was. The old gun IRA man was smiling and Bomber looked at him hard. *Now who does he remind me of,* pondered Bomber. Putting it to the back of his mind, he turned his thoughts back to locating O'Halligan.

The other men, Bomber had ordered to be cuffed and taken out to the pig. Bomber spoke to Jones and Armalite, "Strange no one has protested about the raid or the cuffing and arrest of the others."

"It's weird, boss," said Jones. "I think they have this rehearsed, let's search the place again. My boys will do the back and the kitchen." Bomber agreed and went and watched the faces of the couple. The old woman had joined her husband at the table, but they were not looking at each other.

There was a brick-built toilet attached to the side of the kitchen, common with all these types of terraced houses. Jones opened the toilet door and Bomber noticed the woman look away then to the man who sat upright, betraying nothing. Jones came out and the woman seemed to relax a little.

Leaving Armalite and Dusty to watch the couple, Bomber went to the toilet, calling Jones to follow. Stepping inside, Bomber studied the room. Toilet with a high-water tank with a chain pull on the back wall. The toilet roll holder on the side wall, nothing unusual. Someone had made the effort to modernise the interior by lining the wall with plasterboard and painting it a lemon-yellow colour. A small window was the only other thing on the outside wall.

Bomber went outside, Jones was looking at him strangely. Bomber paced the outside, two and a half long strides; stepping back into the toilet he measured two not so long strides.

Bomber pressed the rear wall on which the water tank was fixed. Then he bent down and felt the toilet bowl. He stepped out and closed the door, then spoke quietly to Jones, who waved over Hotboy Burns and Harris. Harris went to the small shed in the yard and came back with an old pickaxe.

Bomber turned as he could hear the old man and woman kicking off, demanding to know by what right the army had breaking into his home. *Bingo,* thought Bomber and nodded to Harris. "Go ahead break it down."

Harris stepped into the toilet and swung the pick at the rear wall, the axe punctured the plasterboard; pulling it back, he swung again, this time ripping a small section away. Before he could swing again, there was a click and the wall moved. Bomber grabbed Harris and pulled him out, then cocked his rifle the sound of which echoed around the small room. "Don't shoot," a muffled voice called. "I'm coming out, I'm not armed." Bomber and Jones kept their rifles trained on the wall as it swung open with ease. The pipe leading into the water tank was attached to a long flexi-hose. The toilet bowl moved to the left and had a concertina pipe, connecting it to the sewer. *Very clever,* thought Bomber but his eyes were fixed on the emerging figure of O'Halligan.

"You can't shoot me, I'm unarmed." He held his hands up and had a smile on his face. Bomber heard the click as Jones flicked off the safety catch on his rifle.

"No, he's not worth a bullet, Cpl." Bomber knew his safety catch was already off and his finger was tight on the trigger, the first pressure almost gone. With a deep sigh, Bomber eased his finger off the trigger. "Out, you fucker, and keep those hands high," he ordered.

"Search him," Bomber snapped and Harris did it with enthusiasm. Forcing him against the wall, fingertips on the wall, legs spread and pulled back. "Nothing, boss."

Bomber went back into the toilet. Someone like him would not move around the Ardoyne without a shooter. It's what made him a big man on his patch and with friction between the IRA and PIRA, he would want to be tooled up.

Looking in the hole, he found nothing, then he looked up, hooked up on the thick flexi hose, he saw it. An army issue Browning semi-automatic pistol. Being careful not to destroy any fingerprints, he lifted the gun down. Stepping out into the yard, he held the gun for O'Halligan to see.

"You're fucking dead; we all have your name, Brown, you shit, and if we don't get you, someone else will."

Harris kicked O'Halligan legs away and he went down on his face. Bomber wrapped the gun in his handkerchief and handed it to Jones. Kneeling down next to O'Halligan's head, he spoke quietly into his ear, "Now who might that be, my friend, someone we both know. Six foot, has long hair, likes holidays in the sun?"

O'Halligan spat blood and a couple of teeth out and lisped, "You'll fucking well find out just before he puts a bullet between your eyes, arsehole. That's if we don't get you first."

"Well, he will have to be a lot better than you! Everyone said you were crap as a soldier and you're even worse as a terrorist."

Bomber stood up and nodded to Jones, who produced a set of cuffs, clicking them on tightly with relish to O'Halligan's wrist.

Bomber could hear the locals kicking off and Dusty said both sections had stone-throwing kids but nothing else. Nodding, Bomber walked back into the house, wondering why they had the meeting with the old gun. What could be bringing them together?

Bomber sat at the table, looking first at the old man who stared back with pure hate on his face. Then he gazed at the woman, whom he could now see was not really a lovely old girl but a hard-line terrorist. There was a hardness about the face and she too showed the hate that her husband displayed so openly.

"So I have to ask myself what is an old, has been, washed up hard-line IRA man doing hosting a meeting between IRA and PIRA shits?"

The old man spat at Bomber, "You know nothing, you fucking wee shit, washed up, am I?" He had started to rise but Armalite pushed him back down.

He went to speak but his wife snapped at him, "Shut up, Seamus!" He looked at her and nodded.

Bomber continued to push, "Well, it's easy to see who's in charge here. What say you lads?"

There were loud chuckles and Harris said, "I'll lay money on who has the biggest balls."

122

"Shut your filthy mouth, you English bastard," said the old man "or I'll have you all killed. I don't need permission from anybody; I run things here. Listen to them outside, do you think they are going to let you take us out of here?"

The old man slumped down seemingly exhausted by his tirade but with a smile on his face. The old woman looked shocked and she would not meet Bomber's stare. Bomber then knew what they were here for, that they were forming a splinter group. They were disaffected with the current organisations and were forming their own action group.

The noise outside had indeed picked up and Bomber heard the *"whack, whack"* of a baton gun being fired.

"Well, you want to hope we get out because if we don't, we have orders to kill you all and not to leave any of you potential killers breathing." Bomber had no such orders but wanted to see the reaction.

The old woman snapped, "You damn fool, Seamus, why couldn't you keep your mouth shut! Scheming with that fucking O'Halligan has brought them down on us." The woman threw the tea cup in front of her at her husband which hit him on the side of his face.

He looked broken but Bomber wasn't finished yet and ordered another search of the house; he wanted every bit of paper work of any kind to be put in a bag.

Without saying a thing, Armalite moved the old man sideways from the table while he was still sitting in the chair. Then he looked under the table, gave a grunt of satisfaction and pulled an A4 sized envelope from beneath. The old man went wild and threw himself at Armalite but Harris caught him by the shirt collar and forced him back into the chair.

The envelope had torn open where it had been stuck to the underside of the table. They could clearly see five and ten-pound notes inside. Bomber opened it and apart from the money, it contained a slip of paper with four columns of numbers and one of letters.

As Bomber was studying the numbers, Dusty called him, telling him the commander wanted them to move out.

The pigs roared out of the street, scattering stone-throwing youths as they went. At the mill, the RUC, including Superintendent O'Neil, were waiting to take charge of the prisoners.

In the briefing room, Bomber related the sequence of events to the commander and the superintendent, handing over the envelope and money. Showing them the paper with the numbers and letters, Bomber speculated that he could be either the paymaster of the IRA or the PIRA. He also gave them the plastic kitchen bag full of other stuff, mostly routine bills and receipts but they might find something useful.

They were now into the tenth day of the covert ops and results were mounting; several wanted men had been spotted and lifted. Out of area cars were now being followed by plain clothed RUC officers when they left the Ardoyne, helping to build a picture of what was going on.

Bomber sat in Paddy's kitchen, talking to the old soldier and sipping whisky-laced tea. Bomber had presented the old soldier with another good bottle of single malt. He had earlier asked permission from the commander to take a small patrol out to check on the ops.

Bomber had to admit he just wanted to get out of the mill and talk to someone other than his fellow soldiers.

Paddy broke the silence, "If you don't mind me saying, son, you are awful young to have three tapes and a crown on your arm and commanding a platoon with men mostly older than you, how come?"

Bomber sipped some more of the whisky-laced tea, feeling the warmth spread through his body. Then he told Paddy his tale all the way from joining the army cadets at thirteen, then junior leaders in the army at fifteen. Pausing to take another sip, he continued his story of fighting in the Middle East at seventeen, then the time in Germany when he nearly quit and went to live with a girl, who owned a family-run bar in Brunswick. In his heart, Bomber knew it wouldn't have worked.

Bomber paused and looked at Paddy, who was looking at him in a kindly way. Bomber told him about Libya and doing long patrols in the desert, about Catterick Camp in a condemned and run-down barracks plus the endless courses and the army's attempt to civilise him by posting him to an army youth team.

Paddy listened patiently, topping up his teacup with medicine as he called it. When he had finished, Paddy looked at him for a long time.

"You have done an awful lot in a very short time, son. The army has had a lot from you and you seem to thrive on it but you need a life outside of the army or when the time comes for you to leave, you will be lost and alone."

Bomber let the words sink in and realised he was that already.

A polite cough came from Armalite, who was sitting behind him. Bomber had forgotten he was there and the others were still outside.

"Thanks for the tea, Paddy, and for looking after the lads upstairs."

"It's a pleasure, son, makes me feel young again." Paddy grinned at him and Bomber noticed that his face was getting back to normal after the beating.

Bomber stood and headed for the back door. He could hear Paddy and Armalite talking but not what was said.

As he headed for the back gate, three shadows moved and followed him along the alley. "Anything I should know about over the radio, Dusty?"

"Nothing, boss, too quiet by half, don't like it at all."

It stayed quiet and Bomber was happy to spend the rest of the night lying on his bed, thinking until sleep embraced him. The dream left him alone that night.

Chapter 11
Set Up!

Three days later, the platoon was back in Ballykinler Barracks for forty-eight hours' rest and recuperation. Not that there was much to do apart from a little sport or the old cinema, which showed out-of-date films each evening.

Bomber preferred a game of squash and his books.

The second morning, the mess orderly told Bomber he was wanted at the medical centre for a medical. Bomber knew the MO and his friend the medical Sgt were still in Belfast and wondered who was standing in for them.

On arrival, he was met by a Cpl medic that Bomber had not seen before, who took his weight, height, blood pressure and a urine sample. Looking round, Bomber was surprised to see apart from them, the place was empty. The Cpl ushered him into the MO office. It was a sparse room with just a desk with a high-backed chair. Facing the table was a hard wood slatted folding chair. No decorations on the wall, just one large poster warning of the consequences of unprotected sex.

"Sit," came from a female in a white coat-over what Bomber guessed to be some sort of uniform. Her hair was pulled back, giving her face a severe look. Large tinted glasses hid her eyes.

Bomber sat. She carried on writing on a pad, not looking at him. After two minutes of absolute silence, she started asking questions. Firstly about his health, then what did he do to relax? Did he have any problems getting to sleep? How much alcohol did he consume? Any disturbing dreams? Now the alarm bells were ringing; she's not a doc, she's a bloody trick cyclist.

"Well, answer the question." She was staring at Bomber, who had not heard the question due to the alarm bell in his head. "Sorry could you repeat the question?"

"I said do you believe in God?" Bomber did not hesitate, his temper was rising and common sense had fled his mind. "Yes, I believe in God but not you, you fucking fraud." As Bomber said it, he stood and pushed the desk back onto her so that she was trapped against the wall sitting in her chair unable to move.

"Now who put you up to this, who?" Bomber hissed at her. Her glasses had fallen off and he could see she had clear blue eyes. Frightened eyes!

Bomber heard the door open and the medic came in, grabbing Bomber in a bear hug from behind. Bomber brought the heel of his boot back into the man's shin bone and he felt the grip loosen. Then he jerked his head back and felt it connect with the man's nose and the arms fell away. Bomber turned and pushed the medic away saying, "Stay where you are, come back at me and I will really hurt you."

The medic now looked less like a medic and more like a hard man ready for a fight. The medic glanced at the woman, then stepped back and Bomber walked out. As he walked, he cursed himself for losing his temper. That was not the way to get information.

Back at the mess, he picked up the phone and called HQ in Belfast and asked for the MO. After a minute, a familiar voice answered; it was Mike. Bomber told him what had happened. Mike was surprised saying he was not due a medical for another six months and the doctor who normally stood in at barracks, while the MO was in Belfast, was an old retired army medical corps major from Newcastle, the town just along the coast. He finished, saying he would look into it.

Bomber redialled and got the guard room and asked if the two of them had left. He was told that they had in a hurry. Bomber took a walk to the guard room and looked at the signing in and out book.

It showed a captain something and a Cpl something else. The writing was a scribble, totally un-readable. Bomber spoke to the RP (regimental police) Cpl on duty and asked about them. He said they produced genuine ID cards, no he could not remember their names or unit. It had been an extra busy morning and it was just himself and one other on duty as everyone else was in Belfast.

As he walked back towards the mess, the CSM hailed him, telling him the commander wanted to see him. *Fuck's sake,* thought Bomber. *What now?*

He knocked on the commander's door and a voice said, "Enter." The commander was sitting at his desk, files scattered on the top. He looked up at Bomber, "Ah, C/Sgt, by the look on your face, something's not right, what's happened?"

Bomber related the morning events finishing with, "You may think I'm suffering from paranoia, sir, but with O'Halligan, Lt Hood, the 2i/c and now this, I'm beginning to think people don't like me."

"Very strange indeed and even if you are not suffering from paranoia, it don't mean they ain't out to get you." He rifled through the files and brought out a green one, handing it to Bomber telling him to sit down and read it. While he was reading, the commander picked up the phone and told the CSM to investigate the pretend MO and Medic.

It contained the SB report on the three that had beaten up Paddy. The one that Bomber had encouraged to talk had, under interrogation, given out a lot of small-time information. He confirmed it was O'Halligan who had sent them to Paddy's but when shown the photograph of Lt Hood and O'Halligan talking, he clammed up tight. The other two were small fry with very little useful information. One was marked with a U-shaped arrow and Bomber asked what it meant.

"Oh, that's a possible candidate for turning as an informant."

A knock at the door stopped Bomber asking another question and the CSM came in. "The medical centre is locked sir and the keys have not been signed out today since early morning sick parade. Cpl Morgan, the duty medic, said he only had two sickies this morning, so he locked up at nine o'clock and handed the key back in to the guardroom."

"Thank you, CSM, have a word with the dog patrol and see if they noticed anything."

The CSM acknowledged and left, closing the door behind him.

The commander slid a red file out and held it out to Bomber, with the following comment, "This, I think will interest you more."

Opening the file, Bomber noticed it only had two pages. The first was headed Rory John O'Halligan PIRA.

It confirmed that he was suspected of training gunmen, bomb makers and devising tactics for the Ardoyne area.

He was to be charged with the murder of the young boy and inciting riots and the assault on Paddy.

It also confirmed that the old man named as Seamus O'Hara and O'Halligan were trying to organise an assassination squad independent of the control of the IRA or PIRA but with their tentative blessing. Top of the list were several police officers listed in a priority order. Prison officers, several senior army officers and at the bottom, Bomber's name along with several others in the regiment.

"They think it's because of the shooting of the nail bombers and the gunman. It appears they were told you were responsible."

"Now who could that have been?" Bomber's thoughts turned to Hood, *Was it him?* There was no evidence to confirm it.

"Well, we don't know that, so we must keep an open mind for now, ah."

The commander sat silent for a moment, gazing at the ceiling then he looked at Bomber and said, "Have you given any thought about accepting the brigadier's offer of joining his little unit?"

The question caught Bomber by surprise. How did the commander know about that unless he was in league with Fag Ash?

"Oh, I should have mentioned he and I go back a long way, did the odd job for him in the past when I was younger and a bit more adventurous. He spoke to me about you and thinking about it, it could be a good boost for your career."

Bomber was silent for a second or two, then looked at the company commander. "I rather like being a platoon commander, sir, and working for you. The sneaky beaky stuff is not really my scene."

"Good, I thought that would be your feelings. However, I have to tell you he has a lot of influence and he can call on any unit for assistance at any time and the CO knows this. So we may well be seeing him sooner than later."

Early next morning, Bomber woke to the sound of everyone in the mess being woken and ordered to be ready to move in thirty minutes. Getting dressed and grabbing his webbing equipment that he kept packed ready to go, he made his way to the company lines where everyone was forming up.

The CSM was ushering all platoon commanders into the briefing room. When the three of them were present, the commander came in looking grim. He informed them of a big shootout in the Falls Road area and that four Prods were dead. The brigade commander had ordered a lockdown of the whole Falls Road area and that house-to-house searches would be carried out.

Then he gave each platoon its task. Bomber groaned inwardly when his platoon got cordon duty rather than house searches.

Three days later, the lockdown was lifted. There had been no one allowed in or out for three days. After three days of the lockdown and dealing with a few minor skirmishes, he knew the lads were drained and needed a break to re-charge their batteries.

Returning to the mill seemed like going to the Ritz Hotel, with hot showers, clean clothes and a bed to sleep on. Bomber was just going to the mess to get a hot meal when he was intercepted by the company clerk, telling him he was wanted in the briefing room.

Bomber had that feeling he sometimes got when he was about to get bad news. Knocking on the door, he heard the commander say "Come in". Bomber hesitated, he could smell cigarette smoke. Opening the door, he stepped in and was confronted by Fag Ash puffing away. Next to him was the bogus doc and sitting slightly further away was the commander with the CSM standing behind him. Over to the left in civvies was his Cpl medic who had two slightly black eyes from Bomber's backwards head butt. Next to him was a gorilla in a suit that looked as if he could crush cars in his hands.

"Ah, come in, C/Sgt, need your expertise, take a seat," the Commander spoke cheerful as if trying to put Bomber at ease.

Bomber looked at the only chair that had been placed in the centre, the others facing it in a half circle. Bomber picked up the chair and moved it to one side so that his back was close to the wall.

He sat down, undoing the button on his right-hand combat jacket pocket; slipping his hand in, he felt the Beretta and slipped the safety catch off. He didn't know why he did but thought it best not to take any chances.

Fag Ash blew out a cloud of smoke, looked at Bomber and spoke, "Sorry for the melodrama, C/Sgt. You know Captain St Claire." He nodded at the woman in the black suit and white blouse. "There you have Sgt Knight, he is not too happy about his nose and the big chap, that's Cpl Small." Fag Ash chuckled at that. "Yes, it's true, his name is Small."

Bomber looked at the gorilla who remained expressionless. And he tightened his grip on the Beretta.

Fag Ash carried on as if everything was normal. "I'm sorry about the charade the other day at the medical centre but these evaluations on everyone who works for us have been forced on me. I'm told it's the way forward and we try to do it, with the candidates unaware it's us doing it."

He paused and opened a file. "Have your report right here, interesting reading, now where shall I start."

"Hmm, C/Sgt David Brown, age twenty-three and seven months. I'll skip the physical bits, we know you are super fit. Now mental state, has a loner's profile but craves close companionship but pushes it away if it gets too close. Oh, I'm skipping all the official jargon; I like it in a language I can understand. St Claire thinks you are a borderline madman, capable of killing without provocation. Seems you frightened her a little at the medical centre."

Bomber looked at the captain who had coloured and she locked eyes with Bomber, then looked away. None of this escaped Fag Ash who smiled.

"Now, what's next, oh yes, your violent tendencies are kept in check by the strict military discipline you have been subjected to since the age of thirteen and your fear of God. Are you afraid of God, C/Sgt?"

Bomber stayed quiet as he knew an answer was not necessary.

"You are troubled by things you have done and seen in the past and try to erase them by immersing yourself in soldiering and not repeating the mistakes of the past." He closed the file then said, "I could go on but it's all very much the same, any comments?"

Bomber wanted to say bollocks and get up and leave but the commander was watching closely.

"Firstly, I would like to know on what authority you authorised this trick cyclist to do this without my consent and if the report is correct, how come I left both of them breathing?"

"Ah," escaped the commander's lips. "How come they are alive, Brigadier?"

"Because as usual, to coin a phrase, the captain has based her findings on what people consider normal. The fact is men like us and the C/Sgt are not normal; we function completely differently—"

"But Brigadier—" butted in St Claire.

"Don't interrupt me, Captain," Fag Ash snapped and she dropped her head.

"I've been selecting good men, hard men, dangerous men, clever men whatever I have needed to do jobs no one else can do or if they were in their right mind would not want to do." He had now raised his voice considerably.

"I do not need people with PhDs and no field experience, telling me what sort of soldiers I need to select for a job!"

Bomber was beginning to enjoy this but a little warning light had gone on. *If I'm one of his selected, he can go take a running jump.*

Bomber looked at the commander, who was smiling. He caught Bomber's eye and did a little shake of his head, which suggested Bomber kept quiet.

The brigadier was busy lighting another cancer stick. The discarded stub of the previous one smouldered in the already overflowing ashtray.

"Now, C/Sgt, you must forgive me; it appears that I too have a temper and only keep it in check by years of military

135

discipline and by smoking myself to death." He smiled but somehow it did not reach his eyes.

"The truth is, in war, we need killers. That's what all the expensive training is for. However, it's killers who stay within the law of the land or Geneva Convention. Men who can tell the difference between right and wrong, who will not obey unlawful commands from a superior officer. You, C/Sgt, are just such a man."

Now Bomber really had a sinking feeling and did not like the way this was going one little bit.

The brigadier had lapsed into silence and the commander spoke, "I think it's a good time for the CSM to take you to the mess for some coffee," indicating to the CSM to take St Claire and the others.

The CSM ushered them outside. St Claire glared at Bomber as she left.

"You see what I have to put up with these days, Christopher. Not like the old days; now I have to answer to bean counters, trick cyclist and brainless committees of politicians. No wonder I smoke like a bloody chimney."

The commander smiled and reaching into a drawer, pulled out a bottle of Glen Fiddich and three glasses, then poured generous slugs into each.

"Do you think we should put the C/Sgt out of his misery before he pulls that gun you gave him and he tops us out of frustration?"

Fag Ash nodded, took one of the glasses and downed the whisky in one.

Accepting the offered glass, Bomber sipped the whisky, feeling the warmth as it slid down his throat. The alarm in his head was still ringing and a voice was saying, *Take it slowly;*

136

any minute now, they are going to throw a sucker punch at you.

The commander sipped his whisky and paused, savouring it. Then he looked at the brigadier and said, "Are you going to tell him or shall I?"

Here we go, thought Bomber.

The brigadier coughed, put down his cigarette and said calmly, "O'Halligan and Seamus O'Hara have escaped."

Bomber was dumbstruck, he looked first at the brigadier and then at the commander, wondering if this was a wind up.

"They were being transferred from the interrogation unit to the Crumlin Road Jail in an unmarked van with four prison guards." The brigadier paused and lit another cigarette.

Bomber felt the anger rising in him and put the whisky glass down on the floor unable to stop his hands shaking with rage.

"It was well planned, they must have had a tip off as to when they would be leaving and what vehicle they would be in. Two of the guards are dead, the others are in hospital with serious wounds. The only good news is O'Hara was found in the abandoned getaway car with a bullet in his head. Seemingly, he had become a liability to someone."

"Any idea where O'Halligan is now?" Bomber realised this was a pointless question at this stage and was surprised when the brigadier nodded.

"Actually, one of my sources south of the border has informed me that a car with four men in, one of them being O'Halligan arrived at a PIRA safe house."

"So that's that then, we can't touch the bastard," the disgust in Bomber's voice was clear.

The brigadier looked at the commander who nodded.

"Not necessarily, we could do a little snoop on the safe house and maybe snatch him. He won't be expecting something like that, now, will he?"

"Right," said Bomber with a sinking feeling. "Sounds like a good job for the SAS boys."

"Exactly," the brigadier exclaimed. "Just one or two problems with that. Firstly, the few SAS available at the moment are all deployed. The SAS are recruiting and training people like never before but that takes time. Also, they have strict instructions not to cross the border. Needs a clandestine operation, nobody to know but us."

Bomber could not believe his ears. "You want me to take my lads over the border and snatch him. I thought I was crazy but that is totally bonkers."

The commander gave a small "ah", then topped Bomber's glass up. Bomber could not remember picking the glass up or even finishing the contents. "We were not thinking of you taking your platoon over, no, no."

Bomber felt a little relieved and started to take another sip of whisky when the Commander said in a quiet, under stated way, "Just you, C/Sgt, just you."

The whisky was caught in Bomber's throat, making him choke. When he got his breath back, he spluttered, "What makes you think I can cross the border, kidnap O'Halligan and bring him back on my own, without getting nabbed and killed by either his mates or the Garda?"

The brigadier took over again. "Oh, you don't have to worry about the Garda, my contact will ensure they stay clear. As for his mates, if they object; well, we don't really want any of them back."

"What about O'Halligan, is he expendable or is he definitely required alive?"

"If he resists arrest," the brigadier spread his hands.

Bomber looked from one to the other. *They must think I am either completely pissed or insane to agree to something like this; they can take a run and jump.*

Chapter 12
South

The transit van drove steadily south in the dark. From Newry, they took back roads and country lanes until they were close to the border west of Fork Hill. At a lone telephone box, the van stopped; Sgt Knight and Cpl Small were in the front seats. Small got out of the van and walked a hundred yards further up the road, then back again. He grunted to Knight who then turned to Bomber. "Don't forget we will be here every night for the next three nights. Dusk to just before dawn; if you can, call the phone box and warn us when you will be here. Oh, and we will be in a different vehicle each time, good luck." With that, he turned away and restarted the engine.

Bomber opened the back door and stepped out. Cpl Small closed the doors and whispered to Bomber, "You're fucking crazy, trust no one, especially the sarge and the quack."

Standing alone, watching the two dim red lights of the van disappear in the distance, he thought, *How did I end up agreeing to this?* The little voice in his head chuckled away saying, *Because you love doing this and you can never resist a challenge. Now stop moaning, you are always going on about being more proactive and now you are.*

Bomber was dressed in civilian clothes, including a pair of lightweight hiking boots. In his left-hand jacket pocket was a map, small torch and a compass. None of which he needed as he had memorised the route which was pretty straight forward. He felt the weight of the Beretta in his other pocket and wished he had asked Fag Ash for a suppressor, just in case he had to do any quiet work with it. The large wad of cheese sandwiches and a couple of Kit Kats made up the rest of his load.

At the phone box, he took the lane south for eight miles where he would take another lane for three miles to the west. Then he would move over the fields for the remaining one mile to reach the old single-story farmhouse that the target was holed up in. Total of twelve miles, allowing a pace of three miles an hour in the dark on the tarmac, he should be there in four hours which would be one o'clock in the morning.

The lights of the single-story farmhouse blazed out, the only light for miles around. Bomber was sitting by a dry stonewall, watching and munching on one of his cheese sandwiches. *Never go to war on an empty stomach, lad,* the voice in his head said.

Bomber knew he should be scared since he was in another country without permission, no back up and just a Beretta pistol for company and up against what? He knew O'Halligan was tough but the other three he knew nothing of and it could be they would eat him for breakfast, given the chance. *Better not give them the chance then,* he thought.

Creeping forward, Bomber was holding his breath, hoping that there were no dogs to raise the alarm. Now he was against the farmhouse wall, not far from the back door. It was clear the occupants were partying. Empty beer cans and whisky bottles could be seen lying on the table in the kitchen and the laughter of drunken men could clearly be heard.

Bomber went round the house and looked into each window. There were three bedrooms, a kitchen, a room that was in darkness and a lounge where the four men were drinking.

At the front of the house, a black Ford was parked. Bomber checked and it was unlocked but without any keys in the ignition.

It was obvious to Bomber that the target and his pals felt completely safe and had taken no security precautions whatsoever.

Bomber decided to let them drink themselves unconscious, then make his move. Two cheese sandwiches later, the noise had died down. Bomber gave it another half an hour, then crept to the backdoor, gently tried it but it was locked. Most of the lights were out, just one in the lounge could be seen through the half open door.

The kitchen window was of the old wooden sash type. Taking out his Swiss army knife, he slid the blade between the two halves and released the catch of the window. Gently, a little at a time, he eased the window up. Bomber had to hold it in position each time he moved it as the weights that should have balanced it appeared to be unattached from their cords. *Probably rotted away,* the voice mumbled in his head. After what seemed an age, he was able to climb through, being careful not to disturb the dirty crockery in the sink.

Standing still, he listened and he could hear snoring coming from the lounge and someone talking in their sleep. His mouth was dry and he had a problem swallowing; on the table, he saw an open can of coke, lifting it he could tell it was half-full. He downed it in one and almost choked; it had whisky mixed in with it. He moved carefully through to the lounge feeling remarkably calm, perhaps it was the whisky. The Beretta was in his hand, ready to fire at the first sign of trouble. The lounge stunk of beer and whisky and something else sour, then he saw it; one of the two lying out for the count on the large beat-up sofa had vomited and it lay drying on his shirt and floor.

Bomber checked the next room, which was in darkness. Taking out his small torch, he shone it round the room. It had a large table in the middle and several dining chairs against the walls, on which hung old black and white photographs of people long gone. On the table was a suitcase, next to it was a semiautomatic pistol. Bomber carefully opened the suitcase, shining the torch over the contents and caught his breath. *There must be twenty pounds or more of PE (plastic explosive) in there,* thought Bomber. On one side was a battery, two wires and an electrical timer, similar to the type he had seen used in demonstrations at Warminster.

Bomber closed the lid of the case and pondered over the find for a moment. Then he went through the rest of the house to locate the target. In the first bedroom was the other goon, lying flat on his front fully clothed snoring like a pig. The next bedroom was empty but in the last, he found O'Halligan fast asleep on his back, mouth open. As he breathed in and out, he made a whistling sound through his two broken teeth. On the bedside table lay a pistol. Bomber had a great urge to put the barrel of the Beretta into that mouth and pull the trigger. Resisting the temptation, he moved back to the dining room.

The little voice in his head was reciting a wicked plan to him, one that appealed to his sense of justice but not his conscience. *Well, if you are not going to do this, what are you going to do?* the voice asked.

Bomber was moving fast over the field towards the lane. It was 4:30 in the morning and Bomber need a place to hole up for the rest of the night and the following day. The explosion was even bigger than he expected; he felt the blast even though he was at least half a mile away and just entering a small wood on the crest of a slight rise.

Having found a thicket at the edge of the trees, he wiggled into it until he was hidden from view. At just before 6:30, he pushed his way forward; it was now light enough to see his handy work. The farmhouse had ceased to exist and was just a pile of smouldering rubble. Two land rovers had driven up and the occupants had gotten out and were pointing towards the rubble. Ten minutes later, a fire engine and a Garda patrol car arrived.

It was then that Bomber realised the enormity and horror of what he had done. He had returned to the dining room, opened the suitcase and connected the battery, setting the bomb timer to give himself thirty minutes to get away. Before he left, he had turned the taps to the gas stove on, thirty minutes should produce a huge quantity of highly explosive gas. He knew he could not possibly carry the suitcase bomb and get O'Halligan walking in front of him all the way back to the border. The bomb he surmised was destined for Belfast or some other luckless town where innocent men, women and children would be killed or horribly maimed, whole families losing loved ones. This way three terrorists would die, and a young boy's pointless death would have been accounted for. With this form of rationalisation, Bomber closed his eyes and slept.

The cold finally forced Bomber to open his eyes; it was two in the afternoon. Looking down to the remains of the farmhouse, he could see firemen and Garda raking through the rubble. Feeling in his pocket, he fished out his last cheese sandwich and a Kit Kat. Munching away, it dawned on him that his actions of crossing the border, blowing up a house and killing the occupants had put him in the brigadier's power completely and had made him no better than the enemy. He had crossed the line. *Bloody hypocrite,* thought Bomber. The voice countered, *You did what you had to do. What was the choice? Shoot them while they lay in bed? Then what would you have done with the bomb?*

If the brigadier decided to shop Bomber, it would be life in some shitty prison with no chance of time off for good behaviour.

Now why would he do that? the little voice would not shut up. "Who knows?" muttered Bomber, playing the game, "These sneaky beakies can't be trusted. They use people, then when the shit hits the fan, they drop them like a hot brick to carry the can."

Stop worrying; you love doing this stuff, taking the fight to the enemy.

Waiting for darkness to descend, he had decided on his course of action. He would set off across country, avoid the roads as much as possible and not use the two phone boxes en route to phone in.

It was two in the morning and Bomber had been watching the parked car, that was about twenty feet from the phone box, for thirty minutes. The unmistakable shape of Cpl Small, he could see in the passenger seat. Sgt Knight stood by the phone box. Either the light in the box was broken or Knight had disabled it.

He could not detect any other presence close by. Working his way to the back of the car, he could see Small's head was on his chest; he was asleep. Easing open the back door, he hoped that they had switched off the car's interior lights as they would have been trained to do. He was right, the lights stayed off. Crouching down behind the seats, he gently pulled the door until it clicked on the first catch and left it. To close it completely would make too much noise. Now he could hear the sound of steps as Knight returned. Opening the driver's door, he wearily slumped into the seat and Small woke up, yawned and said, "Nothing yet?"

"No," answered Knight with a touch of irritation in his voice. "Guess we're fucking well stuck here until dawn. Your turn to stag on by the box; off you go and don't forget if and when he gets here, thump him and take that bloody gun off him."

Small grunted and got out of the car, walking slowly to the phone box.

Knight let out a little squeal as Bomber ground the barrel of the Beretta into the back of his head saying, "Keep your hands on the steering wheel or your brains are going to be all over the dash board." Knight complied. "Now why would you want to have me thumped and the gun taken off me? Got a little treat in store for me, have you?" Bomber forced the barrel so hard into Knight's neck, his head was touching the steering wheel. "I am only doing what I was told."

"Told by whom, the brigadier?"

"St Claire."

Bomber nearly lost control of his bowels when another voice said, "Yes, St Claire." It was Small. He was standing close to the side of the car and Bomber had not heard or seen a thing. Small stood with his arms held out to show he had no weapons.

"Fucking get him, Small, break the cunt's neck."

Oh, shit, thought Bomber. *Can't get both in time even if this pop gun could stop Small, Knight would be on me.*

In answer, Small wrenched open the driver's door and lifted out Knight. Knight was not a small man, probably twelve and half stone and five ten, but Small lifted him out with one hand and with the other hit him hard in the face before letting him go. Knight fell to the ground unconscious. Then Small removed a Browning semi-automatic pistol from Knight's shoulder holster. Walking to the back of the car, he opened the boot, picked up Knight and tossed the still unconscious Sgt in like a sack of spuds.

Bomber found he could not speak. He had no fear, he just felt amazed at the ease and speed Small had done it. He moved with the grace and speed of a tiger. The giant of a man slid into the driver's seat started the car and drove off.

Still seated in the rear, Bomber managed to find his voice, "What about Knight?"

"The double-dealing bastard is going to jail. I'm the brigadier's man; that shit belongs to St Claire and she was shagging Hood. That not his real name, he's Captain Briggs but he likes to masquerade as something else all the time, the prick."

"So what had they got planned for me?"

"Oh, they were going to drop you off at the RMPs with a statement of what you had been doing. Then you and the

147

brigadier would take the can for crossing the border plus killing O'Halligan and his team."

Bomber digested this as Small drove carefully along the darkened lanes.

"What's to stop her still doing it?"

Small chuckled saying, "The brigadier had her arrested about an hour ago for passing classified information to the IRA."

"And did she?"

Small shrugged. "It matters not, she and Hood were trying to bring the brigadier down. He's smarter than the lot of them put together and has been one step ahead of them the whole way. He had me keep an eye out for you and to watch your back if you returned. I heard you get into the back of the car, I was only pretending to be asleep. I thought that was a nice touch."

"If I returned, was there any doubt?"

Again Small chuckled. "Not with the brigadier and your company commander, they seem to think you have a charmed life. Incidentally, they know about the explosion the Garda seem to think it was an own goal. Nice eh!"

Bomber sat back in the comfort of the rear seat, his mind whirling, struggling to come to grips with the events. He felt drained, exhausted, just wanting a hot shower, food and sleep, not necessarily in that order but his mind would not let him relax.

Small drove carefully back to Ballykinler Barracks. There Bomber was sent straight to the briefing room with Small in tow. In the briefing room, he was given a mug of tea and he drank it quickly. The door opened and in came the CO (Commanding Officer), Lt Col Williams, who had been a company commander in Bomber's old regiment when they were in Germany together. With him was the brigadier, the company commander and the ops officer Captain Bass.

Fuck me, thought Bomber. *Are the press and television people outside as well?*

"Welcome back, C/Sgt, the brigadier tells me you have been up to no good. That is no good to PIRA." The others smiled politely. "Tell us how it went, take your time and leave nothing out."

Bomber took a deep breath and related the events including what had happened at the pickup. He finished by thanking Fag Ash for having Cpl Small watch out for him. The brigadier smiled and inclined his head and Bomber noticed for the first time that the brigadier was not smoking.

There was a moment of silence, then the CO spoke, "Excellent, the brigadier tells me the Garda are officially putting it down to an own goal. Naturally, I don't have to tell you this stays strictly inside these four walls. It does not get mentioned ever again."

"Yes sir," intoned Bomber.

Then they all trooped out except the brigadier. As the door closed, the brigadier spoke, "Well done, young man, I had no doubts you would pull it off. The bomb, well that was inspirational."

Bomber looked at him. "You knew I would not be able to bring him out, so I guessed that it was a one-way ticket for one of us. The bomb; well, I couldn't leave it and as I couldn't carry it, I had to get rid of it, end of story."

"Yes, it was probably the only solution. Part of me thought you might have found a way to bring O'Halligan back. Then we could have grilled the bastard for information but in the long run, it is better he is dead."

"One question, what about St Claire, Hood and Knight?" asked Bomber.

"Oh, I have cleaned ship. Left it too long but I like to get all the ducks in a row before I open fire. Only loose end is Hood, someone is still protecting him and he has gone to ground so keep your eyes open."

Bomber nodded.

"Best go and get some rest; the company is back to Belfast tomorrow. I'll be in touch if I have any news."

Bomber walked from the room and outside, he saw Small waiting by the car. Bomber walked over to him and put out his hand saying, "I owe you Cpl, thanks for everything."

Small's hand completely engulfed Bomber's but the touch was gentle. "Think nothing of it; we are the brigadier's men and we look out for each other." There was a muffled cry from the boot of the car.

"What are you going to do with him?"

"There's a very nice RMP warrant officer waiting for him in Lisburn."

Walking back to the mess, Bomber realised what had been said, 'We are the Brigadier's men.'

Oh God, what have I got myself into? Bomber knew now he would be at the old devil's beck and call.

"Hi boss! Good walking trip?" the cheery voice was Thorny, who fell in step with Bomber as they marched to the mess. "The lads are well rested and everything is ready for tomorrow's start at 0600."

Bomber groaned inwardly, not much time to catch up on rest. *Stop whingeing, you'll be all right*, the little voice chimed.

The next two weeks went by without any major incidents other than bombings in Belfast city centre. PIRA were trying to make the general public too frightened to use the shops and businesses there but the people were having none of it.

To ensure that PIRA could not turn the city centre into a ghost town, it was slowly being turned into a fortified area. Every person and vehicle going in was searched and vehicle barriers were erected to stop cars and trucks. Hundreds of police and soldiers were being deployed in the task and it was beginning to pay off. The number of bombs getting through was dropping and several arrests had been made. Life in the city centre carried on as normal. The people had decided on 'no surrender'.

Chapter 13
The Chasm, August 1970

The regiment had been given a week's break and rather than fester in Ballykinler, Bomber took the opportunity to attend a climbing course at the army centre in Scotland. The courses were run by a retired Royal Engineers' major, who was something of a legend in army mountaineering circles. He had a misfit selection of several army instructors and a couple of civilians employed by the army. All were top climbers who knew the mountains and Scottish climbing well.

Bomber travelled in civilian clothes to Fort George on the east coast of Scotland, all the time feeling that he was under-dressed without a rifle or the Beretta close at hand. Once in the old fort with its thick walls and drab grey granite buildings, he began to relax, exploring the fort built by Colonel William Skinner in 1748 on a spit of land on the Moray Firth. The idea was to control the approach to Inverness and stop any sea borne invasion. One advantage for the rock climber was that the walls provided great climbing practice.

A short briefing was followed by collecting kit and rations, then they moved to the west coast to the village of Ballachulish and camped out in the old TA drill hall. Ballachulish was close to the village of Glencoe on Loch

Leven and since the 17th century, the people had made a living by quarrying slate for roof tiles for both Edinburgh and Glasgow.

The first few days, they enjoyed the sun and the climbing in Glen Nevis. Bomber soon felt he was climbing well. The dry rock felt good to his hands and the old feeling of living on the edge with the challenge of the next move absorbed his whole being. The climbing had wiped all thoughts of Northern Ireland from his mind, climbing was a total commitment and nothing else at this time mattered except finding a good hand or foothold.

Several summers previously, Bomber had climbed Crowberry Gully and Agag's Grove on the Buchaille Etive Mor, a mountain of majestic proportions that guarded the entrance to Glencoe from the landward side. It towered over Rannoch Moor like some giant sentinel. Since that time, he had had a yearning to climb 'The Chasm', a classic 1,500-foot route on the flank of the mountain. The Scots at the time took sadistic pleasure in giving minimal description of Scottish routes and under-grading the difficulty in their guidebooks. Officially, this was because they thought real mountaineers did not need to be told every detail of a route. They also considered the English and Welsh climbers over-graded their climbs and were pansies when it came to real climbing in Scotland.

In the Clachaig Inn, one evening over a few half and halves (Beer and whisky), Big Ian the barman and local hard climber confided in Bomber that it was really a legal way to kill the English. This statement was met with great laughter by the other Scottish climbers present and cost Bomber a round of drinks.

Bomber read the two-paragraph description in the Scottish guidebook to several other guys on the course. Finishing with the grade, "It's only severe, a walk in the park."

"Yep, but a walk of one thousand and five hundred vertical feet plus a hike to the summit, then the main gulley all the way back to the road. It will be a long day and night most likely," quipped a Cpl from the Royal Signals.

"Aye and you know if the Jocks have graded it severe, it will be at least very severe or harder," said Willie, a tall Royal Engineer from Ripon. There was silence for a moment and Bomber thought he was not going to get any takers to climb with him.

"I'll give it a go providing you do all the leading." This came from the third member of Bomber's audience, an RMP Sgt called John, who, like Bomber, was over from Northern Ireland for a break.

Later that evening, Bomber put his suggestion to the major, who paused before saying, "I know from your logbook you have been on the Buchaille before. However, the Chasm is a lot harder and longer. What makes you think you can climb it?"

"Well, it's been a long dry spell so far, this will ensure the normal wet sections are in relatively good conditions. I've been climbing well so far and I have another good climber, John, who has agreed to second me."

To Bomber's surprise, the major agreed that they could do it, providing he came with them to the start to ensure they started in the right place. Then he said, "Dawn start, forecast is good until late afternoon when showers are forecast and believe me, you do not want to be on that route in the rain."

The 120-foot hawser laid climbing rope snaked down below Bomber's feet. Looking between his legs, he could see John belaying him from a precarious belay stance. Bomber had run out all the rope and had only managed to place two runners that would hopefully stop a long fall, should he become detached from the rock. Now he couldn't find a place to belay, to bring John up to him. Looking right, he couldn't see anything and he silently cursed the Jocks for being so mean with their route descriptions. After a precarious traverse left, he found a small ledge, where at shoulder height, he found a thin vertical crack. It was too small to take the chocks he had with him so he fished out two knife blade pitons and hammered them into the crack. Securing himself to these, he was able to bring up John. As he reached Bomber, they both realised at the same time it had gone dark and looking up, they could see thick black clouds spreading from the west over the top of the mountain.

"Better get a move on, it looks like the rain is arriving a lot earlier than forecast," Bomber's comments were met with the first splatter of rain.

"Well, we must be three quarters of the way up now so hopefully it won't be too bad." A crash of thunder punctuated John's words, and they both ducked as if a bomb had gone off.

"Fucking hell, that's all we need!" shouted John over the din. "Let's get the blazes out of here."

"Well, it's too difficult to try and abseil back down now. So it's the top or nothing."

The final pitches to the top were a blur. Every time Bomber raised an arm to find a handhold, water found its way through the cuff of his jacket under his armpit and down inside his shirt. Despite this, he felt elated, man against the element. The rain blinded him and the wind threatened to tear him from his holds but he didn't care. This was living, a fight for survival, every move had to be carefully calculated. The rock was getting slippery and there was a high risk of taking a onetime flying lesson. Bomber felt great!

At the top of the climb, they still had a long way to go to the summit and then their descent route from the col down the gulley. Heading uphill, they bowed their heads into the teeth of the storm. Bomber said a silent prayer of thanks that the thunder and lightning had ceased. More mountaineers got killed by lightning than any other means according to the mountain rescue handbook and Bomber was not keen to add to that statistic.

As they descended, the rain became lighter and eventually they broke out of the cloud layer, which, up to then, had blinded them. Below them, they could see the river and the small footbridge and the Land Rover that had been left for them on the other side. As they sat in the vehicle, removing waterproofs and sodden clothing, another Land Rover pulled up.

"Well, you made it, good." It was the major leaning out of the side window of the Lanny. "I suspect it was a little hairy at times near the top."

"That's an understatement, sir," shouted back John, "but it was bloody fantastic, especially now we are down." Bomber joined in the laughter and that night over a few beers that tasted like nectar they talked about the climb and others like it in the area.

The change in the weather meant that any climbing was out of the question as the rain was relentless. Instead they did some Munro bashing (mountaintops of three thousand feet or over) regardless of what the weather threw at them.

On the last day, they stood on the summit of Ben Nevis with the cloud swirling up the north face like a living monster. Whipped up by a blustery west wind, it wove wild patterns around them. Suddenly, as if by magic, the clouds parted and just for a glorious moment, they could see other mountains stretching in what seemed an endless vista of peaks in colours of mauve, blues and green. It reminded Bomber of a book title, *Blue Remembered Hills*. Then the clouds closed in again like theatre curtains saying end of act one.

Chapter 14
Blue on Blue

It was raining; the heavens seemed to be unloading rain in Biblical proportions and the night was as black as a witch's hat. Bomber led the patrol slowly away from the mill and into the Ardoyne. The company commander had decided that there would be no, 'no-go areas' in the Cath's or Prod's areas under his jurisdiction.

Everyone wore cam cream on their faces so they blended into the shadows, where they could become almost invisible. Only movement gave them away. There had been a number of random shootings in Catholic areas, mostly drive-bys. It was not clear who was responsible but it was generally believed to be the work of the protestant UVF (Ulster Volunteer Force).

Bomber signalled the patrol to halt and everyone melted into the shadows. It was a low noise that had alerted him and now he could hear it clearly. It was a car driving at slow speed with its lights off. As he waited, a door opened on a house not fifty yards from the patrol. Suddenly, the car became visible as it raced forward in the darkness. Shots rang out from at least two semiautomatic weapons. The figure dropped to the ground and the air was ripped by the sound of SLR's firing at the car. There was a horrible grinding sound as rounds tore through the engine block and the car swerved to the right smashing into a redundant streetlight before side-swiping the front of a house.

Dusty was already sending a contact report, asking for back up and medical support. Bomber ordered two men to the downed figure while he and several others surrounded the car. The door to the house that the car had rammed opened and a man appeared. Seeing the armed soldiers, he slammed the door closed and Bomber heard a key turn in the lock.

"Don't shoot, don't shoot," came from within the shattered vehicle and two Browning semiautomatic pistols came out of the passenger window. The driver was slumped over the steering wheel groaning. His left shoulder was soaked in blood. "Get them out!" ordered Bomber.

The lads dragged out the two uninjured ones while the wounded driver was carefully eased out and laid on the tarmac. Field dressings were strapped to the front and back of his wound and he was searched. In a shoulder holster was another Browning handgun.

The larger of the two was making a lot of verbal and demanded to speak to who was in charge. Bomber approached and the man lowered his head and said, "We are on your side; we're MRF." He spoke it in a conspiratorial way as if Bomber should know what it meant. He had heard the MRF mentioned by the brigadier but he wasn't letting on.

He went on to say, "You are in big trouble opening fire on us; now you will escort us out of here fast."

By now, doors were opening and people were gathering and Bomber knew trouble would start as soon as the locals figured out what had happened.

"Oh, I will get you out of here all right."

Bomber turned to Armalite and said, "Cuff them; they are under arrest."

"No; you can't—" but the argument was cut short by Armalite introducing his rifle butt to the man's stomach.

"How's the other one, Cpl Jacobs?" Bomber asked, indicating the figure that had dropped to the ground.

Jacobs brought the man to him saying, "The luckiest guy alive, one bullet has gone through his hat." To emphasise the point, Jacobs had his finger through the peak of the flat cap. "Another one had nicked the sleeve of his rain coat."

Bomber recognised the man as one whose car he had stopped occasionally on routine checks. "Mr Doherty, bet you don't get this much excitement in the dockyard now, do you?"

Doherty looked shaken and steadied himself by holding onto Jacobs. "I never thought I would say this, son, but thank the lord you were here tonight."

"Amen to that," Bomber said shaking Doherty's hand. "Now while I get these shits properly arrested and taken away, I would be grateful if you could speak to your friends and tell them to go home."

As Bomber spoke, two teenagers forced their way towards him shouting, "What are you doing to our da?"

Doherty calmed them but now people were beginning to form their own opinions of what had happened and their anger was being turned on the patrol and the three from the car.

Doherty showed great courage holding up his hands and saying, "Leave it to the soldiers. They saved my life and have shot one of the buggers, so no trouble." Turning to his sons, he said, "I want to go home now, boys."

This seemed to pacify the mob, which was timely, as at that moment, the backup and ambulance arrived. The RUC officer with the backup wanted the other two taken to the Crumlin Road Police Station but Bomber insisted that they were taken to the mill first. He thought there were questions to be asked by the ops officer about why these MRF idiots were operating in our area and why they seemed to think they were our buddies.

In the mill, the ops officer and the CSM set about grilling the two men in separate rooms. The resident RUC Sgt and the RUC officer who arrived with the backup sat in taking notes.

The only information either would give was that they were part of MRF and working directly for GHQ. Bomber wished he could have half an hour with them, certain that he could get the larger of the two men to talk as he seemed to get off on the fact that he was some special agent. After a phone call, the ops officer at GHQ denied any knowledge of them.

Bomber made his own call, leaving a message. If anyone knew what was going on, it would be this man.

"Who do you think they are, boss?" Thorny asked as he passed a mug of tea to Bomber, who was sitting in the best of the broken armchairs in the mess.

"Christ knows. They are not SAS; I've already worked that out."

"How?" Thorny looked puzzled.

"Well, if they were SAS, firstly, Doherty would be dead and secondly, they would not be acting as if they were something special. They would sit quietly and wait for their own team leader to come and pick them up. We have had them for two hours and no one has arrived or even phoned to help them."

They both sat sipping the tea until Thorny broke the silence. "Then who the fuck are they?"

161

The phone rang and Bomber picked it up guessing who it would be. "Tell me," the voice of the brigadier said.

Bomber related the events to him and waited. The phone was quiet for a moment. "Can't talk on this phone, not secure enough, can you get to a secure phone in the ops room?"

"Yes, give me five minutes."

In the ops room, Bomber selected the secure phone furthest away from the operations table where two clerks and the platoon commander from three platoon were fielding the radio calls.

Bomber dialled the number and the brigadier answered, "Going secure now." Bomber and the brigadier pressed the secure button at the same time on their respective phones. Now anyone listening in would only hear a garbled mess. Only the listener at each end could hear what was actually said.

"The silly ideas' boys have come up with this MRF nonsense against my advice and they, like Hood's group, seem to have a freehand to do what they want. I have suspected that they have been behind these drive-by shootings but no proof until now. I have already made a protest to the brigade commander, who has spoken to the general."

"But why let them do this? We could have killed all three of them."

"It's a lack of having a real strategy to deal with the situation and the powers that be are desperate for a way of combating what is becoming a major terrorist war."

"Bloody hell, it's bad enough fighting the enemy, now we have to fight our own terrorist group as well."

"I agree. Anyway I have spoken to your CO who will ensure that it's my people who collect these clowns. It will be

O'Neil and a couple of RUC; oh, and Small will be with them. Now I have to go," with that, the phone went dead.

Bomber sat thinking, going over what had been said, then he realised that three platoons commander was standing close by looking at him.

"Any chance you know what's going on and might enlighten me?"

Lt Harris was the sort of man that the ladies adored. Six foot, athletic with dark good looks; well spoken, with an air of unflappability.

Bomber told him as much as he could and said that they should expect Superintendent O'Neil shortly. As he stood up to leave, the door opened and in walked the CO, looking like a man who wanted heads on poles, so Bomber slipped away before he became the target for the CO's anger.

Bomber sat in the mess, thinking that it was not that many years ago when he and others like him had sat in filthy alleyways waiting to take out bombers and gunmen and no one knew they were there. They too faced the possibility of being shot at by their own side. However, they were not gunning down innocent civilians.

Were these MRF idiots trying to fan the flames between Caths and Prods? Possibly, but to what end? They certainly did not seem to have any qualms about doing it.

His thoughts were interrupted by the CSM coming in and telling him there was a company commander's brief in ten minutes for all platoon commanders and Sgts.

The commander looked seriously hacked off and it transpired he had been ordered to release the so-called MRF pair into the custody of the RMPs who had arrived from GHQ. As it was happening, Superintendent O'Neil arrived and a dispute took place as to who had authority. In the end, O'Neil won but it had caused the company commander a lot of grief with GHQ.

"Now," said the commander in a loud voice to ensure he had everyone's full attention, "As of tomorrow night, we will re-start the covert ops. Each platoon commander is to liaise with the previous house owners and see if they will allow us back in. If not, then our RUC Sgt has a list of potential house owners who might oblige." He paused took a pointer and pointed to the street map indicating three areas. "Each platoon will be responsible for the areas allocated thus." He tapped the map, "One platoon, two platoon and three." Replacing the pointer, he went on. "I want a patrol in each area twenty-four hours a day ready to react to whatever the ops spot without delay. The rest of each platoon not deployed will be divided into two groups, one at fifteen minutes notice the other at thirty minutes. I know this is demanding but we have three more weeks here before a break back in Ballykinler and I want it high profile. Results, gentlemen, can be measured in two ways. One, those trouble makers we catch or kill and two, that the IRA, PIRA, UVF lack the will to try anything while we are on the streets."

The commander looked at everyone's faces, then snapped, "Questions?"

Several routine questions were dealt with. Then the one Bomber was expecting came from three platoon commander.

"What about these chaps driving around shooting at people, are they on our side or what, sir?"

"Anyone driving, walking or even coming by bloody kite who starts shooting in your area gets the same treatment as per the yellow card orders. Clear!"

Everyone was clear and the meeting ended with the new ops room stag list for platoon commanders. Even after a patrol, all had to do a stint manning the radios, responding to what was going on and passing it to the patrols on the ground.

Later, sitting in Paddy's kitchen, drinking tea with a dash of Glen Fiddich, of which Bomber had brought Paddy two new bottles, they talked about local affairs.

Paddy indicated that the Prods were getting more hard-line, arming themselves into two groups, the UVF (Ulster Volunteer Force) and the UDA (Ulster Defence Association) both of which co-operated with each other and had good contacts throughout the RUC and other security agencies.

"Where are they getting the weapons from?"

Paddy paused, sipped some medicine and said, "No one has said these organisations are illegal, so a lot of shotguns, target rifles and handguns are licensed through the RUC for anyone who wishes to buy one. Rumour has it they are now buying stuff from gun catalogues and then smuggling them home from Belgium. I'm not talking sporting stuff here but serious hardware."

"Smuggling in how?" asked Bomber gently.

Paddy looked sideways at Bomber. "That I don't know and would you really expect me to tell you if I knew?"

"Guess not. Who's doing these drive-by shootings?"

"Nasty business, rumour has it that the UDA has a special task force UFF (Ulster Freedom Fighters), only the top men know who they are. They get special training and weapons but what they are doing is going to backfire, that's for sure."

Bomber left Paddy's, pondering on what he had learnt. Back at the mill, he briefed the CSM who said it very much confirmed what was coming in from all the sources.

Three evenings later, as he was getting ready to go out on patrol, he was called to the briefing room. On entering, he was met with the sight of the commander and the brigadier studying a street map. The CSM and Cpl Small were standing close by.

Oh shit, what now? was the first thought that went through Bomber's mind, *What are they setting me up for now?*

The commander turned and saw him. "Ah, C/Sgt, we have had a sighting of what we believe to be Hood or Captain Briggs here." He stabbed the map with a pencil at a building right on the edge of their area then circled it.

The brigadier took up the reins, "Seems he may have run foul of his friends on the other side. My source has it he was dragged into the building in rather a roughed-up state." The brigadier looked thoughtful and Bomber noticed once again he was not smoking but constantly fiddled with a pack of Polo mints.

"What's the building?" Bomber asked but thought he already knew it was a burnt-out shirt factory.

"It's the old shirt factory, roof's gone but the walls are good and the first floor is intact," interjected the commander.

"We want you to take your platoon there and get Briggs and whoever is with him. You have to leave now. Mind, we want him alive if they have not already killed him."

"Yes sir," replied Bomber and raced out to Thorny who was getting the patrol into two pigs. Including himself and the drivers, there were fourteen in the patrol. A quick huddled brief, then he sent Armalite and Harris to go and change into civvies while Thorny drew out two 9mm semiautomatic pistols for them.

The pigs stopped a block and a half from the target. Bomber then sent Harris to wander around to find out who was about. He returned in less than three minutes, reporting that there were two dickers near the front of the building. This time, Bomber sent both Harris and Armalite walking down the street doing an impersonation of two who had had a skin full. It looked quite comical, Harris had a cigarette which he wanted Armalite to fire up but neither of them could co-ordinate enough to achieve it. The dickers thought this hilarious and were openly laughing. As they drew level, Harris and Armalite sprang into action, grabbing the two teenagers and clamping large hands over their mouths.

Bomber had sent four men under Cpl Jacobs to secure the rear of the building. Now that the dickers had been neutralised, Bomber and the rest raced towards the building in the pigs. As they hit the brakes, they dived out tearing the rickety, corrugated iron makeshift door off its hinges. They charged in with cries of "Army, drop your weapons or we fire".

Inside, it was dim and dank. Water dripped from the ceiling. In the middle of the space, which had once held the machinery for making the finest shirts in Europe, stood a large bench. Naked and tied to it was a shattered figure. Standing near him holding his hands in the air was a nasty looking cretin. In one hand, he held a heavy ball hammer. The hammer, his hand and his shirtsleeve were covered in blood.

Three other figures were disappearing into the gloom at the back of the building. Thorny and two others went in hot pursuit. Armalite and Harris, having secured the dickers by cuffing them and placing them in the pigs, now joined Bomber by the bench.

"Is he dead?" Harris asked.

The body shuddered in pain then answered in a blubbering whisper, "No, I'm not dead; is that you Brown I'm having trouble seeing?"

Before Bomber could answer, shooting erupted from the back of the building. It lasted for several minutes, then Thorny appeared with the rest of the team dragging a body and frog-marching another in front of them. "One dead, one alive, but one got away boss," announced Thorny. "Sorry."

Bomber nodded. He had been looking at Briggs' body. His feet had been smashed into a pulp as had his right knee. Blood was leaking from his groin area and Bomber winced at the thought at what they had done there. His right hand was just a red lump and his face was swollen and one eye was completely closed. The hammer man had been enjoying his work.

"Fuck me, what a mess," Thorny broke the silence. Harris had the hammer man on his knees and was cuffing him.

Indicating Briggs, Bomber said, "Cut him loose, be careful. Dusty have you called for the ambulance?"

"Already done, boss."

"Brown, Brown," the face croaked.

Bomber moved closer. "What do you want?"

"I had a feeling it would be you turning up here. Did you get them all?"

"One got away."

"That would be O'Donohue, the fucking bastard, trust you to let him get away."

The sentence took a lot out of him and another shudder of pain raked his body.

"Why did they turn on you, what happened?"

"O'Halligan's team. They knew it wasn't an own goal and they thought I set it up." Briggs shuddered and coughed then spat blood.

"I gave them your name, said you and that old bastard Rogers did it."

Bomber felt himself go a little cold. "Why did you do that, it could have been the SAS boys?"

"Of course it was the fucking SAS, but they wanted names and you and that fossil Rogers pissed me off and caused me all this trouble." What passed for a laugh came from him followed by another spasm.

Dusty interrupted, "Ambulance is here, boss."

Bomber carried on looking at the broken and smashed body of Briggs. As much as he wanted to, he couldn't feel any compassion for the man. *You are a real bastard,* the voice said in his head.

The medics came in with Sgt Mike Smith. Mike took one look at the figure before him, then took a morphine syrette out of his pack and jabbed it into Briggs left buttock before having him put on the stretcher and covered with a blanket.

Having sent the stretcher to the ambulance, he turned his attention to the body. After a brief examination, he produced a body bag and asked who shot him. Two of the lads raised their hands. "Good, well done," said Mike with a smile. "Now you can put him in this and load him into the ambulance."

With a few grumbles, the job was done and while the ambulance set off for the hospital with its escort, Bomber and the team returned to the mill. The two dickers, the gunman and Mr Hammer were trussed up nicely in the back of the pigs, getting a blow for blow account from the lads of what they could expect once in custody. None of it true but it would have them shitting themselves by the time they arrived at the mill.

While Thorny handed the prisoners over to the duty RUC officer, Bomber reported to the commander and the brigadier, telling them what Briggs had said to O'Donohue and how he had got away while his henchmen had a shootout with the platoon.

"O'Donohue eh," the brigadier popped a Polo mint into his mouth. "His name keeps coming up rather too frequently for my liking." He crunched the mint and no one spoke for a minute. "Did you get a look at him?"

"No afraid not, he scarpered fast when we went in, sacrificing his two gunmen to ensure his getaway. So they must think him important."

"Indeed, I will get my contacts working on identifying him."

A knock on the door was followed by the CSM and one of the clerks coming in. The clerk carried a tray with mugs of tea and a packet of Jammy Dodgers biscuits on it. The clerk set the tray down, then left. The CSM opened the biscuits and they all tucked in.

Bomber broke the silence, "What's going to happen to Briggs?"

The brigadier munched his Jammy Dodger. "From your description of his injuries, he is not going to be fit to answer any questions today. However, I have managed to persuade the powers that be to shut down these autonomous groups. Now everything with the odd exception will be under one person's control."

"Your control?" Bomber asked.

"Oh, I'm just a retired old war horse. A new man, very good one as well, will co-ordinate all the intelligence and action groups."

Action groups, thought Bomber, *sounds just like the thing we don't need.*

"So, sir, where do you fit in?"

The brigadier smiled and looked at the commander, who also smiled. *Jesus fucking Christ*, thought Bomber. *Is this some sort of joke?*

The commander spoke, "The brigadier and his team are still sort of independent; they have been in country a long time, mid-fifties I believe." The brigadier nodded.

"The IRA were active in the mid-fifties doing cross border attacks on the RUC. Not large scale but enough to warrant us investigating and building a net-work of contacts on both sides of the community and border. Basically, the brigadier saw the possibility of this all happening and on a very tight budget built a network that he alone handles. That way the contacts all stay safe."

The brigadier gave a cough and the commander stopped. "No need to bore the C/Sgt with history, Christopher. All we need to say is business as usual."

They all drank some tea, then Bomber spoke, "So you have given up smoking, sir."

"Doctor said if I don't, he would not give me five years. So I had some hypnosis and it's worked, I'm smoke free."

Bomber was shocked and must have looked it.

"Oh, don't worry, C/Sgt, I had the hypnotist killed afterwards." He and the commander burst out laughing at Bomber's expression.

"Guess I asked for that."

The brigadier stood, "Now must go and check on Briggs. Sgt Small, yes he has been promoted, is babysitting him at the moment."

With that, he shook hands with the commander. As Bomber stood to salute, the brigadier grabbed his hand and shook it firmly saying, "Keep up the good work. I know you won't join my team but I consider you my most able part-timer."

Then he was gone and Bomber found the commander looking at him. "What sir?"

"You could do a lot worse than join his team you know. He has been in this business a lifetime and he answers only to the government for his actions but he is very good at keeping the GOC on his side as well. The troubles here are going to drag on for a long time."

Bomber felt if he accepted, he would be trapped with no way out. He liked being in a regiment with people who he could trust. They were his family and to leave was almost unthinkable.

"Think about it, no need to rush into anything."

Bomber nodded saluted and left the room.

Chapter 15
Money

It had been three weeks since Bomber had last seen the brigadier and the regiment was now back in Ballykinler. Two days of R and R had been followed by range work and fitness training. Now, during close quarter combat, Bomber was just wondering how to get out of a stranglehold from behind, being applied a little too enthusiastically by Blackman, when a voice called out, "C/Sgt, you are wanted by the CO now!" The summons distracted Blackman who loosened his hold just enough for Bomber to stamp on his foot and ram an elbow into his midriff. As Blackman grunted in pain and let go, Bomber kicked him on the side of his knee and watched him fall to the gym mat, cursing and holding his leg.

"Good work but you mustn't let yourself get distracted, Blackman," Bomber said, laughing, then stepped over him narrowly avoiding a kick aimed at his groin.

When the CO said now, he meant now and Bomber knew he would have to go straight there in his physical training kit, sweat and all.

At the HQ, the adjutant whisked him straight into the CO's office. Bomber marched in and halted. The CO sat behind his desk which was covered by mounds of paper work. In the only arm chair in the room sat the company commander. Standing beside him was a young lieutenant who looked nervous.

The adjutant closed the door and the CO said, "Relax, C/Sgt." Bomber stood at ease.

"Now there are some changes afoot," he pointed to the young officer, "this is Lt Nixon who will take over the platoon from you as of tomorrow. You will have a couple of days to do the handover."

Bomber felt himself sink. What, hand over his platoon! His little family of rough necks and what of me, dumped in some stores? A vision of himself counting blankets passed before his eyes.

The CO was still talking and Bomber forced himself to listen. "After you have done the handover, you will report to Captain Bass, the Recce Platoon commander, who as you know is really the regiment's ops officer. C/Sgt Pillar is being promoted to WO2 (Warrant Officer Class two) and moving on in two weeks. You will take over the Recce Platoon. Questions?"

Bomber was a little too stunned to think of any question so simply said, "No sir; thank you, sir."

"No need to thank me. You have earned the job and you will be ideal for the Recce Platoon's new role. Now take Lt Nixon and introduce him to his new platoon."

The handover went smoothly. Nixon seemed a good man. A little raw but he listened to Bomber and Thorny which was a good start. Bomber relaxed sure that the lads would be in good hands.

The next evening, Bomber was having farewell drinks in the NAAFI with the platoon. Later, after a few tall stories and too many drinks, Bomber and Thorny headed back to the mess. Over a final nightcap, Bomber urged Thorny to stay close to his new platoon commander and give him all the help he could. Thorny promised to take care of him until he found his feet and then they both weaved their way to their respective bunks.

Bomber was up early, running kit on he jogged his way through the sand dunes, wondering what the Recce Platoon's new role would be. The sea air helped to blow away the hangover and the exercise got the blood pumping the alcohol out of his system. He had a meeting with Captain Bass at 9:30 in the ops room. Plenty of time for his run, shower and breakfast. More importantly, time to think.

Captain Bass was a six foot two, white East African. His father still managed a farm in Kenya not too far from Lake Naivasha. For lack of any suitable work in Kenya, Bass had travelled to England and joined the British Army.

Bomber knocked on the ops room door and a voice said, "Come." Entering, Bomber saw Bass and one of the clerks pinning photographs onto a pin board mounted on the wall.

Seeing Bomber, he asked the clerk to leave and invited Bomber to sit down.

"Coffee?" he asked.

"Yes please, sir."

Bass poured two mugs from a percolator that sat in one corner on the floor.

"Milk, sugar?"

"No, just as it comes, sir, will be fine."

"Good, just the way I like it. Taste the coffee that way."

"So firstly, I would like to say I'm very pleased you are taking over from C/Sgt Pillar. He lobbied very hard for you to assume his mantle. He will be a hard act to follow; the lads in the platoon would do anything for him." Bass paused and moved some files until he found the paper he wanted.

"Now the first thing you will notice from this," he thrust a platoon strength return into his hands, "the platoon is under strength and the new role demands we are at full strength. The CO has given me the authority to plunder the other platoons for experienced men. Partly due to the fact we have a shed load of new recruits arriving next week from the depot."

He paused as one of the phones started ringing; it clicked off as one of the clerks in the next room picked it up. "Anyone you would like to include from your old platoon?"

Bomber nodded and said without hesitation, "Cpl Jacobs, L/Cpl Zika, Pte Brown, Miller and Harris. Harris is a fairly new boy but has all the makings of a top soldier and works well with Brown." Bomber had a momentary tinge of guilt about plundering his old platoon of good men but then pushed it to the back of his mind.

"Good, I'll work on that. Two names I want you to take note of." Bass had underlined two of the Recce drivers. "O'Brian and O'Carroll. They are both local Catholic lads and have put in their tickets to leave the army. They were held up, which has caused some resentment from them. However, now we have new recruits coming in, they are to be released in three weeks."

He paused, looked at the names again, then carried on. "Our new role, we will be working in sections of six men, four each in the new Macron armoured Land Rover and two in the Ferret armoured car armed with a .303 machine gun. Total of five sections plus an extra command Land Rover for me if I deploy."

He stopped talking and pulled a buff colour file from a tray. Opening the file, he handed it to Bomber, who read the covering letter. It was from the brigade commander, instructing the CO to have a combat-ready platoon equipped as per the Recce Platoon to be available for any task the brigade commander might wish to employ them on. Half the platoon was to be at one hour's notice and the rest at four hours.

"Do we have any idea what these tasks will be?" Bomber asked.

"No, but I'm sure it will be any shitty job no one else would touch with a barge pole. In the meantime, we carry on with our normal unit tasks."

The meeting closed with Bomber being instructed to go and liaise with Pillar and to start the handover.

Bomber walked over to the Recce Platoon stores and tiny office where he met Steve Pillar, who greeted him with a huge handshake, pumping his arm like he was jacking up a three-ton truck. Bomber thanked him for putting his name forward for the job.

"Christ, you should have seen some of the names put forward, tossers the lot of them. Well, Bassy and I made sure none of them got a look in."

They were in the armoury, checking the registered numbers of the platoon weapons when a breathless HQ company clerk arrived, informing Bomber he was wanted at the double in the ops room.

Arriving at the ops room, he found it occupied by the CO, the brigadier and Captain Bass.

"Ah, C/Sgt, take a seat," the CO ordered.

Bomber looked at the CO who was now talking quietly to Bass. The brigadier was fiddling with his packet of Polo mints.

The CO turned to the brigadier and said, "Perhaps you would like to do the honours, Brigadier."

After popping a mint into his mouth and crunching it, the brigadier started, "The IRA is desperately short of funds for weapons and explosives. They are pushing hard in the USA fundraising but that is taking time. They are building up a cigarette and petrol-smuggling operation from the south to the north to raise money. However, in the short term, they have resorted to kidnap and ransom. Their first victim is a twenty-year-old girl from a wealthy Protestant family of factory owners. She was snatched leaving Queens University where she is studying law. The family have received a ransom demand for one million pounds to be paid within forty-eight hours of which we have thirty-eight left."

Bomber interrupted, "Can the family raise that sort of money?"

"Yes, they can, given time, but we do not want it paid. If the terrorists are successful this time, we will be inundated with kidnappings."

There was a pause during which Bomber realised that someone, namely himself, was going to be given an impossible job in an equally impossible short time.

"All the powers to be are insisting that no ransom is paid but the girl is the family's only child and they have a lot of clout with the government and want to strike a deal. Thanks to my contacts, we know where she is being held and by whom."

"So," said Bomber, "send in the SAS; end of story."

"There lays the problem, she is being held in the south. The GOC is under pressure from Westminster which has strictly laid down that no cross-border action will be taken. The Southern Irish political view is to leave the IRA alone as they hope the troubles will result in the north being ceded back to the south."

Oh shit, here it comes, thought Bomber.

"I, and I say I, take full responsibility for what happens next. I want you to go and get her."

"You don't have to do this, C/Sgt, and no one will think the worse of you if you refuse," the CO said with a sincere tone and Bomber wanted to say 'find another sucker', but instead he heard himself say,

"Where is she being held and how do you know they really have her?"

A map was produced and a building had been circled in red about thirty miles south of the border. Bomber smiled to himself as it was almost in a straight line with his other cross-border trip but much deeper into hostile territory. Perhaps the IRA felt safe being further away from the border.

"In answer to your second question, they sent a locket that her grandmother gave her and she was never without it. It came with a message stating next it would be a finger and so on," the brigadier said calmly but they all knew what the IRA was capable of.

"I'll try and get her. Now what size shoes and clothes does she wear?"

"Why do you want to know that?" Bass asked.

"If you take a hostage, the first thing you do is take their clothes and shoes away. Makes them feel vulnerable which makes them compliant."

"We can get them from her digs at university without anyone knowing," said Bass.

"No," said Bomber, "we can guess her sizes. No one must get even the faintest idea we are doing anything. The NAAFI sells trainers, fleece tops and walking trousers and we can do that in minutes."

Two hours later, Small was driving Bomber towards the border. The CO's final words echoing in his head, *Don't get caught; everyone, and I mean everyone, will deny any knowledge of you being given this job.*

Here we go again, great fun, the voice in his head sounded happy. *How could I refuse to help,* thought Bomber. *You are just too stupid to refuse,* the voice chuckled.

"Perhaps I do need to see a real shrink when, if, I get back," Bomber said aloud to Small.

Small laughed. "You are not the only one, Bomber, most of the people I work with are crazy bastards."

"Does that include the brigadier?"

Small paused for a moment then said, "He's incredibly clever. I sometimes think he can see into the future. Is he crazy? Maybe, like taking this chance with you. If certain people found out what he is up to, they would be baying for his head." They lapsed into silence, Small concentrating on the driving and Bomber brooding on what he had said.

Small had proved to be super-efficient in helping Bomber plot a route. He had identified a farm over the border where he assured Bomber that there would be a car left with the keys in the ignition, courtesy of the brigadier's contacts.

When Bomber asked, "Won't they mind me taking it?" he was told, "Don't worry; they stole it in Dublin yesterday."

Bomber set off over the fields, following the hedgerows into the south. He had estimated an hour to reach the farm and collect the car, meaning he would arrive at the target house with just enough light to study the building and the lie of the land. Crossing fields had its dangers. Cows are curious creatures and the herd would always start to investigate a person walking on their turf. After the second cow encounter, Bomber abandoned the fields and followed the country lanes.

After thirty minutes of watching the farm, he had not detected any sign of life, not even a dog. He could see the car and if it was a setup, it would be perfect, like a piece of cheese for a rat. Bomber did not have time to waste so he circled the farm for the last time, then walked along the farm lane to the car. He looked under the car and then carefully opened the bonnet and the boot. He was thankful to find nothing there that could blow him up.

Leaving the driver's door open, he started the car. It purred beautifully so, sighing with relief, Bomber closed the door and drove off. In less than an hour, he was sitting in a hedgerow five hundred yards away from the house, having abandoned the car a mile away behind a hedgerow, planning to use it later to get back to the north. He only carried a small rucksack containing the clothes for the girl, some sandwiches and a flask of now just warm tea. In his jacket pocket, he had the Beretta. Tucked in his trouser pocket was a cosh that he had made by putting one sock inside another and half filling them with sand, knotting them to keep the sand tight. One smack on the head from it would knock out anyone without killing them.

Bomber shifted uneasily in his hedgerow. Through his monocular, he could see there were two vehicles outside the house. A beat-up old Land Rover of dubious vintage that had a hard roof over the driver's section but no screen or cover at the back. Next to it was a smart dark-green Range Rover. So far he had only seen one person, who was sitting on a dry stonewall watching the lane with a shotgun cradled in his arms. *Surely,* thought Bomber, *they would have more security than this after the O'Halligan affair?*

As the light began to go, the door to the house opened. Out came five men, of whom two climbed into the Range Rover and drove off. The three others stood talking for a while, then one strolled over to the dry stonewall and swapped places with the one already there.

The three then turned together and went back in the house. *Christ four of the buggers to deal with. This is not going to be easy*, thought Bomber. *Well, if you can't take a joke you shouldn't have joined up*, the voice in his head muttered.

Scanning the area one more time, Bomber decided that there was no one else guarding the house. After two more hours, Bomber considered it dark enough to move closer to the house. He knew where the outside guard was by the glow of his cigarette and hoped he was a chain smoker, which would make it easy to keep him spotted.

Bomber was now less than a hundred yards from the rear of the house. The lights were on in all the downstairs rooms but none upstairs. Edging closer, Bomber had to freeze as the rear door suddenly opened and out stepped another sentry complete with shotgun tucked up under his arm. Bomber slowly crouched down behind the dry stonewall that led to the outhouses attached to the main house.

Now he could hear footsteps coming towards him. *He can't have seen me. His night vision will still be adjusting,*

Bomber thought. He could feel his heart pumping and he was sure his breathing was so loud, it would surely be heard.

The footsteps stopped and the man sat down on the wall just above Bomber. Then Bomber heard the wrapper of a sweet being removed. *Wait*, thought Bomber, *just a minute.* He slid the cosh out of his pocket, then holding his breath, he stood up, grabbed the back of the man's coat collar and swung the cosh; it connected with the side of the man's head with a dull thud. Bomber yanked the man back and he fell onto Bomber's side of the wall. For good measure, he smacked him one more time, then ducked down, feeling for the electrical plastic ties he had pinched from the camp electrician. Hands then feet followed by a strip of masking tape over his mouth. He unloaded the shotgun and jammed the barrels into the earth, blocking them both. Anyone firing it now without cleaning out the barrels would blow their own face off.

So one down now for the two in the house. Creeping to the back door, he was relieved to find it was not locked. Regardless of the plea from the brigadier that killing was to be the last resort as his contacts in the south were twitchy after the last incident, Bomber had the Beretta firmly in his right hand. He had no illusions as to his ability to overcome two men in the close confines of the house. In a stand-up fight, he would lose. He stopped dead; he could hear the dull thud of someone going up stairs. The footsteps stopped and he heard a man say "Put the hood on", then a door opened and closed and he heard no more.

Through the gap in the doorway, he could see another man, a fat man sitting at a table turning the pages of a newspaper in a bored fashion. Bomber swopped the Beretta from his right to his left; hefting the cosh in his right hand, he pushed the door open. Stepping quickly into the room, he swung the cosh down hard, aiming at the back of the man's head. As he did, the man half-turned in the chair: Seeing Bomber, he opened his mouth to shout but the cosh struck him on the side of his face, spinning his head away from Bomber, who struck again this time getting him square on the back of the head.

The man collapsed face down on the table. Bomber felt his legs shaking and his mouth was so dry, he couldn't swallow. Then he heard the sound of someone coming down the stairs. He forced himself to walk to the stairway door and stand behind it. As the man came through, he saw his mate with blood spreading on the tablecloth. He dropped the tray which had a plate and mug on it and pulled a gun from his waist band. Bomber struck with the cosh hitting him just behind and above the right ear. It was all that was needed; he slumped to the ground out for the count. Bomber felt his legs go from under him and he sat on the floor. He felt sick with tension and thought he was going to throw up.

Get a grip, you wimp, the voice was strong in his head. *You need to cuff and gag them.* Forcing himself up, he set about securing them. Once he was satisfied, he went to the kitchen. Leaving the light off, he went to the sink, turned on the tap and rinsed his face. Filling a mug that was on the draining board, he drank some water. Feeling better, he set off carefully up the stairs, Beretta in hand. He had not ruled out the chance that someone else might be sleeping upstairs. There were three doors and two were open, one being the bathroom the other an empty bedroom. The third had a key in the lock. He turned it, then pushed open the door. "Wait," a female voice cried. "I don't have the hood on."

"It's okay, you don't need it; I'm a friend." As Bomber stepped into the room, he could see a figure sitting on the floor, shivering under a blanket that looked as if it had seen better days.

"Who are you? Who sent you?" she said in a timid voice.

"I'm nobody, just someone sent to take you home. Now; put these clothes on." Bomber tossed the rucksack to her.

"Turn around then. I'm naked under the blanket."

Bomber turned saying, "Hurry, we don't have much time."

She quickly dressed and Bomber could see she was a tall girl with fair hair and beautiful but frightened eyes.

"Okay now," said Bomber, putting his hand on her arm to re-assure her. "We are going downstairs, okay?" She nodded and Bomber led off.

When they went into the lounge room, she gave a gasp. "Are they dead?"

"No, just knocked out." Bomber scooped up the Land Rover keys from the table and led the girl into the kitchen. "Okay, what we are going to do is walk quietly in the shadows to the Land Rover; we will get in but do not close the door until I start the engine, then you can slam it shut. When you have done that, I want you to crouch down on the floor. There is one more guard; he is about a hundred yards away with a shotgun, but I won't let him stop us, all right?"

"Yes," her voice sounded much stronger, "but what about the other two; they are coming back. I heard them say they were going to make a phone call."

Shit, thought Bomber, *there's only one road out of here for a mile until we get to the crossroads.*

"Okay, they are not here now so our only worry is getting past that clown out there."

Bomber squeezed her hand and she squeezed back.

They walked quietly with confidence to the Land Rover and gently opened the doors. Getting in, Bomber searched for the key hole and finally got it. As he did, so a voice called out.

"Patrick, is that you?"

Bomber in his best Irish shouted back, "Who else would it be?"

There was a second of silence and Bomber turned the key starting the Lanny. The engine sounded like a jet taking off. *Must have a dodgy exhaust,* thought Bomber.

The voice called again, "Patrick, get out of the Land Rover."

"He's coming towards us," the girl said quite calmly.

"Get on the floor." Bomber slammed the gear stick into first and put his foot down and the Lanny sprang forward.

Bomber drove straight at the shape of the cigarette glow that was his target. Going through the gears at a rapid rate, Bomber saw the flash and ducked down as pellets smacked into the windscreen, filling it with mini stars. The figure threw itself sideways as Bomber swerved at it. There was a clunk as the Lanny lurched over the figure's legs and as he drove away, he could hear the man screaming.

"Okay get up and put the seat belt on," Bomber instructed the girl. "It may be a rough ride."

"What seat belt?" the girl replied.

It was clear to Bomber the Lanny had had a hard life and was older than he thought. Only one headlight was working, the dashboard lights were dead and the vehicle's top speed seemed to be about forty. He instructed the girl to feel in his pocket for his small torch to shine on the dash and see what petrol they had.

"Just under half a tank," she said, sounding much better. "Who are you?" she asked. "I don't mean your name, are you police, army or did my dad hire you?"

"I told you I'm nobody. I don't exist and nobody sent me."

"Well, nobody, thank you for saving me."

"Save the thanks; we are not north of the border yet, look."

They were a couple of hundred yards from the cross roads where a set of lights were turning into the lane. The lane was just wide enough for two cars to pass if both squeezed as far as possible to one side.

The other vehicle was now flashing its lights at them. "Hold tight," said Bomber and swung the Lanny at a wooden gate which went into a field. The gate parted with a crash and Bomber paused long enough to get the vehicle into four-wheel drive before driving hard with the engine and gear box screaming in protest. Any thoughts of getting to the other car were now abandoned.

"Look for another gate on that side of the field." Bomber waved his arm to the right struggling to avoid some cows, why would they not get up out of the way. Looking in the rear-view mirror, he could see the more powerful Range Rover gaining on them.

"Over there, over there!" she shouted. Bomber could just see it in the dim single headlight, another wooden gate. Swinging the wheel hard to the right, he hit the gate and it crashed apart. Bomber heaved the Lanny into a hard left onto the lane.

This time the old Lanny did not escape undamaged. He could hear metal rubbing on a wheel and what was left of the exhaust pipe clattered onto the tarmac.

Looking in the rear-view mirror, he could see the Range Rover had been held up by the cows. *This is your chance*, the little voice said. *Put your foot down and go for it.*

"In this heap of shit, it's flat out at forty."

"What did you say?" the girl asked. Bomber had not realised until then he had spoken out loud.

"Nothing, just wishing we had a Range Rover instead of this old heap."

They now had about a two-hundred-yard lead on the Range Rover and by pushing the Lanny as hard as he could, he hoped to maintain it to the border.

The girl was looking behind her at the Range Rover, "They're gaining on us."

Bomber felt in his pocket and pulled out the Beretta, pushing off the safety catch. "Have you fired a gun before?"

"A shotgun but not a pistol."

"Okay, use two hands and just point it at the centre of their vehicle if it gets too close. Then just squeeze the trigger."

She took the Beretta and turned in the seat to face backwards and Bomber hoped she would not have to use it.

They were now on a straight section of lane which would suit the powerful Range Rover. The lane led to the border still miles away and a T-junction where they would turn left.

"They're gaining fast, shall I shoot?"

"Not yet." Bomber watched the rear-view mirror. The Range Rover was almost on them, its powerful engine giving them a turn of speed that made the old Lanny seem like a three-legged camel.

Hearing the cracks as shots whizzed past them, Bomber shouted above the roar of the engine. "Okay, let them have it."

The girl fired, once, twice and then three more times in quick succession. "I got them, I got them," she cried.

The Range Rover backed off and Bomber thought, *We are going to make it.*

Suddenly, the Range Rover surged forward and before the girl could fire again it struck the back of the poor old Lanny. Bomber fought to keep it on the road as it swerved violently from the impact.

Bomber could hear the girl screaming, "You bastards, you bastards," as she fired again until the Beretta clicked on empty.

The Range Rover backed off again this time giving them more space.

Catching his breath Bomber said, "In my pocket, another magazine of ammo."

The girl found it and he told her how to change the magazine and to cock it. One of the Range Rover's headlights had gone out. *Good shooting*, he thought. The Range Rover kept its distance and no one fired at them. *Must have scared them*, thought Bomber, *or are they plotting something?*

Finally he saw the sign, 'leaving Eire'. *Only two hundred to go but will they hold back once we cross.* Bomber had his answer as the Range Rover again roared up behind them. This time it hit them hard and the girl let out a cry as she fell against the door post.

"Hold tight," shouted Bomber. They were at the junction and he swung a hard left, the Lanny rocking dangerously, almost tipping over. They both heard a crash as a small truck without lights on hit the Range Rover. The Range Rover spun, hit the grass verge and then crashed into the ditch, stopping with its one headlight pointing to the heavens like an accusing finger.

Bomber hit the brakes, took the Beretta from the girl and ran back to the wreck. He could see the giant figure of Sgt Small walking to the Range Rover, an old fashioned Thompson sub-machine gun cradled in his hands.

Small covered Bomber while he looked into the vehicle. He saw two bullet holes in the windscreen on the passenger side. *So that's why they had stopped shooting,* he thought. The passenger had a hole in his head. *The girl did good*, thought Bomber, *but I won't tell her*. The driver was slumped against the steering wheel, his neck clearly broken. He had not been wearing a seat belt. "Clear," said Bomber quietly to Small who stepped forward and produced a small camera and took headshots of both.

"Need it for the log."

There was a strong smell of petrol and Bomber went to turn off the ignition but Small stopped him saying,

"Car in a lay-by on the right fifty yards on. I'll deal with this." He spoke in a staccato manner and thrust a set of keys into Bomber's hand. "I'll be with you in a minute."

"What about the truck?"

"Borrowed it from a builder's yard last night," Small said in an offhand manner, "so no problems."

Bomber went back to the Lanny; the girl was standing by its side.

"What happened?" she asked.

"A friend was waiting. Now let's go. There's a car up the road."

190

They found the vehicle and Bomber put the girl in the back and he got in the front passenger seat, feeling he had had enough of driving for one night. Besides, the driver's seat was set for the giant.

There was a sudden whoosh sound and flames lit the sky behind them. The driver's door opened and Small got in passing the Thompson to Bomber who put it on the floor between his feet. The car settled to the right as Small's considerable weight tested the springs. Bomber clapped him on the shoulder and said, "Thank you, pal, that's another one I owe you."

"Yes, thank you so much, er, what's your name?" said the girl.

"No names," said Bomber a little too sharply. Then in a kinder voice said, "Sorry, it's for your own protection as well as ours."

"I understand but it's a shame I don't know the names of my rescuers except Mr Nobody here," tapping Bomber on the shoulder. "However, my name is Jenny, hope that's not breaking any rules?"

"No miss," said Small, who was now driving the car carefully heading north. "It is a pleasure to have been of help." Bomber noticed for the first time that Small was well spoken, no accent, just good Queen's English.

"So what happens now?" Jenny asked.

Bomber answered, "We take you home and drop you at the start of the driveway to your house. There are police at the house and we don't want to meet them."

"I have to phone in to let the boss know we are on the way. He will warn the police we are dropping Jenny off," Small spoke quietly, seemingly distracted by the thought of having to phone in.

A couple of miles further on, they pulled into a lay-by at a crossroad where there was a lone telephone box.

The call took less than a minute, then they were driving again. Just under an hour later, they pulled up at an impressive set of open wrought iron gates. "Here we are," said Small.

The girl undid her seat belt, reached across the front seats and put an arm round each of their shoulders. "Thank you so much. Remember my name, Jenny Morrison, and in a couple of years, I will be a lawyer, so if you ever need one, call me."

With that, she jumped out of the car and Bomber could tell she was crying.

"Better go," said Small, nodding in the direction of torches coming towards them. They sped off with just a little wheel spin to make it all sound dramatic.

Bomber woke with a start; he had fallen asleep almost as soon as they had left Jenny. "Where are we?" queried Bomber.

"Lisburn HQ, the boss wants to talk to us in private."

Bomber handed the old Thompson sub-machine gun back to Small saying, "Where did you get that antiquated thing from?"

Small laughed and said, "Oh, you would be surprised at what the brigadier has collected over the years."

The brigadier's office was the size of a large cupboard with just enough room for a small desk, three hard backed chairs, a tall five-draw filing cabinet and a safe that looked like it was of Victorian vintage.

"Come in, come in," the brigadier greeted them like long lost brothers. "Sit down." He pulled open the bottom drawer of the filing cabinet, removing three mugs and a bottle of Johnnie Walker. Pouring a generous slug into each mug, he handed one to each of them. "Doctor said I have to give up drinking as well as cigarettes. Cigarettes are one thing but good whisky, never!"

He raised his mug and said, "To you both for a job well done."

They drank deeply; Bomber immediately felt the whisky go to his head and his stomach growled in protest at not being fed. *Oh, for a cheese sandwich,* thought Bomber.

"Now tell me all about it."

Bomber explained, finishing by saying it was a close-run thing but thanks to Sgt Small, it worked out fine.

The brigadier sat silent for a moment, then downed his whisky, smacked his lips and said, "Good work. The proverbial will hit the fan in a little while when the powers that be realise someone has been south of the border. But we just keep quiet and act completely innocently, then it will die down quickly. Hopefully, the IRA will get the message that kidnapping won't work and we will always find them. You didn't, by any chance, check to see if any of the men you disabled had any ID on them?"

The look on Bomber's face said it all.

"Of course not, don't know what I was thinking of," the brigadier said quickly.

They sat quietly for a while, then as if a switch had been flipped, the brigadier stood up saying, "I can see you are all in, C/Sgt. Sgt Small has sorted you a bunk in the mess so off you go and get a good night's rest, what's left of it, that is."

Bomber was on his second helping of bacon and eggs when Sgt Small came into the mess dining room in the morning. A pile of newspapers was tucked under his arm. "Did you sleep well?" he asked.

"Very well, but could have done with another six hours at least."

Small plonked the papers on the table in front of Bomber, exposing the front pages. The top one was the Belfast Telegraph. The front was all about the return of Jenny Morrison to her family and the death of two IRA men involved in her kidnapping. No mention of a border crossing and who was involved in the rescue.

"A bit quick off the mark coming up with this, don't you think?" Bomber said to Small.

Small looked around to see if anyone was in ear shot. "The boss's doing, wants the public on side to stop any in-fighting on our side. The politicians love a success story, especially if it takes the public's mind of other issues."

Bomber nodded as if he really knew what it was all about, then asked. "Can you to take me to Ballykinler this morning?"

"No problem, give me an hour and I will have a car at the mess ready to go."

"Great," said Bomber. "By the way, I can't keep calling you Sgt or Small, what's your first name?"

Small smiled saying. "It's Saul, my mother's idea, but since I've seen the light, everyone calls me Paul." He laughed then finished by saying, "That was the boss's idea, Saul of Tarsus and all that."

Bomber laughed. "Okay, Paul it is," and they shook hands.

Paul left and Bomber settled down to more tea and toast while he scanned the papers.

Chapter 16
On a Bomb and a Prayer

Bomber had now been looking after the Recce Platoon for ten days, most of which had been spent on KP duties (Key Points). The KPs could be anything from radio communication masts to remote unmanned TA centres. Anything that was important to the establishment that the IRA might consider a target. The two drivers, O'Brian and O'Carroll, who Bomber had interviewed had been told he would keep them on camp duties until they were discharged. O'Brian seemed surly and unimpressed but muttered a "Thanks". O'Carroll was more relaxed and happy to be left in camp.

Bomber had two reasons for doing this, one was to spare both of them having to do anything unpleasant against their own community, friends or family. Secondly, he did not want them privy to the new tactics and drills he was introducing to the platoon.

Returning one morning to Ballykinler, having spent a fruitless night, watching a country cross road for any night time activity, he was informed he was to go straight to the ops officer. Handing over to his number two Sgt Mason, he went straight into the regiment's HQ.

Captain Bass was looking a bit harassed when Bomber arrived and went straight into what had been happening. "C/Sgt, the IRA has a new tactic; they are targeting our bomb disposal chaps. Phone call to the RUC from IRA, stating bomb in so and so building will explode in one hour, then when the building has been evacuated, in goes our chap complete with screwdriver and pliers, then bang, dammed gunman shoots him. No bomb, just whack, end of the bomb disposal man."

"How often has this happened?" asked Bomber.

"Twice, the first time they missed and our boy got away. Then it wasn't tried again for five or six bomb calls. Then last night, it happened again. Suggestions to counter this?"

Bomber thought for a moment. "Off the top of my head, I see three options which are, one after receiving the call, we seal off the building and wait for it to blow. If it doesn't, then we wait out the gunman or flush him out with some CS gas."

"Don't think that's an option as the powers want the destruction stopped, not wait and see if it happens."

"Well, the second option is the bomb disposal boy waits outside and we go in and clear the building of any possible gunmen first."

"Any more options?"

"Yes, we leave everything as it is and hope that it doesn't happen again."

Captain Bass was silent with his head bowed. "Okay," he suddenly said, "it's the second option, we go in first. Let's discuss how?"

Again Bomber thought, *Cost of training a bomb disposal man against an infantryman got to be at least five to one.* PBI (poor bloody infantry).

They sat and discussed the different ways they could do this. Having chewed it over for an hour, they could only come up with one way. Straight in with normal house-clearing drill but only two would go in, not a full team.

Bomber found Sgt Ian Mason in the stores, checking that all the loose kit from the vehicles had been handed in. Bomber took him to one side and explained what was happening.

"Fuck me," said Ian. "I hope every time we go in it's a gunman. Fancy my chances that way but not against a ticking bomb."

"My sentiments exactly. Let the lads get breakfast, then we will go through the drills for an hour or two before they get their heads down. Mine and Cpl Well's section will deploy to Belfast at 1400 hours and take the first three days."

Ian nodded and went out to tell the lads the form.

It was raining, the sort of hard rain that makes you want to stay in bed and say to hell with the world. They were on their second day of babysitting the bomb disposal team, consisting of a captain and his Cpl, who also drove their Land Rover.

Bomber was shocked to see what little equipment they had to deal with the bombs. A bag of tools, a camera and just the standard army issue helmet and World War Two flak vest.

Bomber wonder where all the kit he had seen demonstrated at Warminster years ago had gone. He mentioned this to the captain who shrugged and said that lots of stuff was in the pipeline but probably would not arrive in Northern Ireland for another year.

Bomber told him about the things they had tried in Aden, such as shooting up a suspect bomb package which tore it apart and rendered it useless. The captain nodded and said he had an idea on that theme for suspect car bombs and was waiting approval.

The lads were just brewing up when the call came, bomb in a clothing factory not far from the city centre. Timing-wise they had fifty minutes if the caller was telling the truth.

They raced to the address, Bomber leading in his Macron armoured Land Rover, the bomb boys next with the ferret-armoured car at the rear. They arrived with thirty-nine minutes left on the clock. The employees were being herded down the street by the RUC away from the factory.

There was no time for finesse. The factory manager had already told Bomber they were ordered out at gunpoint by three hooded men, one carrying a suitcase. Where he had put the case he didn't know but it must be on the ground floor because they hadn't been in there for long.

Bomber, concerned that time was against them, took the manager to one side. The man looked shaken and pale, so Bomber spoke gently, "Now I want you to think, did you see all three go in and all three come out?"

The man looked a little confused, then he pulled himself together. "One stayed by the door with a pistol, making sure we stayed in the yard. Two went in but I don't know if two came out; I was busy trying to keep the girls calm, some were crying—" Bomber cut him off and briefed the lads. The Ferret had already gone to cover the rear of the building. Harris, he put to cover the right side where there was a fire door.

"Let's go!" snapped Bomber and he and Armalite went through the doorway like scalded cats. Inside, they leapfrogged through the workstations. Bomber risked a look at his watch; thirty-two minutes left.

Armalite was pointing in the centre of the workroom. A large suitcase sat on the floor between two work stations. *Shit, thought Bomber, is it real or a set up?* Sweat trickled down his face and his legs told him to turn around and run. But they still had to clear the rest of the room. They moved on and then Bomber saw it, a shadow. Someone was standing behind one of the pillars that supported the ceiling, his shadow faintly outlined on the floor by the ceiling lights.

Bomber mouthed to Armalite to go left and he would go right. Bomber moved quickly right and behind the figure. Hiding behind another pillar, he steadied himself, the safety catch was already off and he had his finger tight on the trigger. He swung round the pillar, rifle pointing at where he thought the gunman was.

Bomber did not know whether to laugh or swear. Armalite had seen it at almost the same time. It was a tailor's dummy complete with clothes. Twenty-seven minutes and they now had to rush the room clearance, checking the two stairways in case anyone was lurking behind the door. Bomber looked at his watch; twenty-four minutes.

"C/Sgt, where are you, we are running out of time," said the Captain, peering round the doorway.

"Here, sir, the room's clear but not anywhere else. The suitcase is in the middle of the room."

"Okay, out you go."

Bomber and Armalite left, relieved to be outside where they took cover and waited. *Nineteen minutes to go,* thought Bomber and at that moment, the captain appeared in the doorway.

Seeing Bomber, he came straight over and without waiting said, "It's a problem one, can't open the case; it's got

199

some sort of wire on one of the catches which could be a trigger. I can't cut into it as may have a trembler device so we can't lift it. So this is what I want to do."

Bomber, Armalite and Dusty were sweating buckets and not too happy but they carried the sandbags from the two Land Rovers and from the back of the Ferret and stacked them as instructed by the captain.

With eight minutes to go, they all took cover outside. The bomb exploded six minutes early and most of the window blew out. The building seemed to shake but Bomber was surprised how well the explosion was contained. They had put a small table over the case, then stacked the sandbags on the top and around the sides, completely sealing the bomb in with a double wall and a triple roof of sandbags. The object of this was to direct the blast into the concrete floor. Going back in, Bomber could see a shallow crater in the floor, sand and tattered bags were everywhere but apart from the workstations closest to the bomb and some of the ceiling lights hanging at a crazy angle, everything else seemed intact.

Leaving the fire brigade and the RUC to declare the building safe for the workers to return, they loaded up and headed back to base.

Later that day, the captain sent for Bomber. "There you are! Any of your chaps know how to fire one of these things?"

The 'thing' was an eighty-four-millimetre anti-tank gun or Carl Gustav. Swedish made, it was becoming standard issue to the British Infantry. It was fired with the gun resting on the shoulder of the firer. It was heavy, noisy and had a large back blast area but was the best infantry anti-tank gun in the world.

"Yes, we are all proficient with it."

"Good, my idea which has been accepted is to fire a non-explosive practice round into any suspected car bomb. The impact will split the bomb apart and save us a lot of trouble, I hope."

"Sounds good to me, sir."

"Yes, only one problem: I and my Cpl have never fired one."

"That's okay, sir, my lads will fight to have the chance to fire it. What distance away from your car bomb would we need to be just in case the bomb explodes?"

"Well, it's hard to be exact but at least a hundred yards, maybe more, how accurate is the Carl Gustav?"

"Very accurate, especially if it's a stationary target, shouldn't be a problem even at two hundred yards."

The chance to use it came that evening when they were called to an abandoned car near the city centre.

The area had been cleared by the RUC. Bomber and his team provided close protection for the captain and his Cpl.

The captain called Bomber to him. He had been studying the vehicle through a pair of powerful binoculars.

"Can't tell if it's a car bomb or not. The RUC have not had any bomb phone call warning but I intend to treat it as a car bomb. Can your lads put a round straight through the boot area of the car from here?"

Bomber judged the range to be about eighty yards. "No problem, sir."

Calling Armalite over, Bomber briefed him. Two minutes later, Armalite was kneeling in the street with the Carl Gustav on his shoulder. Harris had loaded it for him with the inert practice round, then he had retired into cover behind the Ferret armoured car.

Bomber watched Armalite make a slight adjustment, then he fired. The Carl Gustav always made a big bang and the back blast covered up to thirty yards in a wide cone shape behind the firer.

The inert, sand filled round struck the boot right in the middle, tearing a hole through it, the contents, the back seat and out through the front windscreen. It skidded to a halt twenty yards further down the road.

Well, thought Bomber as Armalite retired to the Ferret, *that shook the old car up a bit.*

They now had to wait twenty minutes just in case there was a delayed explosion. When the captain went forward, the lid of the boot hung off at an angle. He gingerly poked around with his screwdriver, took out some snips from his tool bag and appeared to cut a wire or two.

"That man is either extremely brave or completely insane, boss," said Dusty, which was exactly what Bomber was thinking.

"You're right Dusty; it takes a special type of courage to do that."

The next day, Bomber handed over the task to Sgt Ian Mason and his team and they returned to Ballykinler with all of them hoping they would not get that job again. It wasn't the clearing of the building or the bomb as much as relying on what information came from the people who planted the bombs. They could easily lie about the time the bomb would explode. They could do a remote detonation when they were in the building or simply not tell them anything. There were too many variables and Bomber and the lads didn't like it.

After a couple of days of routine patrols in the surrounding countryside, they were given their first of the direct brigade tasks.

They were to hit a large house and outbuildings on the outskirts of Twin Brook, on the southwest side of Belfast. The building had previously been a slaughterhouse, with the outbuildings used to butcher the animals. The owner was a fifty-year-old man with known IRA connections by the name of Ryan O'Reilly and believed to be the quartermaster for the Belfast Brigade. Bomber wondered why they gave themselves such titles or was it our own Int boys sticking the labels on.

Bomber would have the use of a four man RE (Royal Engineers) search team and two RUC SB (Special Branch) one of whom knew the target by sight and the layout of the buildings. He also told them the man kept a large German shepherd dog in the house at night and that it was let loose in the yard by day.

Dogs were a problem when it came to trying a silent approach and when you did get there, they were often hostile. Not just big dogs but ankle snappers who got in the way and distracted you, which could mean the difference between life or death for any of them.

Bomber was not keen on killing a dog whose only thought was to protect its home and master, with no political or hate agenda, just true loyalty. However, he had to be prepared for that eventuality and not put his men's lives at risk because of his sentimental feelings as a dog lover. They were to hit the target house at two o'clock in the morning when, hopefully, there was no one around.

The vehicles crept along in low gear with only side lights on. The house stood at the end of a row of other houses with open country to the rear and one side. Cpl Wells had already circled to the rear of the house to block any escape and had informed Bomber by radio that they were in position.

The vehicles gradually halted, adopting a double T-formation to block the front and sides of the house and to provide protection from any outside interference.

Because of the dog, Bomber had decided not to crash through the door but to give the owner a chance to secure the dog and let them in. Standing at the door with his lads, covering every window in case someone decided to fight it out, he banged loudly on the door. After several good thumps on the door, one of the RUC men shouted out, "Police and army, open up." The dog kicked off barking and growling and throwing itself at the door.

Lights had gone on and Bomber could hear someone shouting at the dog. Then a voice from the other side of the door said, "If you come in, the dog will have you!"

Bomber replied, "Secure the dog and open up or we will break the door down and shoot the dog. Your choice. You have twenty seconds to comply."

Apart from the dog barking, there was silence for a moment, then some whispered voices.

"Ten seconds," Bomber shouted.

"Okay, give me a second; I'll shut the dog in the kitchen."

The door opened and Bomber was confronted by the sight of an overweight man in a dirty vest and boxer shorts. The lads rushed in, pushing the fat man aside to clear the rooms. He started to protest but was told to shut up by the first RUC man and a paper was thrust into his hands. Fat man looked at the paper, then screwed it up and threw it on the floor.

In the room that obviously served as a living room sat a girl with a flimsy dressing gown wrapped around herself. The fat man that the RUC SB man had identified as O'Reilly sat down on the sofa next to her. A glass-panelled door led to the kitchen where the dog was still kicking off. The RE search team needed to go through the kitchen to get to the out buildings but were reluctant because of the dog. O'Reilly seemed amused by this but before Bomber could say or do anything, Armalite had opened the kitchen door and spoken gently to the dog. At first, the dog backed away growling and Bomber heard O'Reilly mutter, "Tear the bastard apart, Regis."

But Regis seemed to like Armalite who was now crouched down stroking the dog and talking in a low soothing voice to the dog.

"Sweet Jesus, you brought your own fucking dog whisperer," the RUC man said to Bomber.

"A man of many talents, some I am only just getting to know," he replied.

Armalite waved the RE boys through and they sidled past him and Regis, keeping their tool bags between them and Armalite's new four-legged buddy.

Waiting outside was Cpl Wells, who reported no one had tried to slip out of the rear of the house. Then he returned to ensure the security remained un-broken at the back.

Harris came into the room and asked Bomber to go upstairs with him to the main bedroom. Leaving Dusty with the two RUC men, who were interviewing O'Reilly and the girl, he followed Harris to the bedroom.

Harris pointed at the bed and said, "None of the other bedrooms have any beds made up but you can see two people were using this bed. That leaves me to believe he and the girl were sharing this bed and if she proves to be over sixteen, I will dance naked in the NAAFI."

Jamieson, who was searching the room, pulled a small suitcase out from under the bed and opened it. He kicked it to one side in disgust swearing, "For fuck's sake, the dirty bastards."

Although the smell should have been warning enough, Bomber still took a look at the contents. The case was full of used sanitary towels. He shared Jamieson's sentiments but then thought about why someone would do that. Using his boot, he tipped the case over, scattering the towels on the carpet. Picking it up and shaking the last of the offending towels free, he examined the case. It was the size of a large briefcase but much deeper, cheap, probably made of re-enforced cardboard thought Bomber.

The inside of the lid seemed slightly thicker than the rest of the case. Finding a corner where he could get a fingernail under the fabric, he found it peeled back very easily. Inside, he found two pieces of paper each of which had numbers and letters in two columns and nothing else. "Seen something like this before at Seamus O'Hara's house," Bomber said to Jamieson and Harris. "Good, keep searching; I will find out something about the girl."

Bomber took the case and papers down with him. He wanted to see the look on O'Reilly's face when he saw the case. Bomber held it under his arm and spoke to the RUC SB men but all the while watching O'Reilly in the wall mirror. O'Reilly nudged the girl and nodded at the case.

Bomber explained both the case and the bed scenario. The bigger of the RUC men said the girl was O'Reilly's niece who claimed she was eighteen years old. However, they did not believe her and had already been on the radio to confirm her ID and age.

A shout from the search team in the outbuildings alerted Bomber and he went outside to see what the problem was. The RE Cpl in charge took him to the largest of the outbuildings, which was the size of a small barn. The lights were on and Bomber stood and looked in amazement. There were bones, bones and more bones stacked from floor to ceiling and cleaned of any meat whatsoever.

"Could take us a while to shift this lot. A lot longer than you have allocated for the search. What do you want me to do?"

Bomber studied the slaughterhouse debris for a moment then said, "You and two of your lads carry on searching the other buildings. I'll send in four of my boys who can clear it with one of your specialists supervising it."

The RE Cpl replied, "L/Cpl Black will be in charge here then. There's a van in one of the other buildings. I want to give it a real going over."

Bomber robbed Wells of two men and then Jacobs, who was guarding the front of the house, of two more to make up the search team.

Four hours later, the sky was just beginning to lighten and the radio was hot from HQ wanting updates. At that point, the finds consisted of the papers from the case, one high velocity .22 semi-automatic rifle complete with telescopic sight and four A4-sized packets, containing one hundred pages each of anti-British literature.

Bomber stalled on HQ saying they needed more time to do the job properly and then he went into the yard to get some fresh air, walking to the outbuilding, where the RE Cpl was pulling a van to pieces. As he entered the building, he heard, "Bingo got you, you fucker."

The Cpl was beaming from ear to ear and pointing at the false compartment in the floor of the van, which contained some sacking. Picking up a piece of the sacking, he said, "Smell that."

Bomber did, gun oil!

"It's taken me ages to work out how to open this bastard. Whoever built it did a good job but not good enough. Now look at this." He walked to the other end of the building where a 1966 Ford Cortina stood. The boot was open and the Cpl shone his powerful Shark torch onto the matting inside. "What do you think that stain is?"

Bomber wet his finger and rubbed it onto the stain, first he sniffed it then put his finger on his tongue. There was a very faint metallic tang, the same taste that blood gives off.

"Okay, well done Cpl," said Bomber, "first-class job. I am going to send out one of the RUC SB boys to photograph all this. Then I will get recovery to take the vehicles."

On his way back into the house, a light went on in Bomber's head. He spoke to the two RUC men and they agreed with his plan.

In the yard, he could see the pile of bones had grown to double-decker bus size and the boys doing the shifting were not happy. Bomber went back to the RE Cpl and asked him if he could put the van back together without any sign that it had been tampered with other than a normal search.

"No problem, boss, leave it to me."

The car was to be back-loaded for the blood to be analysed. The RUC men had already arrested O'Reilly for the gun and other bits plus they had a charge of having sex with a related minor.

The girl was to be taken in and handed over as a welfare case as she was only fifteen.

The search was now getting the attention of rent a crowd despite it being out of the main housing area and Bomber was not sure how long it would be before it changed to rent a mob.

Time to wrap this up and leave, thought Bomber and that's what they did, leaving the bones piled high in the yard. The van was left and the RUC would flag it as a one to follow.

"What the hell are you going to do with that dog and stop him licking my boots for God's sake?" said Bomber.

Armalite and the rest of the lads, including the RUC boys, were all grinning like Cheshire Cats.

"I couldn't leave him, boss. Who would give him food and water and take him for walks?"

The dog had now rolled onto his back and was waiting for its stomach to be rubbed.

"For Christ's sake," roared Bomber, "get the mutt over to the stores and out of sight. You know how the RSM (Regimental Sergeant Major) hates dogs shitting on his grass areas around the camp."

Armalite clicked his finger and Regis went straight to his side and walked beside him towards the stores.

Bomber felt a little envious at the sight, then shook his head and told himself not to be soft.

That night, Bomber slept like a baby, his best night's sleep in weeks, so he was up early and the sky was only just beginning to show signs of the dawn. Bomber jogged slowly towards the range and sand dunes when he realised someone was following him. Reaching into the waist holster under his T-shirt, he gripped the Beretta and spun round only to see Regis coming towards him. Bomber stood still and Regis came to him, sniffed his feet, then licked his hand.

"Regis, Regis, here boy," came Armalite's voice out of the sand dunes.

"He's over here," shouted back Bomber. Regis was now sitting quietly by Bomber's side when Armalite came up panting.

"Oh, hi boss, he seems to like you."

"Don't think you can get round me that way! Come on let's run."

They ran for another twenty minutes until the soft sand had their calf muscles screaming.

"Seriously, Armalite, what are you going to do with him? Our lifestyle isn't conducive to looking after a dog even one as good as this."

"I've already entered him in the dog register in the guardroom and Susan, the Drum Major's wife, has said that when I'm out of camp, he can stay with her. She said she would be glad of the company."

"Worked it out already then, except what are going to do with him at night when you are here? You can't take him in to the barrack block."

"The unit chippy is knocking me up a kennel for a few pints and if it's all right with you, he can stay in the stores' area at night, as a guard dog like."

By now, they had walked back to the barracks and Bomber could see he would probably have a mutiny on his hands if he got rid of the dog. Bomber looked down at Regis, who looked up at him before sitting and cocking his head. "All right but you better take good care of him." Bomber tried to sound stern but he couldn't help but pat Regis on his shoulder and smile.

"Thanks, boss, you won't regret this, I promise you; come on, Regis, breakfast." Bomber watched them jog away and again he felt that pang of envy.

Chapter 17
King

There were other dogs at Ballykinler, which were used to guard the large ammunition complex. Unlike Regis, these were not dogs you could get to like. The boys called them war dogs. Most were very large German shepherd dogs and had armed handlers to look after them, who, if the truth was told, were probably just as scared of the dogs as everyone else.

Bomber was on standby. Their vehicles were parked in the compound at the guardroom, which made up a quadrangle of the company armouries. Just before midnight, he had a call to deploy. Racing to the guardroom with the rest of the lads, they found the place in chaos.

"This is all your fucking fault," a bloodied and bandaged dog handler shouted at Bomber. "How many times do I have to tell your fucking moron drivers not to park too close to the guardroom wall?" Then, the medic jabbed a large needle in the handler's uninjured arm, causing him to curse even more loudly.

"What the hell has happened?" Bomber asked the guard commander.

"You know that big bastard, King?" Bomber must have looked puzzled as the guard commander went on.

"The black war dog. Well, he has been trying all night to get onto the guardroom roof by running and jumping on to your Land Rover, then on to the Ferret's turret. Finally, he made it."

The guard commander paused and suppressed a laugh. "The first I knew of it, the sentry had thrown himself down through the trap door and broke his leg. That's him being carted off to the medical centre now." He indicated a body on a stretcher being carried by two of the guard.

"Anyway, I told the dog handler I couldn't have a mad dog up there with a fully loaded machine gun ready to fire. So I told him to do his job and get up there and sort the dog."

This time he did laugh. "The fucking idiot is half through the trap door, King ripping his arm off and dragging him up." Bomber had to shake the guard commander to stop him laughing.

"I'm sorry but two of my lads are hanging onto his legs trying to pull him down when suddenly King lets go and…" Now he was completely helpless with laughter.

Bomber left and spoke to the medic who nodded. Next, Bomber sent Dusty to the cookhouse. When he came back, he gave a large lump of raw meat to the medic who took a couple of syrettes from his pack and injected them into the steak.

Bomber tossed the steak up onto the roof, then they waited. After a while, the guard commander gingerly pushed the trap door up. Just to one side lay King snoring gently and making, 'I'm having a lovely dog dream' noises.

Bomber went into the compound behind the guardroom which contained his standby vehicles loaded and armed. He looked up at the roof and the gap between his vehicles and roof. He couldn't help but admire King's determination and his courage in making the leap. *Some dog that*, thought Bomber. *I wonder if he has been turned by the IRA?*

They left Ballykinler en route to investigate a suspicious vehicle near one of the KPs, a main communications mast. Blow it up and half of the area's phones, TVs and the security forces communications would be offline.

The mast was at the top of a hill with one narrow lane leading up to it which was used by the maintenance crews. At the start of the lane by the main road stood three houses; opposite them was another lane leading to a farm. One of the houses in a former life had been an inn and it was the occupants of this building who had phoned in the report of the suspicious vehicle.

With lights off on the vehicles, they approached slowly and stopped, blocking the road and lane. They quietly got out of the vehicles. They were all conscious of the fact that two RUC men had recently been killed by a car bomb attending a similar call out.

Bomber had been wondering how long it would be before the IRA and PIRA started laying culvert bombs to blow up vehicle patrols. Culvert bombs equalled large amounts of explosives placed in a drainage pipe under the road and detonated by wire or radio signal by an operator lying up nearby. He had discussed this at length with Captain Bass and what drills they could employ to counter the threat.

One of them they would employ now. Leaving the Ferret and Land Rover to block the junction, Bomber took Armalite and Harris with him. First job was to gently knock on the ex-inn's door and ask the occupants if they had seen the vehicle return. As Bomber went to knock on the door, it opened and a man in his late thirties appeared, shotgun in his hands.

"Been waiting for you boys to turn up, where've you been all this time?"

The speaker turned out to be the stockman who worked on the adjacent farm and had been awake at the time of the car turning into the lane.

"It's still up there, couldn't tell who was in the car," the man said, speaking rapidly like a Vickers machine gun so Bomber had to tell him to slow down.

"Did the car have its lights on or off?" asked Bomber.

The man thought for a moment. "The lights were off."

Bomber thanked the man and left. Instead of driving up, they would go on foot using the field to one side of the lane. It was about half a mile to the mast with a climb of about three hundred feet.

Moving quickly but carefully, Bomber led the other two to the mast. Near the top, Bomber circled out wide to the left so that they could approach from the opposite side to the lane. The mast was protected by a high chain link fence, re-enforced by coils of barbed wire. Inside the chain link fence was a small brick building which housed all the sensitive equipment while the mast soared above them.

Creeping slowly past the fence, Bomber could now see the car parked in the turning circle. He could make out a man standing by the car on the driver's side. He was talking quietly to someone in the driver's seat.

Bomber cupped his hands first over one of Armalite's ears and briefed him. Then he did the same with Harris.

The two men's first inkling that anyone else was there was when Armalite kicked the standing man behind the knees and then pinned him to the floor. Harris yanked the driver's door open and dragged the man from inside and onto the floor. He started to fight back but Bomber's rifle barrel pressed hard into his chest with the words, "Army, stop struggling or you're dead." Not the words on the yellow card thought Bomber but effective.

They quickly cuffed the pair and sat them on the floor with their backs to the car. They were both protesting that they were a plain clothes patrol sent to check on KPs. Their accents were Northern England and both had standard issue 9mm semi-automatic handguns in shoulder holsters. In the boot of the car was a Sterling sub-machine gun and five loaded mags of thirty rounds each. Bomber looked into the car. Shining his torch onto the dash, he could see that a radio of sorts had been fitted into the glove compartment and a set of head phones were hanging loose.

While Harris went round the mast area looking for anything suspicious, Bomber searched the two men and found their ID cards. One, the taller of the two was called Green and the other Deanly. After checking the car carefully to ensure it wasn't carrying anything that could go bang, they set off down the lane. Harris drove the car at the rear with the side lights on and Armalite marched the two in front of him down the hill.

Bomber walked by the car all the time, wondering why two of their own men were up on the hillside waiting in the dark. What this was about defeated him at the moment but that could wait until he had radioed in to HQ.

A couple of hundred yards from the junction, Bomber walked to the front and halted the team. He then walked ahead, whistling a few bars of the regimental march and after a hundred yards, he got the same tune whistled back. He then called the team to follow and they were back at the road junction loading up the prisoners into the Land Rover. Bomber asked Dusty to have a look at the radio inside the car. Dusty sat in the seat, put the headphones on and played with the dials.

"I think it's some listening-in system and when you pick up a signal, you can go to the strongest signal, look." He pointed to the display. "There you have a bearing. Do this from two or three different locations and you can pinpoint the transmitter." Dusty smiled and seemed pleased. "Wouldn't mind one of these myself."

Green and Deanly had clammed up and seemed just a little pissed off that they were being treated this way. The lads couldn't care less. It was because of them, they had spent the early hours of the morning away from their beds, so there was no chance of any sympathy.

Before they left, Bomber went back to the house to thank the man for calling it in. His wife opened the door and said he had left for milking but would pass on the thanks.

When they arrived back at Ballykinler, a military police warrant officer was waiting to take charge of the prisoners. Captain Bass was also there and instructed Bomber to release them, explaining that some bright spark in GHQ had thought it a good idea to check on response times and if we were doing our jobs properly.

Releasing the prisoners and returning their weapons, Bomber cautioned them that their little trick almost cost them their lives. When asked to explain this by the RMP warrant officer, Bomber said, "Very suspicious car, two men, at night by a KP. Just had two RUC officers killed not too far from there. You are lucky my men are well trained and experienced, less experienced men might have shot first and asked questions afterwards."

The warrant officer nodded and added, "Better to be alive and wrong than the other way around, yes?"

"That's it," Bomber replied and walked away thinking, *Checking up on us, bollocks. They didn't even know if they had been spotted or that we would turn out, more likely a fucking smoke screen for someone playing silly buggers.*

In the ops room, Bomber voiced his concerns to Captain Bass. He replied he had thought the same but GHQ were sticking to the story.

"What about the strange-looking radio in the glovebox and come to think of it, the car had two antennas."

"I will keep digging and if I find out anything, I will let you know."

Bomber walked to the mess, passing Armalite and Regis on the way. Armalite was throwing a tennis ball for Regis who would chase and catch it taking it back to Armalite, dropping it at his feet, waiting for it to be thrown again.

In the mess, all the living in members were having breakfast and the talk was of King and the guardroom incident.

As Bomber was ordering his breakfast, the RSM came in and sat next to him. The RSM had been on stag in the ops room most of the night.

"I've just seen Brown out there with that dog. Seems better behaved than that brute King. What did you give him to make him fall asleep like that?"

"Just some steak with a good dollop of morphine in it."

"How did you know that it would put him to sleep?" he asked.

"I didn't, just thought it worth a try. It was that or shoot the dog and no one seemed too keen to get onto the roof to do that."

"No, I don't expect anyone would have been after what it did to its handler."

After breakfast, Bomber went for a shower and a rest. He was back on duty at midday.

Sleep was not kind to him. The dream was back, just the same as always and no matter how many times Bomber shot the figure, it would not die. It just looked up at Bomber, mouthing words he could not hear. But now there was a difference, a banging noise getting louder and no matter how much Bomber tried to shut it out, he couldn't.

Suddenly, a hand was shaking him. He woke looking up at Ian Mason, his Sgt. "Been banging on your door for ages. Thought you had died in your sleep."

"What time is it?" Bomber asked groggily.

"Eleven fifteen; Captain Bass wants the whole platoon ready to go in thirty minutes. I've already got the lads up."

"Do we know what's happening?"

"No, but he said it's a brigade task, not a unit one."

Bomber quickly shaved and put on fresh combat kit. *No time for a shower,* he thought, *but just enough to have a cup of tea and a sandwich in the dining room.*

Mason had the platoon and vehicles lined up ready to go. Bomber and the section commanders waited in the small office for Captain Bass to arrive.

He arrived in his own Land Rover, driven by one of the Provo Sgts men.

Bass called all the platoon together and briefed them, telling them they were to deploy to a village called Moy.

Bomber fiddled with his map as did the Cpls, trying to locate it. *There*, thought Bomber, *it's in County Tyrone.*

They drove out in convoy. Later, when nearer the village, they would have an army air corps helicopter overhead, watching for signs of trouble.

There had been a murder, a local Prod had shot a Cath in broad daylight outside his home and the RUC knew his identity but were reluctant to try and arrest him without military support.

The only intelligence they had on the village was that it was about seventy percent protestant and the rest catholic.

Their plan was simple; the target worked in his family shop in the high street and they would just drive straight in block the street and arrest him, then drive straight out. Simple but hopefully effective. Once out of the village, they would meet with an RUC detachment and hand over the target to them.

As they drove into the village, Bomber thought, *What a lovely place.* No graffiti supporting one side or the other. No curb stones painted red and white or orange and green. Nice 18th century buildings, people going about their normal business, except now they were standing and staring at the convoy of military vehicles.

They pulled up outside the shop and Bomber could see the target looking through the window. Bass and three others went in while Bomber coordinated the screen of vehicles and men to stop any interference.

"It's not going well in there," Armalite said to Bomber, who looked through the window.

It was clear the target was not coming quietly and another older man was trying to punch Bass. Two women in the shop were now also joining and he could see that Bass was getting attacked by both the older man and one of the women. They had also attracted a large crowd outside and they were far from friendly.

Bomber gave the order, "Armalite, Harris, in you go and get them out here fast."

"What the fuck are you soldiers doing? You are supposed to be on our side!" a shout came from the crowd. "Fucking bastards are arresting Danny." Bomber could see that some of the men in the crowd were beginning to rally some very aggressive support for the target and it would soon kick off.

"Let's stop the bastards," someone yelled and scuffles broke out. Outnumbered ten to one and at close quarters, Bomber knew strong action was required. He stepped in front of the nearest vehicle and fired two shots into the air. The crowd scattered and ran to the corners of the street, watching and shouting. Bomber positioned three baton guns to cover the crowd, then went to see how the arrest was going.

Captain Bass was coming out of the shop, his beret was missing and he had scratches down his right check. The target and the larger older version were in cuffs and being marched out. The women stood in the doorway, one hurling insults and swear words at them that would have made a drill Sgt blush. The older woman was crying and wailing. Suddenly, she ran at the older man as he was being put into the Land Rover and wrapped her arms around his shoulders with the grip of a boa constrictor. Two of the lads struggled, trying to prise her free without success. "You two push her in with him; we need to go," Bomber ordered.

With both the older man and woman now firmly wedged into the vehicle, they could drive away.

There was no time to waste; the crowd had regained its courage and rocks and bottles now crashed around them. With everyone loaded, they pulled out and drove back the way they had come, quickly leaving the mob behind. As they passed a street on the left, a crowd cheered and clapped. *Must be the Caths*, thought Bomber. *At least they are happy.*

"Gunman," cried Harris who was standing up looking through the Lanny's hatch. They went straight into an immediate response drill. Bomber's driver swung his Land Rover onto the pavement and stopped. His escort Ferret did the same on the other side of the street. Bomber heard the crack of rounds passing overhead. No one could see the gunman and the only reason that Harris had cried "Gunman" was that a round had cracked past his head burying itself in the Macron armour. A close call for Harris but no more shots came and no one could locate the gunman. Bomber waved the rest of the vehicles through and as the last one passed, they jumped into their own vehicles and left in a hurry before someone decided to have a real go at them.

On the drive back, Bomber wondered how such an idyllic village could harbour so much hate. No wonder the RUC didn't fancy the job of picking up the target. Bomber had the feeling that they would be seeing a lot more of the village of Moy.

Chapter 18
Getting the Willies

On one of Bomber's wandering vehicle patrols, not too far from the border and looking for anything suspicious, Bomber had a feeling of dread. Now he just wanted to stop the patrol and order all-round defence, put himself in the middle and sit quietly. So he did!

Got the willies, have you? the voice in his head said. *Frightened of your own shadow now'?*

Bomber hated to admit it but it seemed very much the case. *Well, what is it that's spooked you?* Bomber stood up from his position by the side of the Land Rover and looked around, fields, fields and more fields. Removing his binos from the vehicle, he walked to the Ferret, aware that the lads were watching him. He rested his elbows on the back of the Ferret, its hard steel feeling cold through his combat jacket.

He studied the road ahead; the autumn had been very cold and wet. Now they were in the first week of December and the winter wind had an Artic bite to it. The leaves had gone from the trees and the hedgerows were bare. Bomber could see nothing odd ahead of them on the road. Then he turned his attention to a small stone barn at the end of a field. Its gable end was facing the road and the only visible opening was a slit high up in the wall, the sort that owls like to use.

Bomber studied it for several minutes. Nothing, or was there? Now he had regained control of his mind; he was beginning to work things out. The road looked clear, nothing there or… "Armalite have you got the list there?" Armalite brought over some cards. On them were the roads and lanes with culverts, small bridges and the like listed. They had started doing this some time ago in an attempt to identify potential culvert bomb sites. This road was not one on which they had compiled anything.

Armalite was leaning on the Ferret and said, "What is it, boss?"

"To be quite honest, I don't know but I just had this feeling. Take my binos and follow the ditches up each side of the road as far as you can see and tell me if you can see anything."

Armalite took his time and finished by shaking his head. "Nothing, boss, except there could be a drainage pipe about two fifty ahead on the left side of the road."

Bomber took the binos and looked. *Yes, it could be,* he thought. Handing back the binos, he told him to study the barn.

He did for a full five minutes, then suddenly tensed. "What is it?" Bomber asked.

"I think someone has just looked round the right-hand corner, then ducked back."

"Okay, this is what we will do." Bomber felt good now that some action was called for.

Cpl Wells was manning the machine gun in the Ferret turret. "Err, isn't that barn just on the other side of the border, boss."

Fuck it, he's right, Bomber thought.

"Okay, you all stay here and cover me; I will go to the barn and if there's a problem, you are all in the clear."

Bomber set off at a jog using a hedgerow for cover. Not great cover but better than nothing. He hadn't gone fifty yards when he realised Armalite and Harris were spread out behind him keeping pace. *Oh well, so you are not the only mad bastard around, get on with it,* the voice said.

They quickly circled the barn, coming from the left side heading to a doorway that was missing its door. They leapfrogged through the doorway, stopped and let their eyes adjust to the dim light.

Bomber could smell cigarette smoke. Someone had been here and smoking not too long ago. A farmer? A dicker? No, what would he be looking out for? A gunman? Possible. A bomber? Maybe.

At the end of the barn with the slit, there was a half upper deck with a ladder to it. Bomber carefully climbed the ladder and peered over the edge. Nothing. Wait! What was that? He edged forward; bending down, he could see half a dozen cigarette stubs. Lying down, he looked through the slit; he could see the road clearly for about three hundred yards in either direction. He could see the Ferret, its machine gun pointing towards the barn.

"Boss, down here," it was Harris.

Climbing down the ladder, Bomber could see Harris had pulled several bales of hay away from the back of the wall, revealing two milk churns and a large role of electrical wire of the type used for telephone connections. The churns were empty but Bomber was sure they were intended to be filled with explosives of some sort and wired up.

Bomber would have dearly loved to booby trap the churns and leave them to take out whoever was setting this up but that would be more than just frowned on by the rules of engagement that had been laid down.

Checking outside, they could see fresh footprints coming into and going away from the barn. There was also a gate in the hedgerow and on the other side, a narrow muddy country lane and in the mud, wheel tracks.

They took the churns and wire, heading straight for the spot where Armalite thought he saw a drainage pipe. They found the pipe and the churns fitted in perfectly. Two churns full of explosives would blow a Land Rover sky-high, killing everyone. An armoured vehicle would not fare much better. It was time to start finding out who used this road on a regular basis.

Back in Ballykinler, Bomber took the half-hearted telling off for going the short distance over the border. The Int boys were more interested in the find as Bomber had taken care not to handle the churns too much, so they thought they may get some fingerprints.

It also turned out that the road was used on a regular basis by an RUC border patrol in an armoured Land Rover. *Time for a change of route for those boys,* thought Bomber. Having sussed the possible bombsite, it would be unlikely that the bombers would return and use it again. But it was marked up in red on the map board as a spot to be extra cautious when approaching the area.

Later in the mess, Bomber spoke to Ian Mason about what had happened. "I don't know what made me stop there and check things. It was the weirdest feeling."

"A feeling worth having it would seem," said Ian. "If you can bottle it, we will all have some."

"When I really need it, it won't happen and I will just go blundering in and wham!"

That night Bomber had the dream again and he awoke feeling washed out. Even a run and extra-long shower could not make him feel any better. Later, on the range, he didn't miss a target and suddenly began to wonder why he let the dream bother him. With a rifle or handgun and plenty of ammunition, what had he got to worry about. *Plenty,* the little voice said.

Chapter 19
Watch and Wait, December 1970

Bomber felt damp right down to his underwear. He, with Armalite, Harris and Dusty, had been lying in the undergrowth for over forty-eight hours. They were one of five covert ops stretched out between Kilkeel and Rostrevor, watching the waters of Carlingford Lough that opened into the sea. To be more accurate, watching for anyone crossing from the south to the north and back again.

Boats involved in any activity had name and number logged. As it had been raining for much of the time, visibility was not great but it was surprising how much water traffic there was. At night, there had been a number of boats spotted crossing and these had been intercepted by the two reaction teams, made up of the remains of the Recce Platoon and the RUC. Bomber could have looked after one of the interception teams but had chosen to put Ian Mason in charge of these and get out on the ground himself.

They had only been able to spot these boats due to being issued with the new night scopes known as image intensifiers. These scopes collected all the ambient light and magnified it into visible images which appeared green in various shades.

They were not any good in areas where there was a lot of street or house lighting as too much light blanked out the images. Bomber had seen them demonstrated in the early sixties but they were only just beginning to reach units for this type of work.

They had another twenty-four hours to go before pulling out and Bomber was guessing that there would be less and less activity as word spread that boats with their contents were being picked up by the army and RUC.

Harris rolled over and spoke to Bomber. "Getting a bit damp in here, boss. Good job we are almost finished."

'In here' was a drab green tarp with a gillie cloth laid over the top where they watched, slept and did just about anything else. Armalite was taking his turn in watching the rear and whenever he moved, one of them got one of his boots in the ribs.

Suddenly, Dusty, who Bomber thought was asleep, but had the radio headset on, opened his eyes and said, "Wilco six two Bravo out."

"We are being pulled out early, boss, pick up at the RV in one hour."

At the RV, they lay in a ditch that was half-full with rainwater but as they were soaked anyway, it seemed the logical place to take cover. They didn't have long to wait before the pig arrived. Throwing in their kit, they joined Cpl Wells' OP team, who were also dripping wet.

"Jesus," said Wells, "do we smell as bad as you?"

"Just as bad," said Bomber. "How did it go?"

"Lots of activity on the road but only a little on the water."

Later in the debriefing room, the ops officer disclosed the extent of their success. Many thousands of smuggled cigarettes had been intercepted. These would have been sold on the black market to fund IRA and PIRA. Over thirty arrests had been made of smugglers and those receiving the cigarettes. It had become so big that the RUC and army had allocated four extra intercept teams after the first eighteen hours.

Bomber asked the question of the ops officer, "If it was so successful, why have we been pulled out early, sir?"

"Good question. Firstly, other units will be taking over the covert ops. Secondly, we have been put on two hours' notice by GHQ to deploy ready for the lead up to the Christmas celebrations. Int believe PIRA in particular will be mounting a huge bombing campaign in Belfast over the next few days to disrupt the final Christmas shopping." The ops officer finally dismissed them so they could get cleaned up and have some rest. Bomber knew any bombings would spark further tit for tat bombings and shootings and they, the army, would once again be in the middle of it.

Chapter 20
Old Friend, New Enemy and Christmas

Bomber was surprised to see an envelope in his slot in the mess. He didn't normally get any mail, just the odd begging letter from his bank manager asking him to reduce his overdraft. The address on the envelope was handwritten in a masculine scrawl and it had a Southern Irish postmark.

Sitting in an easy chair, he opened the letter. It was from O'Brian who had been discharged some eight weeks or so earlier. It simply read:

As you showed me some consideration for the time I had left in the army, by not deploying me on the streets, I feel it's only fair to warn you that I am now a member of the IRA and I will not stop until Eire is united and free of you Brits. I have told the IRA you personally should be targeted, as you are completely dedicated to stopping this happening.

The next and only time I see you again will be over the sights of an M1 rifle. YOU HAVE BEEN WARNED.

Mick O'Brian

Bomber sat for a moment, digesting the words. Was it an idle threat designed to put the wind up him? Was it for real? Within the past eight weeks, O'Brian could have been away on an IRA indoctrination course. He was probably in touch with the IRA while he was serving anyway. The thoughts flowed through Bomber's mind.

His next reaction was to throw the letter in the bin and say 'do your worst, shithead' but common sense prevailed. He was already targeted because of Briggs, so no sense in not taking some precautions.

In the ops room, he gave the letter to Captain Bass who looked at it, then took an identical letter off his desk and handed it to Bomber. The letter was from O'Brian and was in the same vein.

They sat and discussed it for a while then Bass picked up the phone and dialled a number and put it on speaker. The voice that answered was that of the brigadier, who listened to Bass. When Bass had finished there was a pause. "Leave it with me."

Bass poured them coffee and they drank in silence, which was broken by the phone ringing.

"Ops officer," Bass said. "Ah, Brigadier, let me put you on speaker I have the C/Sgt here."

The brigadier's voice echoed out of the speaker as if he was not in the same room as the phone he was using.

"From the heads up you gave me on O'Brian and O'Carroll, I had them on the radar when they left the army. O'Carroll has gone south and is working as a postman in the village where his family live. O'Brian also went south and then disappeared on holiday to Spain. He returned six weeks later which is about the average time for an indoctrination course in Libya. We now believe he is a member of the IRA, working from over the border into the Armagh area as part of a very aggressive section."

"Thanks Brigadier. I take it we can consider the threat that we are targeted as real."

"Oh, very much so. We know they are targeting individuals. The only comfort I can offer you both is that you are not as high profile as all the others on whatever list they have compiled."

"Thanks sir, that's a real comfort," Bomber said with a laugh.

"You are welcome," the brigadier chuckled back. "Oh, by the way, I have a little job for you both on Christmas day. Smart civvies for you both; your CO knows about it and will brief you." With that, the phone went dead.

"Well, if he thinks I am playing Father Christmas south of the border on Christmas day, he can think again," Bomber said and meant it. The last escapade had left him feeling a little unwelcome down south.

"No, I have an idea what it will be, so you can relax on that score."

Christmas day found them in the very smart country house of a prominent Northern Irish family. The platoon had been allocated five houses of prominent families to guard over Christmas. In the grounds were four of the lads in a covert position, watching and waiting in the freezing cold while Bass and Bomber provided the close protection inside the house. The same format was being applied at the other four houses. Normally, this would have been an RUC or RMP task but they, like everyone else, were fully occupied over Christmas.

Their hostess was charming; in her forties, she displayed an elegance and grace that made Bomber feel he was not worthy to clean her shoes. He could see she was a beautiful woman but such was her poise, it seemed to be as natural as a rose in full bloom.

Bass was completely comfortable but Bomber was worried that his lack of social graces would make him look a complete fool.

He needn't have worried, the husband was so relaxed, it made Bomber feel completely at ease. They had two daughters, both in their late teens, who were home from college in England and they added a light heartedness to the whole day.

The family had received death threats like many others in the province but the security forces were determined that the IRA would not have a killing spree on this day.

"Just waiting for an old friend to arrive, then we can enjoy lunch. Meanwhile, just help yourself to a fresh drink. I know you are really on duty but feel free to enjoy yourselves." said the husband.

Bomber and Bass had previously taken a tour of the house and seen the shotguns at various locations in the house. The house staff consisted of a cook, a formidable-looking woman, who light heartedly scolded them for getting in her way when they went into her kitchen and her daughter Penny, who helped her along with her husband George, a stocky ruddy-faced man, who normally looked after the garden but today would help to wait on. Finally, there was a tough-looking ex-Irish guardsman, who introduced himself as John. He was an unofficial bodyguard, who prowled the house, checking doors and windows constantly. He didn't seem put out by Bass and

234

Bomber being present and was quite chatty, asking how things were in the army at present. Bomber suspected he missed the comradeship of his old regiment. Bomber also noticed he carried a .38 revolver in a belt holster at his waist, hidden by his blazer but if you knew what to look for, you could spot it when he moved.

Just before one o'clock, a black car pulled up and Bomber couldn't fail to recognise the giant of a driver; it was Sgt Paul Small. Out stepped the brigadier and the ex-Irish guardsman opened the front door to let him in, relocking it and replacing the three large steel bolts to secure the door. Small took the car to the back of the house where the stable block served as a garage, then came in through the kitchen.

The brigadier and the host obviously were old friends and the brigadier greeted each member of the family as if they knew each other very well. Bomber later found out that he was godfather to the two girls.

Once the greetings were over, the brigadier cornered Bass and Bomber by the large French windows of the lounge, which looked out onto the immaculately manicured lawn.

"Everyone in place outside?" he said quietly and cocked his head to one side as he spoke.

Bass replied, "Yes, sir, everyone is in place."

"Excellent, I hope they won't be required but it's possible, despite unofficial promises of no violence today by the IRA. PIRA cannot be trusted nor any of the small hard-line splinter groups."

As the brigadier sipped his sherry, Bomber studied his face. Bomber was thinking that he looked less stressed than previously and reflected it could be due to his laying off the cigarettes or simply the fact that he had got rid of a number of very annoying people.

"What's going on in that head of yours, David?"

Bomber paused and said, "I was just thinking how relaxed you looked, sir."

He chuckled. "Yes, I do feel more relaxed than I have done for some time; thank you, David."

Bass followed up by asking, "Is there particular reason for that, sir?"

"Oh, let's just say bits of the jigsaw are beginning to fit nicely together at long last. Now enough shop. You are both in for a real treat. Mrs Murphy is an outstanding cook, none of your fancy fiddly stuff, real food cooked to perfection."

As he said it, a gong sounded in the hall and they all went to the dining room. Small was there waiting and Bomber quickly shook hands with him before they sat. The older daughter Mary said grace and Bomber noticed she was a perfect mirror image of her mother, except younger. The other daughter, Jean, seemed full of mischief and was a little more like her father but still very pretty in a tomboyish sort of way.

Bomber had asked the host if he could be seated so that he faced the large bay windows that looked out onto the garden. He had obliged and Bomber kept half an eye on the garden while still enjoying the food and joining in with the small talk.

The brigadier had not been kidding when he said Mrs Murphy was an outstanding cook. A soup the likes Bomber had never tasted before had him wanting more. This was followed by fish, a sole cooked with a variety of herbs that seemed to make it melt in the mouth. Then a traditional roast goose with roast potatoes and a host of other vegetables.

After this, everyone sat back and tried to relax their bulging stomachs before the traditional Christmas pudding was brought in. When the lights were dimmed, in came Mrs Murphy holding a flaming pudding aloft to great applause.

Later, they played games with the family, cards, Monopoly and snakes and ladders, a family favourite.

Later, Bomber felt a twinge of guilt that his lads were outside in the freezing cold, watching over the house but he quickly dismissed it as they would be having a slap-up Christmas dinner the next day. Everyone would stay in position overnight but Bass and Bomber would leave at ten in the evening, going on to stand by in the ops room, leaving the close protection to Small and John.

Bomber could hear the phone ringing in the hallway and the ex-Irish guardsman answered it. He came into the room and waved Bass over. Bomber followed Bass, picked up the phone and listened, then asked, "Any of our boys hurt?" He listened some more then put the phone down. The brigadier had joined them in the hallway.

Bass looked at both of them. "Six two Charlie had a contact and a shootout. Two baddies killed, a third in a car got away but the RUC have road blocks out, so hopefully they will get it."

"All our lads okay, sir?" Bomber asked with some trepidation fearing the worst.

"Cpl Jacobs got nicked on the arm but will be fine."

The brigadier spoke for the first time, "Which location is six two Charlie at?"

"It's the manor, the Deacons place."

Bomber knew the Deacons were an important Catholic family who had spoken out against the violence and had a lot of sway with the Catholics in their area.

"Please excuse me," said the brigadier, picking up the phone. "I need to find out a bit more about this."

Bass and Bomber left him and returned to the lounge. As they entered, all faces were turned to them. Bass nudged Bomber and smiled his best 'everything's all right' smile and said, "I think it's my turn to win all the money at Monopoly. Who's for a game?"

Bomber went and stood to one side of the French windows and looked out.

"Has someone been killed?" Bomber turned and looked into the face of the oldest daughter, trying hard to remember her name.

"Only bad guys, Mary, only bad guys."

"If it's only bad guys, why do you look so sad?"

"Oh, just thinking if whoever died thought it was all worth dying for before life left them?"

"They must have known they might get killed doing what they did."

"No one thinks it will happen to them, only to someone else. But that's enough of such things, let's see who's winning at Monopoly."

The rest of the Christmas passed relatively quietly; all sides, it seemed, wanted a breather. However, that did not stop Brigade HQ wanting more patrols and roadblocks. Bomber was returning late at night to Ballykinler from one such patrol when they had a call from the ops room to check on the local TA centre. It was not manned at night by the TA but a section from the regiment guarded it. Apparently, all communications had been lost and Bomber was sent to investigate.

Firstly, they did a wide circuit of the area to see if anything or anyone suspicious was lurking close by. With that all cleared, Bomber put the Ferret at one end of the road and the Land Rover blocking the other end. Bomber and Armalite approached on foot covering each other.

The centre was enclosed with a high chain link fence reinforced with barbed wire. The main entrance consisted of double chain link gates. The centre itself was not large, a garage area, office block, drill hall and a canteen area. A large quadrangle was at the front and this too was in darkness.

Kneeling at the gate, they studied the building and the sentry post, which was a sandbagged emplacement. No lights on anywhere and no sign of a sentry. The signs were not good so Bomber was not feeling good about this. What the hell was going on? What would they find inside?

Armalite produced the bolt cutters and he cut the chain securing the gates. Moving quickly but quietly, they first checked the sentry post, no one. Past the office block that was in darkness but secure. Then the armoury, locked and the alarm was on but not tripped. The canteen was next, this would be where the section would eat and sleep. Bomber looked through the window and he could just see eight bodies laid out like mummies in sleeping bags on camp beds.

Bomber shook his head and indicated Armalite to look. He too could not make out if they were dead or asleep. Then one of them turned over and Bomber felt his temper flare. No sentry on, all asleep on duty; who the fuck was in charge of this rabble?

"The shits are asleep, let's give them hell, boss," the anger in Armalite's voice was clear.

"Let's do it!" Bomber replied. The door was unlocked and they went in shouting and turning over camp beds, kicking and cursing the bodies inside the sleeping bags until everyone was awake and up.

Armalite grabbed the first two and sent them to the sentry post. Bomber had identified the Cpl in charge and placed him in close arrest. He looked as if it was a fuss over nothing and perfectly normal to put everyone's lives at risk and hold open house for the IRA. Bomber had to send Armalite to signal the Ferret and the Land Rover to come in, as he was all for giving the Cpl a good smacking.

When they arrived, Bomber put the Cpl in the Land Rover, hands cuffed and told Harris to guard him.

He then briefed Cpl Wells to take over the section and the guarding of the centre.

"Make sure you have half on guard at any one time and the rest cleaning this shit hole up." Bomber knew he was being hard on the soldiers but they all had a responsibility. Any of them with a bit of guts could have stood up to the section commander and taken it on themselves to guard the centre.

"Don't worry, boss, they won't know what's hit them." Wells looked stern and in no mood to be messed about by a bunch of layabouts, especially as he was not going to get to bed that night now.

Bomber informed the ops room what was happening and that Cpl Wells was now the commander at the centre.

Armalite took over the command of the Ferret and after a final check with Wells that he had communications with

Ballykinler, they drove off towards camp. Bomber knew he was now in a black mood because of this Cpl's lack of any sense of duty. He could not understand why anyone should behave so and he considered they deserved the severest of punishment.

At the guardroom, the Provo Sgt took charge of the Cpl, placing him in one of the cells pending charges of dereliction of duties. Bomber went into the ops room and brought up-to-date the duty officer, who phoned the CO, who was not going to be a happy teddy when he heard the news.

Bomber went to his bunk and stripped off. Throwing himself on the bed, he dropped into a deep sleep.

After four hours, he woke with the rain beating against the window of his bunk. A full gale was blowing and Bomber had a feeling that it wouldn't just be the weather blowing a gale in the HQ.

Bomber was half way through his very late breakfast when he received the summons to go to the headquarter company commander. Bomber had not had much to do with him as he always reported to the ops officer, Captain Bass.

He knew the company commander was an ex-ranker and had been with the regiment for all of his career. He was a big man who had played rugby for a long time and prided himself on his fitness.

"Come in, C/Sgt," the voice boomed out as Bomber approached the open door of his office. Bomber went in, halted and saluted. "Have a seat; just need to finish this return, give me a second."

Bomber studied the office, pictures of the regiment's rugby teams from the past hung on the walls. Several others of different barracks, Germany mostly, took up the wall behind the desk.

"Right, thank you for coming so quickly. Didn't think you would be up yet after a long night's patrol." He paused, looking at Bomber who sat looking back.

"Bad business last night, not the sort of thing the regiment expects from its JNCOs (Junior non-commissioned officers)."

"Or its soldiers," Bomber added.

"Yes, I agree. Their own company commander will be talking to them about that later."

"What will happen to the Cpl now, sir?"

"Well, the charge you have put him on will require a court martial. A great embarrassment to the regiment of course." He let the words hang and Bomber now knew what this little chat was about.

"He is protesting that his guard orders did not state that he was to have a sentry on during darkness but that he was just to occupy the centre."

Bomber could not help himself and burst out laughing and said, "The useless toe rag; what did he think he was there for, to catch up on his sleep?"

Bomber realised that the commander was not laughing and remembered that he, Bomber, was a new boy in the regiment, 'an outsider'. *Play it cool*, the voice said in his head.

"Okay, sir, what is it you want from me?"

"Hmmm, really we need you to drop the charge." The commander dropped his head not wishing to look at Bomber and waited for a response.

For fuck's sake, I'm not letting the bastard get away completely free, thought Bomber. *The shit will get people killed.*

"Okay, sir, I will drop the charge but he must be removed from his post and not allowed to look after soldiers in Northern Ireland because next time the embarrassment will be him getting our soldiers killed." Bomber thought blackmailing the CO might not be the best way to go but he wasn't going to let the fucker get away unpunished.

The commander stared at Bomber for a long moment. "All right, I will speak to the CO. Clearly, he cannot be seen to let this go unpunished. I also intend to see those centre orders are rewritten. No more loop holes for the likes of him."

Bomber stood to go but before he could salute, the commander spoke again. "Strictly between you and me, C/Sgt, I would wring the bastard's neck for him but they have rules against that sort of thing these days."

"I know just how you feel, sir." Bomber saluted and left.

Bomber went to the Recce Platoon stores, where he found Sgt Mason getting ready for his patrol and brought him up-to-date on what had happened and told him that the bastard would most likely get away with it.

"I don't think he will," replied Mason. "The word's already out and the Cpls Club is hopping mad and they may well decide to deal with him, unofficially of course."

The Cpls did not get a chance. The culprit was on a plane and back to the depot before the end of the day but that was not to be the last Bomber would see of him.

Chapter 21
Honey and Death, January 1971

The constant patrolling in their small sections was beginning to make the sections somewhat insular, so when Bomber had the chance to get the whole platoon together at the same time either for a job or training, he made the most of it.

It was even better when Captain Bass was free of his ops duties and could join them. They had the opportunity to discuss the current situation with the lads, rehash tactics and IAs. (Immediate action drills). Time on the range was always well spent and the lads loved firing off the Browning machine guns of the Ferret armoured cars. The orders forbade them from using bursts of fire from the machine guns when in contact with the enemy. Some bright spark had decided that they had to take every other round out of the belt so it would only fire one round at a time. This caused a number of problems and the Ferret commanders normally only did this with two or three rounds at the beginning of the belt after which they would fire bursts. The problem with the machine gun was it could not be aimed as accurately as a rifle due to the way it was mounted in the vehicle. Nor was it meant to be.

It was an area weapon, which, in a firefight, made it very effective and fatal if you were on the receiving end.

It was a crisp February morning with a light frost lying on the grass. For once, there wasn't a gale blowing in from the Irish Sea.

Bomber was confirming his range booking by phone for the platoon when Captain Bass came into the tiny platoon office, looking hassled and tired. Bomber knew he spent very long hours in the ops room, dealing with incidents and planning operations for the regiment and it could and did take its toll on those who did this.

Bomber could tell by the look on his face something had happened and he must have been up all night. Bomber stood and saluted him. Bass returned the salute and then slumped into the one and only chair.

"Harris," Bomber called out and Harris stuck his head round the door. "Some strong tea for Captain Bass in here at the double please."

"Coming right up, boss." Harris disappeared into the stores next door where the makings were kept.

"Bad night, sir?" Bomber kept his voice low and Bass just nodded as if too tired to speak.

A knock at the door and in came Harris with two mugs of tea and a half packet of Jammy Dodger biscuits.

When Harris had left and Bass had drunk some tea and consumed three biscuits in quick succession, Bomber asked, "No breakfast yet, sir?"

Bass shook his head. "Not had time; it's been a shit of a night."

"Harris," Bomber shouted, Harris must have been trying to earwig at the door because his head came round the doorway in ultra-fast time.

"Yes, boss?"

"I want two bacon and egg sarnies here in double time for Captain Bass."

"Coming right up, sir." Harris disappeared and within seconds, Bomber could smell bacon cooking. The lads always had stuff ready in the Ferret storage bins in case of being deployed at short notice. The petrol cookers could turn out a brew or a meal like lighting in the right hands. Harris had those hands.

Bomber watched Bass. His eyes kept closing and his head would suddenly jerk up as he felt himself nod off.

Harris came in with a Dixie lid serving as a plate. On it were two very large sarnies and Bass seemed to come alive at the smell. He tucked in like a man who had not eaten for a week. A second mug of tea and Bomber could see him come back to life.

"Okay, sir, tell me what's happened?"

Bass outlined the events of the previous evening and night and Bomber realised why he looked so down.

Three off duty soldiers from another unit had gone out in civvies to what was considered a safe area. They had been taken and killed by the IRA. There had also been another attempt on a soldier being lured by a girl with the offer of sex to a house, where a gunman was waiting. Fortunately, he had escaped by jumping out of a window and running like hell.

A mobile patrol had narrowly escaped death when a car bomb exploded just after they had passed the car. A shootout in the falls had been put down to a fall out between an IRA fraction and PIRA with one killed and another in hospital with gunshot wounds. Plus, a bomb had gone off just outside the city centre in a clothing factory. A warning had been received so there were no casualties.

"So, all in all a busy night and as usual we have to come up with some response to counter these developments."

Bass outlined the tactics for both the kidnapping and the honey trap. The platoon would work in groups of nine, going to places such as the Deer Park Hotel dressed in civvies for a night out. The Deer Park Hotel was famous for its showbands and dances. A group of three would be the bait, seemingly drinking and having a good time while the other three would fade into the background acting as watchers and bodyguards.

The watchers would all be armed with 9mm pistols hidden under jackets. The one enjoying himself would be unarmed as any girl worth her salt would soon detect a large pistol hidden under clothing at the first dance or hug.

A response team would also be in the vicinity in civvies using an unmarked car, able to close in and bring more fire power to bear if needed.

Two other locations would also be targeted. Each one involved bands, dancing and a big mix of the two communities using them. So if off duty soldiers were being targeted, either with kidnapping or honey traps, these were the places most likely to be favoured by the IRA and PIRA.

The response teams were commanded by Bass, Bomber and Mason, one at each of the locations parked close by. In each vehicle, they had two others, both armed with SMGs. Bomber had his car parked on the edge of the Deer Park's car park, where he could see the entrance to the hotel.

The main problem with this sort of operation was communications. They lacked any sort of small easy to conceal two-way radios. The only thing they could lay their hands on were some Motorola handheld radios. The leader of the body guards would have one which had to be turned on only when he needed to contact the response team. Hiding it on his body was a problem as it was about the size of half a house brick and just as heavy. The problem was solved by wearing a large shirt and carrying the radio next to the skin. Then a jacket was worn over the top of this, effectively hiding it.

Everyone else was working on a wing and a prayer. Simple hand signals or gestures had to suffice.

"The place is packed," Armalite said almost to himself "Never seen so many girls. Hope those dozy buggers of ours remember what they are there for."

Harris who was in the back seat, half-turned so he could watch the rear. "They have to blend in so it would look odd if they ignored the birds. I'm told there are four times more females than males in Ireland but I'm not sure if it's the same both sides of the border."

"Well, if it is, even the ugly mugs we have put in will stand a chance of pulling," Armalite said with some envy in his voice.

The conversation slowly died as time ticked by. They could hear the showband clearly, even from where they were sitting on the other side of the car park.

Bomber saw the white van pull in near the front door. It was 22:30. The bouncers were now inside watching for any trouble.

"This could be us, stay alert." A van with a sliding door was ideal for kidnapping. Easy to get people in and out at gunpoint and two or three gunmen could hide in the back.

Bomber had the car positioned so that they could pull forward and quickly block the exit before any vehicle could drive round the car park and out.

"Get ready to start the car when I say." Armalite had his fingers on the key ready.

"There," said Armalite. Bomber brought the binos up to his eyes and studied the figures coming out of the hotel doorway. A young girl and a boy but not one of our men. He could be a local or another off-duty soldier.

The girl waved at the driver in the van and ran towards it. The boy stayed at the top of the steps. The girl got into the passenger seat and the van drove away while the boy waved.

Bomber studied the driver as he drove towards the exit. "Some concerned dad collecting his daughter I guess."

The clock on the dashboard seem to tick louder as the time crept to midnight. Harris yawned loudly in the back. "Sorry, boss, but I wish the band would pack up and go home."

Ten minutes later, the band announced the last song and people started leaving. "Okay, everyone this is where it gets tricky. Lots of people leaving don't want to miss our guys in the crowd."

Armalite spotted their bait coming out. Each had a girl with them and once in the car park, they gave each of them a kiss, then the girls parted, getting into a new looking Ford Escort.

The guys waved as they drove away then they too went and found their beat-up old Vauxhall and got in but did not leave.

The body guards emerged separately. One made his way to Bomber while the other two collected a motorbike. Dusty, who owned the bike, figured it was the best thing for the job should they have to chase anyone.

Bomber was not sure because he hated the things. Noisy, dangerous and what was worse they only had two wheels.

They now had a routine tactic to check to see if they were being followed. The bait's car drove out of the car park after the bike followed by the bodyguards, who would, after about half a mile overtake and get ahead, then pull in somewhere to watch for a tail. Bomber followed two cars or so behind. Dusty on his bike, who had got ahead, would then wait for all to pass, then tuck in behind. All had to note other cars and check that they were not tailing anyone.

Eventually, after a roundabout route, they arrived back at Ballykinler, handed in the weapons and did a short debrief. The other two teams had had a similar experience and they were to repeat the operation again over the next two evenings, which were the Friday and Saturday. This pleased the three guys with Bomber, who were the bait, as they had got dates to meet with the three girls they had met that night.

Bomber had to carefully explain that was not the object of the exercise and because of that, the bait teams were swapped around. However, just in case they were setting the lads up, the names of the three girls were run by the Int boys, who confirmed that they were all Prods from a hard-core Prod area, so very unlikely to be involved in anything more dangerous than looking for a boyfriend.

Friday night proved to be very much the same except a patrolling RUC car took a look round the car park and started to take too much interest in Bomber's car. Bomber did not want any attention so slipped out of the car and intercepted the RUC on their third circuit and identified himself. After that, the RUC left them to it.

Saturday night would be a big one. If Armalite thought the place was packed on Thursday, he had a revelation on Saturday night.

"Jesus, there must be ten girls to every guy in there. What about popping in for a quick drink, boss? I'll make it a coke if you like."

"Easy, boy, we are working; keep your mind above your waistline. It's going to be a long night."

It was ten o'clock when the radio came to life. It was Cpl Wells' head of the bodyguards. "Boss, Dusty going to the back exit with a bird, I'm following."

"Okay, on our way."

The three of them left the car and ran for the back of the building. At the back was a garden area, open during the day but normally closed at night. It was a large lawn area with tables, chairs and plenty of bushes to conceal someone.

Running round the side of the hotel, they passed the kitchen with all its bins overflowing with uneaten food. Stopping at the corner, they were just in time to see the girl come out followed by Dusty. As Dusty walked out, a figure stepped out of the shadows and raised his arm. Bomber brought his pistol up to fire but before he could, Dusty went into a forward roll and two shots rang out.

The figure collapsed and Bomber and the others raced to the doorway. Standing there, gun in hand, was Cpl Wells.

"Sorry, boss, no time to give a warning; he was about to top Dusty." Bomber had forgotten about the girl but Harris and Armalite had chased after her.

Bomber turned to Dusty, "Are you okay, Dusty?"

Dusty stood brushing himself down. "Think so, boss. God, she had me following her like a dog after a bitch on heat. Thank God, we practiced those drills."

Bomber knelt by the body on the opposite side to where a pool of blood was gathering. The bullet had hit him in the middle of the back. *Straight through the heart I think,* muttered Bomber to himself. He tried for a pulse but couldn't find one and he could feel the body was cooling rapidly. He resisted the temptation of removing the gun that had fallen from the lifeless hand and which now lay less than six inches from his outstretched arm. Needed to leave that for the RUC.

Standing and turning to Dusty, he said. "Yes, nice forward roll, the bullet must have skimmed you by an inch or two."

"Felt a lot closer, thought I was a goner. Thanks, Cpl Wells, I owe you big time."

"No problem." Wells said with a shrug.

Just then, Harris and Armalite appeared. Between them they held a very beautiful young girl, who was trying hard to kick each of them in turn and using very unladylike language.

Bomber tried the radio with little hope of raising anyone due to the range. "Need to get to a telephone and report in. Cpl Wells, get one of the others out here to guard the body with you and everyone else, to the cars. Armalite, take her to our car with Dusty and make sure the other cars RV at our car once they are all out. Harris stay here until Cpl Wells returns."

Due to the noise from the showband, no one had heard the shots. Bomber went round to the front door, where, in the reception area, was a phone. The phone sat on the counter with a large guy standing behind the counter.

Bomber produced his ID card and said, "Army, need to use the phone to report an incident."

The man put his hand on top of the phone. "No one gets to use it but me in case of an emergency, so fuck off!"

Bomber felt his temper rise and pulled out the Browning pistol; pointing it at the man's head, he snarled, "I can make it a real emergency if you want, shithead?"

The man pulled his hand from the phone and held both of them in front of his face, which had changed from a drinker's red to a pasty white. It may have been the gun or it could have been the look on Bomber's face that convinced him to back off. "Go ahead, no problem, man."

Bomber phoned in and asked for army and RUC support including an ambulance. Having briefed the duty officer on the incident, he turned his attention to the man.

He had been listening and started calling out to one of the bouncers standing at the ballroom door. But they couldn't hear him over the band beating the hell out of a 'Girl from Ipanema'. Anyway, they were far too busy watching the young girls dancing to look into the reception area.

Bomber didn't need their attention or a stampede of people if word got out of a shooting.

Acting on impulse, he vaulted the counter. The man was somewhat overweight and was backing away from Bomber until he was stopped by the end of the counter. There was a door that went into a windowless office about the size of two-broom cupboards. Bomber pushed open the door, "In and keep quiet."

The man obeyed, watching the gun in Bomber's hand. "Are you going to kill me?" he asked in a trembling voice.

"Not if you do as you are told, now sit in the chair and be as silent as a lamb." The man complied. Bomber unplugged the phone from the wall and took it out and put it on the counter outside. Closing the door, he locked it with the key that was in the lock, checked it was secured and then put the key next to the phone.

"Boss, are you okay?" it was Harris, SMG held down by his side, standing in the main doorway.

"Yes, just stopped someone raising the alarm and causing a stampede."

Harris was trying to see through the glass panel in the door. "The RUC have just turned up and we can hear the ambulance."

Bomber nodded and walked out with him; the cars were now all parked together and the lads were facing outwards. Armalite was talking to an RUC Sgt, who, on seeing Bomber, came forward and shook hands.

"Got the girl in the car but I hear you had a shooting. Where's the body?"

Bomber led both officers to the back of the hotel. Wells was sitting on one of the chairs and Moss was blocking the doorway in case anyone came out that way.

Wells stood and Bomber waved him down. The RUC Sgt checked the body and spoke to the other officer, who took out a notebook and wrote some stuff in it. Then the Sgt produced a plastic bag, turned it inside out and picked up the pistol. Expertly reversing the bag so the gun was inside without any contamination with his own fingerprints.

Harris now appeared with two army medics, who had a stretcher and a body bag. The RUC Sgt had assumed control and ordered the body to be taken away quickly, as it was getting close to finishing time for the band and people would soon start leaving.

"We can do statements at the station, don't want to hang around here too long."

Fifteen minutes later, they were driving away in a convoy of three cars, the RUC Land Rover, Bomber's car and the ambulance with its siren turned off.

The girl had lapsed into silence but when they got to the RUC station, she kicked off, swearing and spitting, her lovely features twisted into a mask of fury and lashing out with her feet at anyone close enough. The RUC officers bundled her into a cell to cool off, saying she could wait until morning.

An inspector and the Sgt took statements from each of them, having first supplied them all with mugs of tea. Bomber sipped his slowly while he watched Cpl Wells give his statement and wondered if Wells would be haunted by the man he had lawfully killed that night? Bomber thought he had better speak to him later to ask if he was okay.

Once back at camp, they sat with the ops officer and discussed how the operation had gone, talking through the problems of the bodyguards trying to blend in but still being able to do the job. The ones who seemed the least concerned about anything were the bait. They all had to have a couple of drinks or more to look as if they were there to just relax and enjoy themselves. They knew they had someone watching over them who would follow wherever they went.

Bomber was concerned with the gap between bodyguard and reaction team. Dusty had Wells close behind him but it was still a close-run thing. The gunman had been well positioned to kill him as he stepped out of the doorway; a second later and Dusty would have been dead.

The girl acting as the honey trap dictated the route out of the ballroom and they all talked about trying to cover all potential routes out that might be used. The problem was they didn't have the manpower or the communication system to coordinate such a plan.

Cpl Wells, who had been silent for most of the discussion, came up with the definitive answer when he said, "Why not just confine every service man and woman to camp and make them take time off on the mainland?"

Bass answered, "That may well happen but until it does, we have to do these operations when we are told. So let's keep working on the drills and I will do what I can about a better communication system."

The meeting broke up and they all made their way out for breakfast which would be followed by some shut eye. As they left, Bomber fell in step with Cpl Wells, who was just short of six foot tall, the sort of man some would describe as rangy in physique.

"Good work last night; if you hadn't been on the ball, Dusty would have copped it."

Wells paused and turn to Bomber. "I nearly blew it, boss, I had stayed too far back and I hesitated when it came to shooting the bastard."

"You did not stay too far back and you timed your shot perfectly. The results proved that. Dusty is alive thanks to you. I was too far away for an accurate shot. You have nothing to beat yourself up about."

"Thanks, boss. Some of the lads were saying you did this sort of thing in Aden. Did it get any easier the more you did it?"

Bomber wondered who had been telling tales about him since he had not talked about Aden to anyone.

"To be honest, it became more of a drill, an automatic reaction to training. But you needed friends around you for support, especially when it came to releasing the tension afterwards. So if you need someone to talk to or sink a few beers with, let me know."

"Will do, boss, and thanks."

They split and Bomber walked to the mess, hoping Wells would be okay. *Of course he will, he's tougher than you*, the voice in his head chanted. *I truly hope so*,' Bomber chimed back.

The platoon did two more long weekends on the same operation but there was no repetition of the honey trap or any kidnap attempts. So it was back to rural patrols and KP duties.

Chapter 22
People Power and Fertiliser, March 1971

Escalating violence by both the IRA and PIRA was beginning to provoke a demand for a more drastic response from the general public. One of which was a march through Belfast by thousands of shipyard workers, demanding the government introduce internment for terrorists. It was aimed at the IRA and PIRA but could equally apply to the Prod terror groups as well.

On the day of the march, Bomber and the Recce lads found themselves on rooftops, watching for any likely attacks on the marchers. They had been in position well before dawn and it proved to be a long day of watching and waiting. Bomber wondered how many hours he had spent in the army doing exactly that. He was trying to remember who said 'a soldier's life was thirty percent sleeping, thirty percent training, thirty percent recreation and ten percent horrific action' when Dusty took a radio call from HQ informing them to stand down. The march had been over for a couple of hours but they had been left in position, watching just in case there was any reaction from those opposing the call for internment. Having called up the vehicles, they descended back to ground, relieved to be off the roof and mobile again. They had only been driving for five minutes when a man ran out in front of Bomber's vehicle, waving his arms and Harris put the brakes on hard.

"They've put a bomb in my filling station. I had to run. They had a gun!" The man was in shock, he was shaking and had trouble speaking. Bomber could see a petrol station two hundred yards or so further up the road.

Ordering Harris and Dusty to stay with the man, he sent the Ferret forward with himself and Armalite following at the run. They stopped level with the filling station on the opposite side of the road. Bomber pushed up the visor on his helmet to aim his rifle. Studying the station, he could not see anyone in the shop payment area or in the vicinity of the pumps. Before he could give any orders, he found himself lifted from his feet and tossed backwards over the pavement and against a wall.

Bomber staggered to his feet, spitting blood that was running down his face into his open mouth which was trying to suck in air.

"Boss, you okay?" Armalite was holding his arm and looking at his face.

"I think so, is there a fire?"

"No, the pumps are intact more than your face is. You've got blood everywhere."

Bomber saw that at the filling station, the explosion had completely destroyed the building but amazingly the pumps were intact. Cpl Wells was out of the Ferret, trying to pull off a metal grill that had originally been covering a window at the station. It was wrapped round the front left wheel arch. After a superhuman effort, he wrenched it free and tossed it in the direction of the wreckage.

Now people were gathering and Bomber was concerned about a secondary explosion from the petrol stored below the forecourt. The RUC had now arrived and between them, they managed to clear the people away from the danger area. A TV news team became a problem wanting to get close ups of Bomber's face. Eventually, Bomber lost his cool and he and Armalite physically removed them from the danger area with the reporter screaming "army brutality".

Once the fire brigade declared the area safe, they returned to Ballykinler, where Bomber sat in the medical centre while Mick Smith carefully removed slivers of glass from his face. After half an hour, he had a dish of tiny splinters of glass and Bomber had a face covered in sticking plaster.

"Keep the plasters on until tomorrow and next time keep your visor down. You were lucky that you didn't get any in your eyes." Mike then handed him a small bottle with some painkillers in. "For the bruising, it's going to be painful for a day or two."

Bomber thanked him and stood up stiffly. His body felt like it had been punched and kicked all over. Trying to walk normally proved a painful experience now that there wasn't any adrenaline racing round his body. At the mess, he ran a hot bath and soaked until he saw his skin starting to wrinkle, then he stepped into a cold shower forcing himself to stay under the ice-cold water for several minutes.

After towelling himself down, he took two painkillers, then dressed and went into the dining room for some dinner.

Some light-hearted banter greeted him and he had to relive the whole thing for those sitting at the table.

In the bar afterwards, there was no shortage of those offering to buy him a drink. Aware that he had taken the painkillers, he just had a couple of whiskies, then excused himself and went to bed.

Bomber woke at dawn feeling like he had been run over by a steamroller. His body ached in places he didn't know he had and thanks to the whisky and painkillers, his head throbbed with every beat of his heart.

Struggling into his running kit, he made his way out of the mess and headed for the sand dunes. A limping jog soon had the blood circulating and his head started to clear. Suddenly, he became aware of Regis trotting by his side. Looking back, he could see Armalite coming up fast behind him.

"Sorry, boss, Regis must have caught your scent; he suddenly took off and raced ahead. How are you feeling?"

"Better than yesterday evening and don't be sorry, I'm glad of the company."

They jogged gently for about ten more minutes before Bomber then turned and took the shorter route back to camp. They stopped near the Recce Platoon stores and Regis sat at Bomber's feet, looking up at him.

"He's a lovely dog, Armalite. Have you checked he has had his jabs?" Bomber said, stroking Regis' head.

"I saw the veterinary corps Sgt and he gave him some shots and a vaccination log for me to keep a record of all his jabs."

"Good! Right, time for a shower and some breakfast." With that, they went their separate ways and once again, Bomber felt that twinge of envy as Regis, happily wagging his tail, followed Armalite.

After a hot, cold, hot shower, Bomber felt a little better and ate a hearty breakfast, downing at least a pint of tea all to himself. *Your bladder is the first thing that will go on you*, the voice chuckled in his head. *Worse ways to go,*' he chimed back.

Once all the patrol commanders were present in the platoon office, Bomber hit them with the new patrol routine roster and drills. He had discussed it at length with the ops officer, Captain Bass. They both knew it would reduce the distance they could cover on a patrol but they considered the price worth paying.

With the new drill firmly established in the minds of everyone, the first patrol left. Bomber was due to go out in the afternoon and cover a route close to the border area.

Bomber studied the map as they drove through the picturesque country side. The cloud for once was high in the sky and patches of blue could be seen. The hedgerows were beginning to show signs of green and Bomber longed to see the Hawthorn break into bloom.

Was that something from my childhood, wondered Bomber, *a longing to see Hawthorn in bloom?*

Getting all sentimental, are you, wimp? the voice in his head challenged, with an edge to it as if he had no right to think of anything other than soldiering. "Fuck off," Bomber must have said it out loud as Harris looked at him and said,

"What's up, boss?"

"Nothing, pull up here."

They pulled up and the two in the back jumped out and took cover. Marked on Bomber's route map was a red circle. It was marked round a small stone bridge so small that if they had been driving over it at speed, they probably would not have noticed it.

This was an ideal position for a roadside bomb and the new drill was to stop and then precede on foot either side of the road in the fields and check to see if there was any IED waiting for them. First though, Bomber would study the area with his binos, looking for anything that didn't seem right.

After a while, he called Harris, who was crouched down beside the Land Rover to take a look.

Bomber was aware that Harris and Armalite were particularly good at spotting things that were out of place. They weren't country boys but both had a good eye and observation skills.

"See anything out of place."

"Nothing, boss, that I can see." Harris handed the binos back and Bomber slipped them back into the case by his seat.

"Okay, we are going to clear the left side first." They set off, Bomber, Armalite and Dusty leapfrogging through in the field along the hedgerow. Fifty yards out from the bridge, they swung out to the left up towards a hedge junction with a few stunted trees growing there. They targeted that particular spot as it would be an ideal position for someone to lay up and detonate an IED. With slightly higher ground, it would provide good cover and was located about the right distance to lay a wire from the IED to the person setting it off so that they would not get blown up or spotted.

Bomber had hammered home that they could do hundreds of these sweeps without finding a thing but they had to treat each one as a possible. If they didn't, they could be the ones getting killed.

The position was clear; no sign of anyone having laid up, no flattened grass or cigarette butts. They studied the area for footprints, nothing. Heading back towards the bridge, they again swung around it in an arc fifty yards out in case there was an IED and they had laid the wire going the other way. Still nothing!

Bomber then checked under the bridge, a tiny trickle of clear water ran under it but no milk churns or plastic bags stacked there. Dusty waved the vehicles to them and they set off once more. They had four more red circles on their route before they could check two KPs. After clearing the second site, Bomber sat in the Land Rover, watching a lorry at a farm through his binos. The lorry had a logo on the side, advertising fertiliser.

"What do you see around us, Harris?"

Harris was taken a bit by surprise and took a look around. "Well, fields, cows and some sheep plus the farm, boss."

"Any crops growing or ploughed fields?"

"No, nothing like that."

"Then why would a farmer need so much fertiliser on a cattle farm."

"He wouldn't; he would use the cattle shit to spread on his fields from the cow sheds. They sort of make it in a slurry that they spray onto the fields to make the grass grow."

"For a townie, you seem to know a lot about farming."

"As a kid, we used to go to my uncle's. He had a small farm in Sussex, dairy cows and I always remember the stink, but they made their own butter, which was delicious."

Bomber began to think. *Shall we stop the lorry and question the driver? Should we raid the farm now? No best let them think we haven't noticed and then move in.*

"Dusty, have you got the A41 radio there?"

"Yes, boss, and a couple of spare batteries."

Bomber called HQ and told them what he had observed and what he wanted to do. HQ told him to 'wait out', then after about twenty minutes, he recognised the voice of Captain Bass giving the okay.

They had been sitting in the hedgerow for three hours, watching the farm and the light was just beginning to fail. They shared out some compo oatmeal biscuits and cheese. Their vehicles had turned round and gone part of the way back to camp, leaving them to watch and wait. The vehicle radio was much more powerful than the A41 and they would act as a relay station to HQ for them, passing messages back and forth.

Bomber was good at the watching but sometimes the waiting could become tedious. Once the light had gone completely, they would move closer to the farm. They had the platoon's one and only image intensifier, so they would be able to spot things from further away. Bomber had managed with Captain Bass's help to persuade the QM tech to hang onto one of the image intensifiers after their last big OP job. QM tech was probably getting flak from the Brigade QM but he had managed to stall brigade and they had kept it.

As the last of the light slipped away, they carefully made their way to a better position nearer the farm. They would be able to see anyone coming in by car or on foot and thanks to the image intensifier, they could look at any place that was in complete darkness and see clearly, even though it was in a weird green light.

They sat and waited. Bomber wondered if he was just imagining things in his head and this was just an innocent farmer planning on doing a lot of fertilising. Better not to take a chance even if it wasn't a lot of fun sitting out at night and missing dinner and a drink in the mess.

At eight o'clock, a motor bike arrived but the rider did not go to the farmhouse but straight to the barn. As he slid the door open, just enough to let himself get in, Bomber saw that there was a faint light on inside the barn.

Twenty minutes later, a car arrived and three men got out and Bomber noticed that the interior light to the car had been disabled. The three, like the motorbike rider, went straight to the barn and entered. There was no sign of the farmer or the two dogs that had been roaming the farm yard earlier. Dusty was reporting the events as Bomber described them and he heard Dusty acknowledge the reply from HQ.

"We are to stay put and keep observing, boss," he said.

"Okay." Bomber felt in his pocket and brought out three hard-boiled compo sweets and handed one each to Armalite and Dusty.

Popping one in his own mouth, Bomber imagined Captain Bass persuading the CO to let him lead a raiding party on the farm. Having convinced the CO, he would then have to wait while the CO got permission from brigade. The rest of the platoon would be sitting on standby all ready to go.

"Boss, one of them has come out of the barn and has moved to the gate," Armalite said in a low voice.

"I didn't see the light when the door opened; they are either working in the dark, which is unlikely or they have fitted a blackout cover for when the door is opened."

"Seems likely, boss. The guy's now sitting on the dry stonewall, smoking." Armalite was holding onto the image intensifier, not willing to share the new toy.

They sat and watched for another hour with HQ asking for updates every twenty minutes. Suddenly, Dusty tensed and acknowledged a message. "The rest of the platoon are going to raid it, boss, they are five minutes out."

"Look at the fields behind the barn, Armalite."

He swung the image intensifier beyond the buildings and suddenly said, "I can see them six, no eight, coming across the field in extended line."

"Okay, watch the sentry and the barn door now."

Bomber directed his binos onto the road and waited. He knew once the cut-offs were in position, the vehicles would charge in on the road.

"They are going in now, boss," Dusty hissed.

Suddenly, on the road, six sets of head light came on and the noise of engines revving came to them.

"What's the sentry doing?" asked Bomber.

"He's standing up and looking, no he's heading back to the barn. Oh, nice one," exclaimed Armalite. "One of the lads has just stepped out from the corner of the barn and downed the sentry."

The lead vehicle must have been a pig as it didn't stop at the gate but drove straight through it, clearing the way for the Land Rovers.

Dusty, who was acknowledging a call on the radio, nudged Bomber, "We are to go to the farm, boss, six zero is there."

Six zero was Bass's call sign. *So,* thought Bomber, *he managed to persuade the CO to let him come out to play after all.*

By the time they had arrived at the farm, there were four men sitting with their backs to the barn wall. Bomber could see that three of them were in their twenties, while an older one, maybe in his forties, sat slightly apart.

"Captain Bass wants you to join him in the barn, boss."

Bomber went in. There was a heavy canvas sheet hanging over the inside of the doorway. It had been pulled back and hooked up to allow easy access. Bomber went inside.

Bass was standing by several bins where opened bags of fertiliser and other sacks where stacked. In the bins, a mix of the different bags was being concocted. But Bass and a bomb disposal warrant officer were examining a selection of detonators, timers and what looked like small radios.

"There you are, C/Sgt, this is a good day's work. Look at this stuff, really up-to-date timers and radio detonators. Could be we have upset a number of bombings or one giant one."

The bomb disposal warrant officer was almost wetting himself with excitement, explaining that with this equipment they could explode the bombs remotely without the need for timers or wires running from the bomb.

Sitting on a sack of fertiliser, Bomber rubbed his hand over his tired eyes and tried to think. *Why would they have the latest detonators, remote devices and stuff but be mixing up homemade explosives instead of using plastic explosives? Where was the PE?*

"What's the matter, C/Sgt?" it was Bass who spoke, breaking into his thoughts.

Bomber looked at the bomb disposal warrant officer and frowned. The warrant officer was a lean man with a weather-beaten face. The sort of face that had seen a lot and spent most of its time outdoors.

"He's wondering where the PE is, aren't you, C/Sgt?" The warrant officer was smiling and looking at him.

"Yes, why would they get all this up-to-date gear, then have to mix homemade shit?"

Bass nodded and clicked his teeth as he sometimes did when he was running things through his mind.

"Maybe they were planning to use the homemade stuff for a trial of the new radio-controlled detonators before committing to using the harder to get PE," Bass said it almost to himself as if Bomber and the warrant officer weren't there.

"That's feasible, sir, but if they have PE, where have they stashed it?"

Two RUC officers entered the barn, interrupting their train of thought. Speaking to Bass, the older one of the two said, "The farmer and his wife are terrified. They were told to expect the shipment and to store it in the barn and then to stay away. They are both staunch Catholics and have family on either side of the border but swear they don't support the bombings and killings."

"So are you arresting them or what?" Bass asked.

"Leaving them for now We don't have any evidence that they did this voluntarily but the other four are known to us and with what we have here they are looking at a long stretch."

"Fine, if you want to take them away, I'll provide an escort while we wait for this lot to be collected. It will also give us time to have a further look around the place."

"Thanks, we'll do that."

"C/Sgt." Bomber jerked himself out of the stupor he was sinking into.

"Sir."

"If you and your team escort the RUC back, then stand down, you have done enough today."

Bomber knew he must look tired. He certainly felt he was running on empty and was starving hungry.

"Will do, sir."

The following morning Bomber woke at his normal time of six o'clock. He didn't have to be at the office until eight thirty so he lay in bed thinking about the day before and where the IRA would stash a load of PE. That's if they had any of course, which he didn't really doubt. Captain Bass's idea of a trial of the new equipment was perfectly feasible but they really did need to find the PE before it could be used.

Trouble was there were over three hundred miles of border and probably even more than three hundred roads, lanes and paths crossing that three hundred plus miles. What they needed to do is to place a 'Cordon Sanitaire' along the three hundred odd miles.

No, the politicians haven't got the balls to do that. Everyone would be shouting 'It's just like the Russian have done in Europe'. Irish Americans would have a field day, the UN would be banging the table. It's not going to happen sunshine, the voice said in his head, *so get out of bed, you lazy shit, come on, up and at 'em.*

Bomber was feeling rested and content after a good sleep and excellent breakfast. He was talking to Cpl Wells, his Ferret commander and number two in their team, about the drills for checking culverts and bridges on a patrol route. Once the IRA realised what they were doing, they would try and counter it. Dusty added the comment that they could easily just load a car with explosives and leave that by the side of the road. The army would see that and deal with it in the normal way but the IRA could leave an ambush in place and hope to take out the clearing team. However, they had the Ferret's machine gun to counter this threat.

The phone interrupted the discussion; it was Captain Bass telling Bomber he was wanted by the CO. Bomber went to the HQ with some trepidation. When the CO sent for you, it was one of two things. A 'well done' or a 'not well done'. Bomber couldn't think of anything he had done wrong or anyone senior to himself that he might have upset, so it must be a well done for yesterday.

The RSM was waiting for him at the HQ and said, "Who have you upset now, C/Sgt?"

"No-one that I know of sir, why?"

"That brigadier of yours and a colonel are in there with the CO."

The RSM turned and went into his own office and Bomber suddenly had the sinking feeling that he was not going to enjoy this.

He knocked on the door to the CO's office and the adjutant opened it. He raised his eyebrows to Bomber and waved him in and then departed as if he was glad to be out of there.

"Ah, there you are, C/Sgt, come in and have a seat." The CO indicated a hard upright chair in front of his desk.

Bomber sat and looked at the other occupants of the office. The brigadier, wearing his normal dark, pinstriped suit was sitting in an armchair, fiddling with a pack of Polo mints while gazing out of the window. In the other chair sat a thin but tall man dressed in combat clothing with full colonel tabs on display. Studying Bomber, the colonel looked him up and down, giving Bomber the impression he was not impressed with what he saw.

"Now, excellent work yesterday," said the CO, "Everyone is very pleased with the results. Now let me introduce you. The brigadier, you know of course but you haven't met Colonel Wilson." He nodded in the direction of the tall man who raised his hand in acknowledgement. The way he reacted, Bomber thought that was probably not his real name.

The CO continued, "Officially, I am going to send you on leave, which you are overdue, but you are going to be seconded to the colonel and brigadier for a couple of weeks."

The way he said colonel first and brigadier second, Bomber wondered if there had been a change in the power on the throne.

The CO paused and looked at the colonel, who cleared his throat before he spoke, "The brigadier tells me you are the man for a delicate job we need doing. Your CO is reluctant to release you without you agreeing to the task. Are you willing to work for us?"

"Well sir, I find it difficult to make a decision without knowing what you want me to do."

"Afraid I can't tell you at the moment, still in the early stages."

Bomber could tell he knew exactly what he wanted Bomber to do but was unwilling to say, but why? The alarm bells were ringing in his head. *He needs a sucker who's expendable,* the voice warned.

Bomber looked at the brigadier and raised an eyebrow. The brigadier responded by sitting upright in his chair and saying, "It's not too dissimilar to your last jobs except you only have to watch what's going on and report back."

Okay, thought Bomber, *South again. Three times could be pushing my luck. Really?* said the voice. *This morning you were thinking how easy it was to cross the border, day or night.*

Bomber conceded the point and knew one way or another, they, or more likely the brigadier, would get him on side.

With a shrug, he said, "All right but only on condition I can look at the plan and make a feasibility study to see if I think I can pull it off."

The colonel looked shocked that Bomber would make such a request and barked, "There are no ifs here, C/Sgt, once you have heard what the task is, you are in!"

Bomber felt himself getting angry. *Who the fuck does he think he is?* The thoughts ran through his head, like a rat in a maze and he was just going to make a court martial level retort when the brigadier spoke.

"Oh, I think we can let him make his own assessment of the job, Colonel. He is quite good on the ideas' front."

The colonel looked a little flustered at first but then said, "Yes, jolly good idea, that's what we will do."

So, thought Bomber, *the power is still with the old warhorse, that's good!*

"That's settled then," the CO said. "The adjutant has a leave pass ready for you. Enjoy yourself, C/Sgt." The CO gave a half smile that said a lot to Bomber.

Bomber stood up and the brigadier said, "Sgt Small will pick you up at the mess in a couple of hours. Is that enough time to get ready?"

"Yes, sir, plenty of time." Bomber saluted and went to the office of the adjutant, who was waiting for him and handed him an envelope. "There is a fourteen day leave pass and some travel warrants, signed and stamped but not made out for anywhere. Take care of them, don't drop me in it by losing them. Use them as you need, those you don't tear up."

"Will do, sir."

Bomber went straight to the platoon office, where he found Sgt Ian Mason, his number two, getting ready for a patrol. Bomber briefed him as much as he dare by telling him he was to be away for a couple of weeks, officially on leave. Mason was already reading between the lines and replied, "Don't worry about anything here, just make sure you get back in one piece from wherever you are going and from whatever you're getting up too."

In his bunk, Bomber changed into civvies and a zip-up jacket that would cover the Beretta. He packed his hiking gear and a pair of jeans, a shirt, trainers, and underwear, plus a torch, knife, compass and a tiny camping gas stove into his green mountaineering rucksack. His waterproof jacket, he kept out to wear.

Going back downstairs, he could see a dark-blue Ford escort through the glass doors. Leaning against it was Paul Small. As Bomber came out, Paul's face broke into a wide grin and he greeted him with, "I wondered how long it would be before they dragged you back into the fold."

As they drove towards Lisburn, Bomber questioned Paul on the colonel's role and where the brigadier fitted in. Paul explained that the brigadier was still very much in charge but that they had put a serving officer as head of the department. All the contacts that the brigadier had built up over the past sixteen years would only deal with him directly to protect their identity. So the brigadier stayed and called the shots but the two got on well together, despite being very different characters.

At the HQ, they headed for a small building set apart from the rest. A security guard stopped them and spoke to Paul. They emptied their pockets of anything metal and walked through a body-sized metal detector. On the other side, the security guard bagged their pistols and labelled them with their names.

Small led the way to a room without windows. The door was locked and he pressed a button on the intercom at the side of the door. A tinny sounding voice asked who it was. Small looked up to a camera mounted above the door frame and said his name.

The door clicked open. Inside, sitting at a table with six chairs around it were the brigadier and the colonel.

"Come in sit down, coffee? Help yourself, biscuits too." The brigadier sounded upbeat as if things were going well.

Small said, "I'll get the coffee."

Bomber sat opposite the colonel. The chair was hard and uncomfortable, designed to keep the occupant awake. Small placed a large mug of hot strong coffee in front of Bomber and a plate of chocolate biscuits before sitting next to Bomber.

"Right, we'll begin." The brigadier was in a hurry and explained quickly what the situation was. Armagh on the north side of the border and County Monaghan on the south side were rapidly becoming the IRA's favourite places to plan and prepare, then use to launch their attacks into the heart of the North.

"This weekend, we believe the IRA higher echelons will be meeting other contacts at a remote farm in North West Monaghan." He stabbed a finger on the map spread out on the table on which a building circled in red was the only building for miles around. Bomber tried reading the map upside down and he could make out Bragan Mountain and below it, Bog.

"We want you, C/Sgt, to watch this farm and record who goes in, vehicle registration numbers and so on. We will give you a state-of-the-art camera with a telephoto lens which will enable you to spot number plates from half a mile away."

The brigadier paused and Bomber studied the map. Uphill of the farm, maybe six hundred yards away, there was forest covering a large area. There were several lakes or loughs as they were named on the map. The brigadier slid onto the table a large black and white photograph of the farm and the surrounding area, obviously taken from a very highflying aircraft. The detail was excellent.

The brigadier carried on, "When any of the vehicles leave, we will want to know how many are in the vehicle and which direction they are travelling in."

Bomber had guessed the answer but asked it anyway, "Why sir?"

"You don't need to know that, C/Sgt," said the colonel, who answered in a brusque manner.

"I do, sir, so I know how to prioritise my messages when there is a lot going on. I mean, if those leaving are to be ambushed and captured, I would send that first, as opposed to those that are only going to be followed."

The colonel cleared his throat with a "Hurrumph". "In that case, yes, those that we believe are heading back to the north will be picked up. The rest we will make other arrangements for."

Bomber went back to studying the map. He needed to be in position by Thursday night and it was already Monday afternoon. The distance was not that great but he could not just go direct by car to the location. Plus he had to get his equipment organised. He started scribbling on a piece of paper, pushing it across the table when he had finished. The brigadier looked at it, stood up and went to a desk, then took out a key and unlocked a drawer. The colonel had picked up the list, then let out a snort. "Five hundred pounds, you are going to do an op, not throw a party!"

The brigadier dropped two wads of notes in front of Bomber, one was of Irish punts, the other Northern Irish pound notes.

"Do you want me to sign for it, sir?"

"No, it's non-accountable and non-traceable; let's hope you don't have to use it. The other items, Sgt Small will get for you and bring them here." The Brigadier paused when he saw the Colonel was fidgeting. "What is it, Morris?"

"I don't see the reason for so much money, what's it for?"

"I imagine that the C/Sgt stuck south of the border would be happy if he had some bribe money or if he had to hole up in a hotel somewhere for a while to be able to pay for it."

"I see, thank you for explaining it." He then looked at Bomber. "Not doubting your methods, C/Sgt, it's just some of this stuff is new to me."

"No problem, sir, I guess we are all learning on the job here. I'm just trying to cover all bases."

"Indeed, indeed. Tell me how will you be able to watch the farm for three days and stay awake?" The colonel looked genuinely interested.

"Well, I expect that the occupants of the house will not stay up all night, so when the house goes to sleep, so will I."

"Very logical when you put it like that."

The brigadier placed a box a little larger than a shoebox on the table and from it, he took out what looked like a normal Motorola handheld radio. "You underlined communication on your list, our boffins have had a play with this and boosted its power output to increase the range but you will need to put up this wire antenna as high as you can. Then you plug in this little box to the radio. It allows you to talk in clear but scrambles the communication so only we, with the other box at this end, can understand what you are saying."

The brigadier paused and demonstrated where to plug the scrambler in on the radio.

"The range is limited but with the wire antenna, you should reach the listening posts I will station on the border. They will act as a relay to me. Now I am going to leave you with Sgt Small to do your planning. I'll be back in a couple of hours."

The colonel left with the brigadier and Bomber turned to Paul. "Any chance of some food, I'm starving?"

Paul nodded and picked up a telephone and spoke into it. Twenty minutes later, the buzzer went on the door. Having checked the monitor, Paul opened it and took a large tray from a man in chef's whites. Closing the door, he put the tray on a side table and said, "Come on, let's eat."

Bomber sat back and rubbed his stomach. Four sausages, two eggs, chips, grilled tomatoes and toast washed down with more coffee and he was feeling much better.

"You don't seem fazed by this job, what are you thinking?" asked Small.

"What's to be fazed about? A ride and walk over a mountain, long rest in a forest and then back home. No one to kill or to kill me if I'm careful. Easy!"

Paul grinned and slapped him on the back. "You hope it will be easy but I don't think it will be."

Chapter 23
Murder Farm

Bomber was pedalling hard and was sweating buckets. He had forgotten more about riding a bike than he could remember. His backside was already regretting the mode of transport and he wondered if he had allowed enough time. It was dark and it was already close to midnight. To add to his problems, he was riding without any lights on, so speed on the downhill sections was not an option. He had chosen the bike as it was silent, easy to hide and he could claim to be on a cycling holiday if needed.

Paul had driven him from Lisburn along the old A4 in a battered Cortina car and had brought along a Cpl called Andy as escort. Andy said very little and sat in the back of the car, cradling a sub-machine gun. Andy was stocky and looked as hard as nails. Paul said he could be relied upon in a fight. Bomber asked what unit he was from and this brought a long look from Paul who replied, "He's not in the army anymore due to a misunderstanding but the brigadier recognises talent and took him on." Eventually, they turned onto a B-road towards the border. Several miles before the border, they stopped. Paul lifted Bomber's bike off the roof rack and they shook hands before parting company. The bike had two rear panniers containing most of Bomber's needs. On his back, in his rucksack, he had his essential gear so if he needed to leave the bike in a hurry, he could still survive and complete the job.

He was on back lanes, heading to the River Fury, where he was assured there was an unmanned bridge crossing the river. He found it and sped across. On the road ahead he could spot the headlights of any vehicles coming towards him and he would be able to get off the road well before they arrived.

Now he could see the beginning of the forest and he slowed down to a fast-walking pace, looking for a forestry track that would take him closer to the farm where he could set up an op.

He found it and lifted the bike over the locked forestry gate. Now the going got really tough. The track was broken and muddy and he was concerned that he was leaving signs of his presence. It was almost pitch black in the forest so after about a mile, where the track came to a junction, he got off the bike and carried it to the far side of the track walking on the edge by the trees to avoid leaving tracks Once there, he was slowed down by having to wheel the bike alongside the trees.

Just keep it going, the voice in his head told him. *You'll get there, keep going.*

Bomber carried on and just before dawn, he came to the end of the forest. He backtracked a couple of hundred yards and worked his way into the forest, aiming for the southern edge. The bike became a real handicap now and so he packed as much as he could into the rucksack and left the cycle covered with fallen branches.

Further on, the mature trees gave way to a newer belt of trees, younger and as yet not thinned out. Bomber knew from the photograph that this line of trees was only about fifty yards wide and would provide excellent cover. He had to move on all fours, pushing his way through the branches which lashed his face when he looked up.

Dawn had well and truly risen when he peered through the last line of tree branches. By luck, he was in the right spot and could see straight to the farm. A few yards in front of his position, there was a good track that seemed to traverse the complete front of this section of forest. Beyond that was a wide stretch of bog land, sloping down towards the farm that had at some stage been worked to reclaim the land around the farm for grazing and probably for growing root crops.

Wriggling back twenty yards, Bomber sorted his kit out into his bivvy site and first priority was a brew. The camping gas stove quickly boiled the water and a hot cup of tea was soon being enjoyed. He would have to restrict his brews as he could only carry six pints of water with him and as yet he hadn't spotted a close supply that he could get to at night without being seen.

Going back to the bike, he emptied the panniers. Taking out a small tin, he worked his way back to near the point he had entered the forest where he then sprinkled pepper. Moving back, he repeated this just before the hiding place of the bike. Satisfied the bike could not be seen, he made his way back to the bivvy site. Now he wriggled his way to his OP and checking the wind was blowing away from him, he sprinkled some pepper out in front of his OP site.

Tired and hungry, he was tempted to have a sleep but he needed to get things set up. The radio needed testing and to do that he had to get the antenna up high so, taking the weighted end of the wire, he tossed it up into the treetops. It took four goes before it stayed up, then unwinding the wire from its spool, he edged towards the OP. Once there, he plugged everything in and switched on the radio. The earpiece crackled a little in his ear, then it was silent. He pressed the send button and spoke. "Zero, this is zero alpha radio check over." Bomber knew he would have to wait several seconds for it to go through the scrambler and relay station.

He was just getting worried when a familiar voice said, "Zero alpha this is zero, are you in position?" It was the brigadier.

Good on you, Brig, said the voice in Bomber's head and he said 'Amen to that'.

"Yes over." Now communications were established and they had the scrambler working Bomber could use it like a telephone.

"Well done, out," the brigadier ended the radio check and Bomber turned off his radio to save the battery power.

Bomber crawled to the edge of the OP position but now he had cam cream on his face, which would allow him to blend in easily with the foliage. With him, he had the state-of-the-art camera and lens that Paul had told him was not yet available in the shops. The lens was labelled Super Telephoto. Bomber knew very little about taking good photographs but the camera, a Canon F1 had an auto exposure system and Paul told him to keep it set on that.

Bomber looked through the eyepiece and focused the lens on the farm. It jumped out at him as though he was actually standing in the farmyard. Bomber studied the building. It was old, built of stone and reminded him of pictures he had seen of fortified manor houses on the Scottish border country. The main house had wings on either side which formed a U-shape at the back. Possibly stables in the past which at a guess were now used for farm machinery and cars. In its day, it must have been a grand building but now it had an air of neglect, probably due to a lack of funds to maintain it.

Parked in front of the building was a Land Rover and Bomber took a photograph of it zooming in on the number plate. He had to jerk his finger off the shutter button as the power winder took three photos in quick succession, taking him by surprise. While he was watching, two figures, followed by two dogs, emerged from the house and walked to the vehicle. Bomber took two photos and he could see that one had a shotgun and the other some sort of rifle. The two dogs, one Springer the other a German shepherd jumped into the back of the vehicle when the door was opened for them.

The Land Rover drove away from the house and Bomber refocused his attention on the house. It was on two levels. The upper had six large windows facing him and he zoomed in to see if he could see into them. He could see curtains of some sort but not into the rooms. Then at the fourth window, he spotted a figure standing, looking out, possibly watching the Land Rover leave. He thought it could be a woman but before he could fine focus on the figure, it moved back into the room. The ground floor had two large windows either side of a double doorway that was framed by two pillars.

Bomber heard the Land Rover coming up the track in front of him, then it stopped. Bomber heard the doors open and slam shut and one of the men talking to the dogs, followed by footsteps on the stony track coming his way. Bomber wriggled further back, easing the branches back in place. From the inside of his jacket, he gently pulled out the Walther PPK with the permanently fitted suppressor to deaden the sound of any shots fired. It fired the .32 ammunition as opposed to the 38-calibre model which had a wicked recoil, which took the gun off target each time it was fired. The .32 was a much more gentle calibre but just as deadly.

He could now hear the dogs sniffing around as the men approached his position. It was the Springer he was most concerned about as it could sniff him out at fifty paces. Then he would have to decide whether to kill both men and the dogs, which would then leave him with the problem of disposing of the bodies or running for it.

The Springer was now close and suddenly it started sneezing and shaking its head. The pepper was doing its job. *Let's hope the two men are too stupid to realise what has caused it,* the voice in his head whispered. Bomber tightened his grip on the Walther. He had never fired it, so he wanted to make sure if he used it, he would be up close so he was ready to jump up and out at the men.

The Springer was now sneezing in rapid succession, Bomber could see the legs of the other dog as it came to investigate the Springer's behaviour, then it too started sneezing.

Bomber flinched and his heart missed a beat as he saw the boots of one of the men right in front of him. "What the fuck is the matter with these dogs?"

From the left, the other man answered, "They're always sticking their noses into something that makes them sneeze. Come on we got the whole bloody track to check before lunch." They moved off to Bomber's right, calling the dogs which ran after them still sneezing.

Bomber relaxed his grip on the gun, pushed the safety catch back on and slid it back inside his jacket. He could feel the blood pounding each side of his head and he knew he was going to develop a headache due to the lack of sleep and the tension of the close call.

Wriggling back to his bivvy site, he sat up and searched the side pouch of the rucksack for the small medical kit. Taking out two paracetamols, he washed them down with a swig of water. *Sleep*, the voice said. *That's what you need.* Bomber wrapped the waxed waterproof cotton sheet around himself, curled up, closed his eyes and slept. He woke feeling chilled and he checked his watch to find it was four o'clock in the afternoon. First job was to have a pee, then to crawl to the OP and see if anyone was around. No one was about, so he wriggled back to the bivvy site and fired up the stove and placed a pan of water on to boil. The wind whistling through the trees would cover any noise the stove made. The exercise had warmed him up and once he had some food and a hot drink inside him, he knew he would feel fine. In the boiling water, he placed a boil in the bag stew. Once that was hot, he could use the water for a brew. Having eaten and finished his tea, he packed the rucksack again. If he needed to leave in a hurry, he wanted to just be able to grab the kit and run. Stuffing a packet of fig rolls in his jacket pocket, he took the camera and the image intensifier and worked his way back to the OP.

He reckoned he had three hours of good light left, so he settled down and watched the house. The brigadier had said he wanted the house covered from Friday through to Monday morning so being in position twelve hours before that would give Bomber time to see what sort of routine, if any, the house had.

The first thing he noticed was that next to the Land Rover was a large black car. Zooming in, he took a photo of the number plate which was a Southern Irish one. Bomber scanned the windows but could not see a thing. Settling down, he waited and watched. After an hour, a car drove in and parked next to the black one. It was a silver Ford saloon and four men got out with one being held by a big man who gripped the man by his arm and marched him towards the house. The other two followed. Bomber took several photos and wished he had a way to send them direct to the brigadier.

Half an hour later, the first two men and the dogs came out and got into the Land Rover again. They drove up to Bomber's track, parking in the same place and walked towards his location. Bomber eased out the Walther just in case. The dogs, being smart, avoided the area to Bomber's front by going off the track and onto the bog. The men stopped about twenty yards away from Bomber and he could hear them talking. Edging slightly forward, Bomber could see them standing, looking into the bog.

"This should do, let's dig it here." Bomber could see the two men. The one who had spoken was tall and thin whereas his companion was shorter and stocky. Bomber immediately named them Laurel and Hardy.

"I don't see why we should be doing this; let them fuckers do it. We're here to patrol, not dig fucking holes," Hardy protested loudly.

Laurel replied, "Well, you can tell them if you want; I'm for staying alive. That fucking O'Brian will kill you as soon as look at you. As for that shit, O'Keefe, he could break your neck with one hand."

With that, they stepped down off the track and walked about fifty feet into the bog and starting digging.

Bomber scribbled the names and time in his note book. Was it the regiment's O'Brian? Clicking on the radio, he called in after several seconds. The brigadier replied and Bomber gave him the two names and what was happening and the brigadier told him to inform him when the men left.

Bomber watched the men and took several photographs. The men made short work of digging the hole in the peat bog. The shorter one, Hardy, was cursing the water as it was filling the hole as they dug.

Bomber could only think of one reason they were digging a hole and that was for a body. Could it be the man who was being held and marched into the house? For a split second, he thought, *They know I'm here and O'Brian's having it dug for me.* He dismissed the thought straightaway and wondered what he would do if they brought the man here to murder him?

The voice in his head said *Kill the bastards* but that would blow the whole operation which would seriously piss off the brigadier and colonel, Bomber countered. *But what's more important, lots of photos or a person's life?* Bomber decided to do what he often did, deal with it by instinct if and when it happened.

He was distracted by Laurel and Hardy coming back to the track. They called the dogs in and went back to the Land Rover. He heard them throw in the shovels and then tell the dogs to jump in. A minute later, they drove off.

Bomber carried on watching and thought about O'Brian. What made him join the IRA? What did he think of his old comrades and friends? Bomber knew he had some friends in the regiment but would he be prepared to kill them? Bomber knew he would kill O'Brian as he was not a friend but an outsider to the regiment. O'Brian would also consider Bomber to be part of the system suppressing the Catholics.

The door of the house opened and Bomber watched as an older man came out followed by a younger woman. The woman walked ahead and opened the rear door of the car for the man. Bomber took photos. The woman closed the door and the car left. Could it have been her he had seen at the window earlier? Bomber called it in but thought the car would not be crossing to the north, not with the plates being from the wrong side of the border.

The light was fading now and Bomber warmed up the image intensifier, scanning the farm but avoiding the two windows that had some light coming from them. Those he looked at with the telephoto lens but the curtains were drawn and the light came from gaps in the curtains.

A flood of light came from the front door and Bomber watched as a figure ran out. It had not gone more than fifteen paces before shots rang out and the figure fell to the floor.

Laurel and Hardy came running from the side of the house, guns in hand, but they stopped abruptly when they saw the big man, O'Keefe, and one other, who Bomber suspected was O'Brian, come out of the doorway and walk to the body.

Something must have been said as Laurel got the Land Rover and backed it up to the body and he and Hardy lifted it into the back and shut the door. O'Keefe was pointing at the house where, sitting on the steps was the third man who had arrived with O'Brian and O'Keefe. He was holding his head. Then a woman appeared from the house and helped the man sitting to his feet and then steered him into the house.

The four men got into the Land Rover which drove up to Bomber's location and stopped, just as before. After a couple of minutes, Laurel and Hardy appeared, carrying the body between them. A short distance from Bomber, they put the body down on the track and then O'Keefe blocked Bomber's view by standing in front of his position. O'Keefe was holding two shovels. Then an argument started because Laurel and Hardy were not keen about picking up the body and putting it in the hole.

Bomber recognised O'Brian's voice when he said, "Patrick, do you think that hole is big enough for three bodies?"

"If it's not, I'll make one of these fuckers dig some more," O'Keefe growled.

"There's no need to be threatening us. We are just a wee bit tired that's all, give us a second to catch our breath and we'll be doing it," Laurel spoke without a tremor in his voice but Hardy spoke with real fear,

"We were only joking, of course we'll put the shit in the hole."

Bomber heard the splash as the body went into the hole and the grunts as the two men filled it in. They were working in the dark, so Bomber was able to use the image intensifier to watch the proceedings.

Finally, they were finished and Laurel and Hardy went back to the Land Rover with the shovels. O'Keefe and O'Brian lingered and Bomber could clearly hear them talking.

"We will have to take care of that pair before we leave; they can't be trusted to keep their mouths shut," O'Keefe spoke with intensity.

O'Brian agreed saying, "Once everyone has gone, I'll deal with it, just need to get the nod from above."

"What's the matter?" O'Keefe asked.

O'Brian didn't answer for a minute or two then said, "Nothing just had an odd feeling, gone now."

They walked back to the vehicle and Bomber gently let his breath out and put the safety catch back on the Walther.

He watched the four go back into the house, then sent a radio report to the brigadier, who left him in no doubt that he was not to risk the mission by killing O'Brian.

Bomber acknowledged and lay watching the house until he could no longer see any lights on, then he crawled back to his bivvy, where he said a prayer for whoever was lying in the unmarked grave. Then he slept a sleep that was punctuated by scenes of the figure trying to run away, then his old dream came back and he woke with a start and a splitting headache.

Chapter 24
Death and Flight

Bomber was chilled and checking his watch, he knew dawn was only an hour away. He decided to take a chance and have an early brew and breakfast but first he forced himself to stay disciplined and crawled to the OP position and scanned the area, then he listened for several minutes but the only noise was a fox call in the distance and the wind in the trees.

After a mug of tea, two paracetamols, a boil in the bag sausage and beans, he began to feel better. A second mug of tea and he was ready to move to the OP position with his headache receding to a dull ache.

The farm was quiet, just the Ford and Land Rover parked at the front; curtains were still drawn and there wasn't any smoke coming from the triple stack of chimneys at either end of the house.

Bomber continued to find his eyes drawn to the grave and he wondered who the occupant was and what he had done to deserve such a fate? He was fully aware that if he was caught, he could end up next to him.

At nine o'clock, he saw Laurel and Hardy come out of the house with their weapons cradled in their arms and being followed by the two dogs. They climbed into the Land Rover and drove off. Bomber heard the Lanny grinding its way up the hill but instead of turning onto the track in front of him, it took the fork off to the right. Bomber had used this track to come in on and was where he had hidden the bike.

Bomber was not too worried; he had over two hundred yards of dense fir trees between the track and him. The trees had not been tended to and they were packed tightly together as only a fir plantation can be. Laurel and Hardy did not seem the type of foot soldiers that would investigate too far from the track or Lanny.

Bomber could still hear the Lanny and it didn't stop. *Must be going all the way to the gate,* thought Bomber. *Hope they don't see the bike's tyre tracks. Should have taken more care over that. Too late now,* the voice in his head said. *Shouldn't be such a lazy bastard, should you?*

Bomber dismissed the voice; he needed to concentrate on the farm. Those two clowns were not out on patrol for fun, they must be expecting someone soon. Bomber checked in on the radio but there was no answer. After a second go, there was still no reply. He turned off the radio thinking, *Great no comms, just what I need. Quit whinging,* the voice said, scolding him. *The relay station will still be having breakfast.*

Bomber waited and tried again at ten o'clock. This time he got a response and sighed with relief. He hadn't realised just how vulnerable he had felt when the first two comms' checks had failed. It wasn't the brigadier's voice but Paul Small's he heard acknowledging the comms check and asking for an update. Bomber obliged.

Bomber heard the familiar sound of the Lanny trundling along in low gear. It was coming from his right, so they must have had a key to the padlock on the gate and completed a circuit. Laurel and Hardy stopped opposite the grave, killed the engine and got out. Hardy opened the back door of the Lanny and the dogs jumped out and had a race around before settling down to sniff. Laurel and Hardy never seemed to notice that the dogs avoided the area in front of Bomber. Hardy took two shovels from the back of the vehicle and walked over to Laurel, who had his head bowed and was mumbling.

"Didn't know you believed in that stuff," Hardy said, handing a shovel to Laurel.

"Wasn't right beating him up like that, then killing him, he was one of us."

"They said he was a traitor informing on us."

"They, who the fuck are they. Just a couple of crazy fucking killers, who enjoy hurting people. They don't care about a free Ireland; they just enjoy the power of killing people."

Laurel's voice had now reached a level that caused Hardy to put his arm on Laurel's and told him to keep it down.

"Sorry, but have you thought that we are the only witnesses to the killing and do you think that when this is over, they will leave us alive?"

So Laurel isn't as daft as I thought, he must be working on a bug out plan and taking Hardy with him.

"Jesus, you don't mean that, I mean they wouldn't dare without it being sanctioned by the council."

"For fuck's sake, Mick, they don't answer to the IRA; they are Provos. This meeting is about a division of power and could easily end up in a blood bath with those two maniacs leading the way!"

Hardy, that is Mick, seemed stunned and didn't speak for several seconds, then said, "What are we going to do?"

"Once the meeting is in full swing, we take the Lanny out on patrol and fuck off to Dublin and hole up."

With that, Laurel walked out to the grave and started to put the finishing touches to the top so that it blended in with the surroundings. Hardy helped him but didn't seem to be putting much effort into it.

Suddenly, Bomber was aware of two eyes staring at him from about fifteen feet away. The German shepherd was staring straight at his location. Bomber could only grip the Walther and pray. Then the dog sprang and Bomber aimed the gun. There was a flash in front of him and a rabbit took off at high speed, outpacing the shepherd but not the Springer that had been waiting further along the track. A rabbit's death squeal is probably the most pitiful sound in the animal kingdom and it scared the living daylights out of Bomber while the two men jumped and cursed the dogs. They stomped back to the Lanny calling the dogs in. The Springer came forward wagging its tail with the rabbit in its mouth.

Once they had gone, Bomber put the Walther away and rested his head in his arms, waiting for his heart rate to come down. Then he crawled back to the bivvy, put the stove on for a brew and tended to his first solid call of nature, which he did into the heavy-duty black plastic bag with the new zip lock seal. Bomber smiled to himself, nothing like a bit of a scare to get the bowels moving. While he waited for the water to boil, he radioed in and made his report. Again it was Paul who answered.

Back in the OP, Bomber felt better. He not only had a brew but another boil in the bag meal of rice and chicken which tasted vaguely of dehydrated chicken that had failed to rehydrate. A packet of Jammy Dodger biscuits in his pocket would see him through now until the night.

It was a little before midday when two cars arrived, saloon cars, one with plates from north of the border, the other with southern plates. Four men got out of each vehicle and Bomber could see they were wary of each other. Nothing more than a nod passed between any of them. Laurel and Hardy came out to meet them and after a short conversation, two from each group went into the house while the others remained outside.

Bomber was taking plenty of photographs when another car pulled up. It was a smart car, expensive, the type you see government officials being driven around in. The driver got out and spoke to the men standing by the door of the house. Then he went back to the car and opened the rear door. A man with grey hair, wearing a suit, got out and Bomber clicked away. The woman had come out of the house to greet the man in the suit with a hug and then, arm-in-arm, they walked into the house.

Thirty minutes later, another car very much like the other one, arrived and this time, two men got out of the front seats. One stood by the car, hand resting on the passenger door and then he opened it. After a pause of perhaps two seconds, a short, swarthy man stepped out. Even through the telephoto lens, Bomber could tell the suit he wore cost more than Bomber earned in a year. The swarthy man stood looking around, then the front door of the house opened and a crowd came out led by the grey-haired man and the woman to greet the new arrival.

Bomber took more photos and then the camera automatically rewound the film as he clicked off the last exposure. He pulled a new roll of film from his pocket and quickly reloaded but by then, they had already gone into the house.

Bomber took the chance to radio in and this time it was the brigadier who answered and Bomber relayed everything that had happened. The brigadier acknowledged and ended the call.

Bomber munched the last of the Jammy Dodgers and waited and wondered why he hadn't seen anything of O'Brian and his two pals. What were they up to? Could be they were going to top the opposition, no that would start an all-out war between the two factions.

Then the doors opened and the grey-haired man walked out talking to the swarthy one. At the cars, they shook hands the swarthy one got into his and it drove off. Grey hair went to his car and that drove off too, followed by one of the other cars with four men in it.

There was no sign of O'Brian and friends. After another hour, the other four men came out and climbed into their car and left. Bomber was on the radio talking rapidly, advising on what direction he thought the cars were taking.

So what have we got left, thought Bomber. *The woman, Laurel and Hardy plus O'Brian and his two goons. I wonder what Laurel and Hardy are up to now everyone has left? Maybe they should have pulled out when the VIPs left, giving themselves a chance.*

It was now five o'clock in the afternoon and Bomber was feeling hungry and in need of a brew when a van pulled in and parked between the Lanny and the Ford. Bomber took photos as three men climbed out and walked to the door. O'Brian stepped out, shook hands with them, then they all went back in. Before Bomber could radio in, he saw Laurel and Hardy being pushed at gun point towards the Lanny by the big man and his pal, who Bomber had last seen sitting on the steps.

The big man forced them into the back of the vehicle and made them lay face down while his pal sat on the backseat guarding them.

Oh shit, thought Bomber, *they left it too late*. Bomber knew the voice would chime in and it did, *So what are you going to do about it?* He knew that the voice would carry on so he stayed silent. *Is it worth the risk trying to save them? Better let them get topped than blow the job and it won't take long for the others to realise they are missing and come looking for whoever did it.*

He heard the Lanny stop and Laurel and Hardy being ordered out. There was the sound of a cry and punches landing on one of them. Bomber felt sure it was Hardy getting a pasting.

Fuck it, why me? thought Bomber. *Because you're here, twit,* the voice replied. *What's worse?* he asked himself. *Let two IRA south of the border guards get topped by two hardened north of the border PIRA killers or kill the potential killers and leave Laurel and Hardy to run for it?*

Laurel and Hardy were pushed along the track. Bomber could see Hardy had taken a beating and his face was covered in blood. Laurel held his head and blood seeped through his fingers from a cut. They both carried shovels stopping just in front of Bomber. The big man said, "Get out there and dig."

They both turned. Hardy looked pleadingly but Laurel had defiance in his face and dropped the shovel and said, "Fucking dig it yourself, you shit."

The big man raised his hand and Bomber could see he had a semiautomatic Browning pistol and Laurel braced himself.

The big man arched his back, then crumpled to the ground. His pal looked at him in amazement, then turned to see where the shots, two *"thufts"* had come from. He had a pistol in his hand and swung it back and forth along the tree line, firing trying to flush the shooter. Bomber ignored the rounds passing harmlessly through the tree branches, then shot him in the face, then the chest. He was dead before he hit the ground. Laurel and Hardy stood with their mouths open as they still couldn't see Bomber or where the shots had come from.

Still they stood there and Bomber was beginning to wonder if they had gone into shock, so in his best Irish he said, "Tell the council about these bastards, now fuck off, move!"

Hardy took off as fast as his legs could go but Laurel walked forward staring into the trees.

"If you want me to kill you, keep coming, otherwise catch up with your pal."

Laurel stopped, nodded and said, "Thanks I owe you, whoever you are." He turned and ran after Hardy who had already started the Lanny. A few seconds later, Bomber heard it drive away, spraying gravel as it went.

Well, thought Bomber, *they're not going to stop until they get to Dublin or beyond.* He looked at the two bodies lying on the track in front of him, leaking blood, which mingled with the mud. Bomber felt numb. He had no regrets, he felt no remorse and it worried him.

He knew he didn't have long to get moving. Firstly, he radioed in and told the brigadier what had happened and that he was pulling out. The brigadier sounded neutral when he acknowledged and signed off.

Don't think I'm going to get a hero's welcome from him, Bomber muttered to himself.

Packing his kit, he moved back to the bike and stopping there, he used the last of his water to wash his face. Riding along with cam cream on might be a giveaway. He pulled off his gillie jacket and stuffed it into one of the panniers and replaced it with a lightweight dark-blue nylon windproof to hide the Walther. His Beretta stayed in his trouser pocket; the precious rolls of film were in his other trouser pocket, the camera, radio and image intensifier were in the rucksack. Then he was off, all the time wondering how far he could get before O'Brian went looking for his pals?

Should have asked Laurel and Hardy for a lift, the voice chuckled.

I think they would have given me one as well, Bomber retorted.

Which way to go was the problem. Once O'Brian found the bodies, would he think Laurel and Hardy had managed to turn the tables? He might for a moment but Bomber knew he would not be fooled for long. He would look at the bodies, work out were the shots had come from, then investigate in the trees. Then he would send the van to check out the tracks through the forest while he would take the car and follow the roads.

East and then north, thought Bomber. He had a road map but he could picture the many lanes and those main roads that covered the area. After half an hour, he was regretting just having the bike and there seemed to be more uphill sections than down. As he came round a bend, he could see several

300

houses. Slowing down, he studied the place. Half a dozen houses, a pub, post office and a single pump petrol station with three cars in the front with For Sale signs on them.

Bomber pulled in and looked at the cars, an old Ford popular with half decent tyres, a beat-up old, short wheel base Land Rover and an even older MG two-seater sports car.

"Are yer looking to buy, son?"

Bomber turned and thought he was hallucinating, standing there was the image of an Irish leprechaun. All he needed to complete the illusion was the hat.

"I just wanted to rent something if possible."

"Are you from Australia, son?"

Bomber knew that sometimes his Cambridgeshire accent sounded a bit Southern Hemisphere, so he went along with it. "Yes, been touring Europe and now Ireland, but I'm tired of cycling." He rubbed his backside to emphasise the point.

"Well, I don't normally rent anything out but how long would you need it for?" The leprechaun had a musical voice and Bomber really did begin to think he was going daft.

"Just a couple of days to drive around the area, tell you what let me test drive the Ford and if it's okay, I'll rent it."

The man's creased face became even more creased as he laughed but before he could say anything, Bomber pulled the wad of Irish money out and peeled off two hundred and said, "Look, I'll leave this and my bike as security while I test drive it. I think there's enough money there to cover it, yes."

The man was already counting the money. Bomber knew there was enough there to buy the car twice over and he would report the car stolen at some stage and claim the insurance.

"All right, son." He pulled a set of keys from his pocket and handed them to Bomber. "I'll just go and sort the paper work while you drive it around the village but don't go far mind."

Bomber threw his rucksack, then the panniers onto the back seat and sat behind the wheel, turned the key in the ignition and to his surprise, the engine started and sounded good. He looked at the fuel tank, over half full, should be plenty. Putting it into gear, he pulled out just as a Ford went past. It stopped, burning rubber on the tarmac as the brakes went on and it slid to a halt.

Bomber didn't need to look to see who it might be but put his foot down and took the left turn heading east. Flooring the pedal, he felt the old car leap to life and Bomber thought if he stayed on the narrow lanes, he might stand a chance against the more powerful car.

It would be dark in an hour or so and he hoped he could stay ahead long enough to lose them in the darkness. He kept the old car going flat out and drove hard around the lanes, often sliding onto the grass verges on the bends. He could see the Ford in his rear-view mirror on the short sections of straight road. Suddenly, he came to a main road junction and without stopping, he swung the car to the left, narrowly missing a car coming the other way. A lorry on his side honked him for pulling out in front of him but Bomber was hoping the lorry would shield him from view and kept going.

He saw a sign saying 'Castle Blayney' but missed how far it was. Then it happened! He saw the car overtake the lorry and race up to get alongside the Popular. Bomber had his foot hard down but the Popular was no match when it came to speed and the Ford came alongside. He saw the gun in O'Brian's hand as he pointed it and then hesitated as a look of recognition came on his face. Bomber swung the Popular into the side of the Ford and O'Brian's shot went through the rear passenger window, spraying glass into the interior.

The driver of the Ford had to brake hard in the face of oncoming traffic and swing back into the lane behind Bomber, who could see traffic ahead. The next second, his rear screen disintegrated and a bullet hole appeared in the roof to the left of his head. A road sign came into view showing 'Castle Blayney' to the left at the crossroad ahead. There was a stop sign which Bomber ignored. Taking the left turn, squealing brakes and horn blasts were soon left behind.

The Ford must have been forced to stop as Bomber could not see it but kept the Popular going flat out. The road was good. The light was beginning to fail and Bomber needed to get to a junction to make a turn to shake off O'Brian.

Seeing it to the right, he took it in third gear with tires squealing in protest. It was a minor road and he slowed the car and drove carefully as he wanted to conserve fuel. He followed lane after lane, hoping he was heading in the right direction when finally he spotted a sign at the next junction, 'Carrickmacross'.

Where the fucks that? he wondered. Pulling up, he reached into the rucksack for the road map and finding it, he studied it by the dim interior light. *Christ, I'm going away from the border, shit where to now.*

Think, what's O'Brian going to do? Cover the routes north to the border, main roads definitely, minor, too many but anywhere there was a crossroad. To do that, he would need help but did he have that sort of help?

What would he not think I would do? The glimmer of a plan now came into Bomber's head and he plotted a route by minor roads as much as possible and set off for Dundalk.

The Popular ran out of fuel just after he arrived in Dundalk. Bomber was not surprised as it had been running on empty according to the gauge for over twenty minutes when it juddered to a halt. Pulling over, he left it at the side of the road. He was not worried about leaving fingerprints as he had had his cycling gloves on the whole time, including when he used the cycle.

Shouldering his rucksack and panniers, he set off for the docks, where the fishing and pleasure craft would be moored. It was 10:30 at night and Bomber knew he would not be able to do anything until morning. He needed a place to hole up but as he had no ID, he was not going to book into a hotel or any hostelry. Spotting a café, he went in and ordered pie, chips and tea. The café was used to feeding fishermen and the drivers who drove the trucks, so the portions were massive which suited Bomber just fine.

After feeding the crowds thrown out of the pubs at closing time, the café locked its doors. Bomber wandered out with the drunks, some still clutching their pies. As they thinned out, he headed for the docks where he found a set of steps going down to the water at the side of the quay. Checking that no one was about, he went down until he was out of sight. There he settled down and tried to sleep sitting on the panniers with his head on his rucksack. He had a cold, fitful sleep, waking up at any sound or extra-large wave hitting the quay wall. The noise of the seagulls woke him and he wondered for a minute where he was. Then he shouldered the rucksack and peered over the quay's edge, no one. Once up, he walked along the quay. His plan, a simple one, was to bribe or use gunpoint for a lift to the North. Then he saw the sign advertising trips around the bay 'See the seals, one pound'. The sign was a bit old and could do with a re-paint but moored close by was a converted inshore fishing boat. Bomber went over to where a mobile café had just pulled up. The driver was also the cook, waiter and general dogsbody and when he saw Bomber, he said. "You're a wee bit early; it will take me a few minutes to get set up." He looked at Bomber's unshaven face and clothes and frowned.

"That's okay. I was told to be here early if I wanted to see the seals."

The man laughed. "Seals eh, Australian, are you?"

"Yes, does it show?" Bomber retorted.

The man laughed again. "Not much but old Pat will be here at about eight o'clock to get the Mary Jane ready but normally he won't go out until he has a full load."

Bomber nodded and once the cafe was ready, he ordered tea and two bacon sandwiches, which he demolished in quick time. He then went and sat where he could see the Mary Jane and the approaches to the quay, aware that O'Brian might still be looking for him.

Old Pat turned out to be a man in his fifties, dressed in sea boots and waterproof trousers held up with shoulder braces over a patterned roll neck sweater. He looked as if he had spent all his days at sea. His face was covered in white whiskers and what you could see of his skin was ruddy. He stepped down into the Mary Jane and started to get her ready for sea.

Bomber waited a while and then stepped onto the boat. Looking up, the man said, "Not going out yet, need at least ten to make it worth my while."

Bomber replied that he was desperate to see the seals now because he had to be back for the bus at midday. He peeled off fifteen pounds from his remaining Irish pounds and asked if that would make it worthwhile.

The man decided it would and started the engine before he cast off quickly, turning the boat into the current. As they edged out, Bomber caught sight of a van pulling up by the mobile café. He was sure it was the same one he had seen at the farm.

The boat rocked and rolled but Bomber did not care. He stood by the old sea dog and watched the quay as they went out to sea. He was sure he could see two men watching the boat.

"Who are you running away from, the Garda?"

The question had caught Bomber off guard but he quickly recovered and decided to work near the truth. "No, a couple of killers who I'd rather not meet."

The old man stared at him for a long time, then he said, "Where do you want dropping? It will have to be inshore somewhere, this old girl can't handle the open sea anymore."

"Anywhere north of the border will do but the further the better."

"I know a place, it's remote but a twenty-minute walk will get you to a village where you can get a bus."

"What will you say when people ask where you have been?" Bomber asked.

"The locals won't ask but anyone else I'll just say you forced me at gunpoint to take you north."

Bomber nodded and then pulled the rest of his Irish pounds from his pocket and put them on the shelf in front of the wheel. "Fuel money," Bomber said.

"Thanks, but it's not necessary."

"Yes, it is; you saved me a long walk and maybe worse."

As the boat laboured north, Bomber wondered about the two men and the van at the quay. If they were O'Brian's boys, they would have spoken to the mobile café owner and guessed it was Bomber on the boat. *So what?* the voice said. *So they will telephone ahead and arrange a reception,* Bomber shot back.

Well, radio in, stupid. "Yes," gasped Bomber. "It might work."

The sea dog looked at him as if he was mad but Bomber didn't care. He got the radio out, hooked up the wire antenna onto the top of the wheelhouse and called in. After the third try, a distant voice that he recognised as the brigadier answered. Bomber explained the situation and asked for support and gave the location the sea dog indicated on the chart stuck to the shelf in front of him.

"It will be there," then the signal died on the brigadier.

An hour later, the sea dog steered the boat into a shallow cove that could only be accessed at high tide. Bomber shouldered his pack and shook the man's calloused hand before thrusting the wad of English pounds into his other hand, saying, "You can put it down to your smuggling income if anyone asks."

The man laughed and said, "May God go with you, lad."

Bomber jumped down from the front of the boat into knee-deep water, turned and pushed the boat as the sea dog put the engine in reverse. It slid back gracefully and turned in its own length and headed out to sea. Bomber waded onto the shore and walked up to the dunes. As he reached them, two figures stood up from the shadows, weapons pointing at him. He stood still and felt a cold calm embrace him. He dropped the panniers and wondered if he could get the Walther out before the first shots cut him down then a familiar voice said, "Having a nice leave, boss."

Bomber felt himself sigh with relief and replied, "I've had better."

Sitting in the back of the Lanny, Cpl Wells explained they were on KP patrol when they were ordered to find him. One of the other sections was now patrolling the roads on the lookout for any nasty boys in cars.

"We have to take you to Lisburn fast, no stopping for a brew."

Bomber nodded and before he knew it, he was asleep wedged against the C42 radio and a pair of legs belonging to the escort who turned out to be Harris.

Chapter 25
Beautiful Eyes

Bomber felt dirty and smelly, sitting facing the brigadier and the colonel who looked as if he was sucking a lemon. Bomber had gone through the complete period of the operation from start to finish and now sat silent waiting for someone to speak.

"I can't understand why you would jeopardise the OP and your own life to save two IRA terrorists." The colonel spoke with a hint of anger and amazement in his voice.

"I considered the main job completed and in my view, the visitors had been and gone, meeting over. Laurel and Hardy would have been murdered in cold blood right in front of me and the two killers had already killed one person I couldn't help. If I had let it happen a second time, I would be just as guilty as those two PIRA thugs."

"That is not the point; your job was observation not participation."

Bomber was now getting pissed off by the colonel's attitude and he could feel his temper rising. He knew if this went on any longer, he would explode and say something that would really get him into trouble.

Taking a deep breath, he replied, "On an op, there will always be something that will not go to plan and whoever is on the ground will have to make a quick decision and deal with whatever shit is thrown up. That's what I did." Bomber looked at the brigadier, who was fiddling with his Polo mints and gazing at a large map pinned on the wall, seemingly disinterested in the conversation.

The colonel's tone softened as he went on, "I see, so you think you made the right decision at that moment in time. Interesting point, anyway I personally think you did a good job in difficult circumstances. Loved the boat trip bit." Bomber looked on in amazement; the colonel was even smiling or maybe he just had wind.

Bomber again looked to the brigadier, who was now looking at Bomber. "Yes, good job, how productive we will find out in just a minute." As he finished speaking, there came a knock at the door. The colonel pressed a button on the table and the door opened.

In marched Paul Small and Andy. Paul placed a file in front of the brigadier and another in front of the colonel. Andy plonked a tray on the table and began handing out mugs of tea.

"My goodness," exclaimed the colonel. "Is that who I think it is?" He had one of Bomber's photographs in his hand, holding it up to the brigadier.

"Yes, I'm sure it is and this one is even more damning," the brigadier said, showing another one to the colonel.

The brigadier then became silent. Studying another photograph, passing it to the colonel, he said, "That's why we haven't heard from him."

Bomber couldn't see who it was but guessed it was the one who he had seen murdered.

The brigadier looked at Bomber. "Just with these three photographs, your op was a complete success. The death of this man," he poked a photograph in front of him, "we will try to follow through and give the Garda some details. The two killers you dealt with, well, that was unfortunate but necessary and I have no doubt PIRA will want to give them a military show funeral this side of the border for everyone to see. Then we will know their names."

Bomber let out a sigh and felt relieved the brigadier thought he had acted correctly.

"We will need to study these in some detail before we decide what to do," he said, indicating the photographs. "In the meantime, you have six days' leave left; why don't you go and enjoy it?"

"Yes sir, thank you."

The brigadier and the colonel both stood and shook Bomber by the hand. "No, thank you, C/Sgt," said the colonel. The brigadier nodded and smiled.

Bomber left the room with Paul and Andy. In the corridor, Bomber felt dizzy and had to lean against the wall. Paul held him and said, "Look, let's get you over to our place and you can have a shower and some food. I went to your bunk in Ballykinler and packed your civvies. You can be on the evening ferry and in England before the cock crows."

After a shower and some food, Paul drove Bomber to the ferry terminal with Andy sitting in the back holding his SMG in his lap, covered by a small blanket so it wasn't visible to anyone passing.

Bomber used one of his travel warrants to get a return ticket with a cabin and once on the ferry, he locked himself in the cabin and did not wake up until a steward banged on the door eight hours later, telling him they were docking in thirty minutes. In Liverpool, he caught a train to London Euston and then jumped in a taxi to Kings Cross. From there he went onto Cambridge, his home town.

What Bomber was hoping to find there, he didn't know. Sure, he had family and some old school friends but he knew he was looking for something else but could not work out what it was. Each day he went out, he carried the Beretta hidden inside his jacket. The thought of going naked, as he called it, made him feel very vulnerable.

On the second evening, he had had enough of family and friends. They were not unkind; on the contrary, the kindness was overpowering but he couldn't handle it. Friends seemed to think him odd, perhaps he was. He was certainly drinking a lot and could be withdrawn, sinking into depths from which he struggled to rise.

It was a fresh sunny day so he had decided to cheer himself up by going to the Red Lion Hotel in the town centre that evening. No more wallowing in the depths, wondering what he was looking for. The Red Lion was an old coaching inn close to the central market place. The coach entrance led into a large courtyard with what had been stables but that had been converted into a bar and jazz room.

Bomber could hear a clarinet softly playing a tune with a piano tinkling along. *This is more like it,* thought Bomber. *Tonight, I'm going to be cheerful and forget all about Ireland.*

Ordering himself a beer, he sat at the bar, watching and listening to the music. The place was filling up with university types, who seemed to be drinking like camels fresh out of the desert.

The music had just stopped and the light applause died down when he heard the voice and he immediately recognised it. *No, don't turn round, you idiot,* he told himself. Then it happened.

"Hello, Nobody, can I buy you a drink?"

Bomber turned round; there was no mistaking those eyes that had made such a lasting impression on him the first time. He had seen her, even though she had been scared and vulnerable then.

Jenny Morrison smiled and placing a hand on his arm, she said, "Well, can I buy my saviour a drink?"

At that moment, Bomber knew what it was he had been looking for, someone who knew, someone who understood but wasn't army.

"I'll have a beer, thank you."

"A beer and a glass of white wine please," she said to the barman. "So tell me, what are you doing here?"

"I was going to ask you the same thing! Have you given up law?"

"Oh no, my father thought it too dangerous for me to go back to Queens, so he pulled some strings and got me into Cambridge."

Before Bomber could say anything else, a six foot four, broad shouldered guy, who looked like he should be on the silver screen, appeared at Jenny's shoulder and said, "Come on, Jen, you are supposed to be with us," indicating a group sitting at a table.

"Sorry, Roger, I've just met the man that I had the most exciting time of my life with and I need to catch up. See you later."

Roger looked as if he had been punched in the stomach by Henry Cooper. "Fine," he said through gritted teeth and walked away to his group of friends at the table.

"Boyfriend?" Bomber asked.

"No chance. He would like to add me to his list of conquests but he is too fond of himself for my liking. Now I can't keep calling you 'nobody', so give me a name."

"You can call me David. Do you mind if I call you Jenny?"

The evening became a blur and they left the Red Lion and went to another pub where they found a quiet table. Bomber felt great. Jenny was easy to talk to and he found himself totally immersed in her presence. He was lost in her eyes when she looked at him. Then she said she had to get back to her digs as she had an early start the next day. He quickly offered to walk her there, not wanting the evening to end. At her college digs, he said goodbye at the gate, having made arrangements to meet for lunch at the Pickerel Inn the next day. She kissed him on the cheek and left, running through the gate and up the steps. The college porter looked on, seemingly daring Bomber to try and follow her. Bomber watched her go.

Then he put his hand in the inside pocket of his jacket and felt the Beretta was free and easy to get at.

Now, he thought, *time to deal with that fucker who's been shadowing us all night.*

Epilogue
The Darkness

By David Brown
1972 No Time to Wonder.

Bomber woke to the sound of his stepfather's voice telling him there was a phone call for him. Still drowsy with sleep Bomber picked up the phone. The voice on the other end snapped, "I need you back here now. We have a problem! Go to Marshall's airport. Show them your ID. There's a plane waiting." The phone went dead.

'Shit,' thought Bomber. *'Why me at this moment in time?'*

Bomber could have walked from his parents' house to the small airport run by Marshalls of Cambridge but he took a taxi as he wanted to leave a message for someone on the other side of the city.

At the airport the security man checked Bomber's identity card and then directed him to a hanger to the left of the main building. In the hanger he found an Army Air Corp Warrant Officer standing by a de Havilland Beaver. The Beaver was a rugged 'go anywhere' single engine, propeller driven plane that could land and take off on a ploughed field if it needed to.

The Warrant Officer pilot introduced himself as Bob and said, "Stow your bag in that open side bin and we will be off."

The plane took off in less than a football pitch length and headed west. Bob had already told him that he had to make one more stop before crossing the Irish Sea. The weather forecast was good with a tail wind so they should make good time he told Bomber.

'Good time,' thought Bomber *'if this thing can do more than a hundred and sixty knots I'll buy Bob a crate of beer'.*

He hoped the message he had left with the college porter had been received. He had made it clear he had no choice but to leave but still it nagged in his mind that he could not deliver the message personally.

Bomber watched the patchwork countryside below as it slid by, which was the sort of thing one missed when flying up high in a commercial airliner.

'I guess this is what makes the Beaver such a good observation aircraft,' he mused.

He must have dozed off for a while as suddenly they were descending and preparing to land at RAF Cosford where they took on more fuel and one passenger. He too was in civvies but it was clear he was army, probably SAS from Hereford. Having met a number of Hereford lads before, Bomber could detect the signs. The air of confidence and the way they moved marked them out as somewhat above the average, beside the fact they always looked as fit as hell. As they waited for the refuelling to finish, the new passenger stuck out his hand and said, "Bill, not seen you before on this run, new are you?"

Bomber was not sure what to make of this so just gripped the offered hand and said. "David, been recalled early from leave. First time travelling this way so something must have kicked off."

Bill nodded, then said, "Don't I know you from somewhere?"

"I don't think so," replied Bomber.

"Oh, I'm sure we must have met! I never forget a face. You're not Regiment so it must have been on a course or a mixed op." Bill stared at Bomber as if trying to see into his mind.

"Well, right now, I can't think where it could have been," answered Bomber.

The conversation ended at a signal from Bob to climb aboard. They lapsed into silence as the Beaver raced along the runway and took off, gaining height quickly. Then Bob pointed the plane westwards and out over the Irish Sea.

Bomber hoped that Jenny had received his note explaining why he couldn't meet her for lunch. He felt a great sadness come over him and he had the silly idea of asking the pilot to take him back to Cambridge.

'You've blown it again,' the voice in his head taunted him. *'She's the best thing to happen to you and as usual you put the army first.'*

'It's my job, I have to go or I would be AWOL' (absent without leave).

'Just another excuse to avoid getting too close to someone,' the voice mocked. *'Think of all the other nice girls you have met and then done exactly the same thing'.*

Bomber dismissed the voice and concentrated on the mountains of Wales below, then it was out over the Irish Sea. The ships and boats he could see below looked like toys on the emerald sea. Everything was tranquil but in the back of his mind he knew the aircraft carried him towards another day of violence and death in a beautiful country that throughout history seemed doomed to suffer the turmoil of religion, war, famine and death. As they approached the coast of Northern Ireland a dark bank of clouds was building up and moving in from the west. As they descended to land the rain started, a driving rain but not hard enough to cleanse the country. Only blood it seemed would do that.

As the Beaver taxied to a halt Bomber could see Sgt Paul Small and Andy there to meet them. They were standing by a beat up looking black, Ford saloon car. Paul ushered them into the car, telling them time was wasting. Paul drove while Andy sat in the front passenger seat cradling his SMG (Sub machine gun). The way Bill greeted him it was clear they were old pals.

"Good to see you back in business, Andy," said Bill.

"It's good to be back in harness. The Brig is a good man to work for, lots of action," replied Andy.

'So Bill is on the team,' thought Bomber.

"What's happening Paul, why have we been recalled early?" asked Bill.

Paul looked up in the rear view mirror with a smile on his face and said, "Oh the shit's really hit the fan, thanks to Bomber here. The Brig is beside himself with joy as he has been given a free hand to sort it."

Bill stared at Bomber who knew Bill wanted to ask questions but was too well disciplined to do so.

'Great,' thought Bomber, *'that's all I need, to be the cause of the trouble and probably the sucker who will be honoured with trying to clean it up but I'm not going south again.'*

'Oh yes, now when have I heard that before,' the voice in his head mocked.

They gathered in the Brig's smaller briefing room, just the six of them. The Brig sat quietly while the Colonel did the talking. He told them all about the consequences of Bomber's last foray south of the border when he had been forced to shoot two PIRA thugs. Not that Bomber regretted doing it. If he hadn't, two others would have died. The meeting that had taken place at a remote farm had resulted in a split in Sinn Fein. Now there was a Provisional Sinn Fein and an Official Sinn Fein, both with members in the Southern Irish Parliament. The split was not amicable. However, it was suspected that several senior figures in the Republic's government supported the IRA and PIRA, if not openly, then covertly, using their influence to help make both factions untouchable south of the border.

The Official Sinn Fein, who were the political arm of the IRA, still followed the Marxist view that had originally cemented them together, while the Provisional Sinn Fein, representing PIRA, followed the traditional Nationalistic line, whatever that meant. Either way they were still both hell bent on reuniting Ireland against the wishes of the majority by any means, especially violent intimidation.

The Brig's informants had indicated that both factions were determined to strike hard in Northern Ireland without delay. Having received weapons and training from Libya and more financial support from Irish Americans, they were keen to flex their muscles.

Bomber, with his Recce Platoon lads, had been given a large stretch of border to watch. While Bill, the Brigadier's SAS liaison and Jack of all trades Sgt, would coordinate SAS cut off teams to back up each of Bombers OPs. Bomber was still not sure if this was a brigade job or the Brig's own operation. If it was the latter, it was an impressive show of his power.

Once the briefing was over, the Brig, who had been silent throughout the meeting, called Bomber to him.

The Brig seemed thoughtful and fiddled with his packet of mints, then told Bomber to sit down.

"How are you, David?"

"Fine sir."

"One of my contacts over the border has told me that PIRA are hopping mad over you topping two of their most valuable men. Questions have also been asked by Sinn Fein in Leinster House, the Irish Parliament, about British army hit squads operating in the south."

He paused before taking out a mint and popping it into his mouth, then in an absentminded fashion offered one to Bomber who shook his head and waited for what he suspected was the really bad news. The Brig sucked the mint, then crunched it before continuing.

"O'Brian has fingered you for it. Apparently he recognised you during the car chase and has made a point of telling everyone he will settle with you, come hell or high water. You weren't named in the questions but they did say a serving British soldier was seen in the vicinity. Of course our government has poo pooed it but there have been a few people sniffing around to see what we have been up to, but I've taken care of them."

Bomber looked at Paul who had stayed in the room when the others left but Paul wasn't giving anything away and just faced front.

The Brig continued, "Your CO wants you posted out of harm's way, as he puts it. Rightly or wrongly, I have advised against it as here you will be surrounded by armed friends. Elsewhere you will be vulnerable with people unaware of the situation. That is partly why I called you back."

He stopped talking and fiddled with the packet of mints, putting them first into one pocket then the other.

"Your thoughts, David?" the Brig asked, looking directly at Bomber.

"I'm not going anywhere, sir. If O'Brian and his dogs want to come after me, fine. I rate my chance better here than in England where I'm sure the police would object to me going around tooled up."

"Yes, quite, but if you do have to go back, I can help on that score."

"It's the politicians I am worried about. You know how they like to offer up a sacrificial goat when the finger pointing starts." Bomber felt himself getting angry and breathed deeply to regain control.

"You haven't any worries on that score. Outside of this room no one knows that it was you and that's the way it will stay."

A gentle knock at the door interrupted them. Bill entered and handed a paper to the Brig who studied it, then folded it and stuffed it into his jacket pocket.

"Well, we will leave it there for now but call me or the Colonel at any time if you need to."

He then walked past Bomber and out of the room with Bill following.

Bomber turned to Paul who sat looking at him with a half a smile on his face.

"What!" Bomber asked, a little too sharply.

"I know what you are thinking but I'm not letting you do it on your own. Andy and I want in. Bill also said he can arrange some extra back up without anyone asking questions."

"It's no good if I don't know where that bastard O'Brian is hiding out."

"Oh, I think the Brig will find that out for us," Paul said, grinning.

A day later, back at the border, Bomber watched a car drive from County Monaghan in the south across the border. The grey Ford Consul with Northern Irish plates drove carefully past the hidden OP. Bomber could clearly see the four men in the car through his binos and they looked grim. The Intel was they were heavily armed and were going to attack the RUC station in Newtown Hamilton.

Bomber listened to Dusty pass the information over the radio to the SAS cut off groups and HQ.

"They have acknowledged, boss," Dusty whispered.

Bomber nodded and waited. It was less than two minutes before the action started. The sound of gunfire shattered the peaceful country air and Bomber thought he recognised the heavy chatter of an AK47. It was immediately answered by the wicked whiplash crack of multiple Heckler Koch MP5 sub machine guns and the heavier thump of SLRs. Bomber timed it, one minute twenty seconds to when the last shot was fired. *'I wonder how many men died in that time,'* he thought.

Dusty listened intently as the radio traffic started to flow and he scribbled in his note book.

"They got them boss, three dead one wounded. One of the cut-off team has also been wounded. Chopper coming in to pick up the casualties."

Without taking his attention away from his line of vision, Bomber acknowledged Dusty with a nod and a grunt. Stretched out before him lay a picture of tranquillity that was the Armagh countryside, matched by County Monaghan south of the border. A complete contrast to the violence and death that had taken place a short distance away.

Bomber's mind wouldn't let him enjoy the view. *'So who else is there coming this way and who supplied them with AK47s? They must have some back up if they were going to attack a police station, or were they hoping surprise would make it easy for just the four of them?'*

All of Bomber's recce Platoon were deployed in the five OPs along this stretch of the border. Reporting anything that crossed the border, truck, car or donkey, it was all passed to the cut-off teams made up of heavily armed SAS. As always it was difficult to identify who the terrorists were until they had been stopped and that was when the shooting usually started.

Dusty nudged Bomber, jerking him back to reality and pointed to the two cars that had pulled up at the border.

"Garda," said Harris handing the binos to Bomber.

Several Garda Officers were now standing by their cars parked at the border. One of them was scanning the area with binos. The others watched the helicopter that was coming in for the two wounded men less than half a mile away.

After a few moments of talking, they got into their cars and drove back south.

Bomber shifted uneasily in the damp hedgerow and camouflage netting that made up their hide. He needed the toilet but couldn't motivate himself to go through the rigmarole required to do a furtive shit into a plastic bag. So he just sighed and clenched his cheeks. The day was slowly drawing to a close, several of the OPs had reported vehicles crossing which the cut offs intercepted but without any results. Once the news was out that vehicles were being intercepted, the terrorists would move to another part of the border or just wait it out.

Dusk was just beginning to make its presence felt when a heavy firefight erupted about a mile north of Bomber's location.

"Contact report from six two alpha, boss. They are under heavy attack," Dusty said into Bomber's ear, as if he couldn't hear over the noise of the gun fire.

"Their cut-off group is responding and so is ours. What do you want us to do, boss?"

Without vehicles there was little point in trying to hot foot it across country to six two alpha. Two cut-off teams were about sixteen heavily armed SAS men who could be there in a flash. Six two alpha would just have to hold on until they arrived.

Harris nudged Bomber, "We've got company, boss and they seem to know we are here."

Bomber saw that three cars had pulled up just short of the border. Men got out, some holding weapons in clear view, not worried about being seen. Bomber told Dusty not to call it in straight away as he didn't want their cut-off team being diverted back from six two alpha fire fight.

Studying them through the binos Bomber thought there was some sort of argument going on. After a further minute of arm waving, they all got back into the cars and drove back south. There hadn't been any point in trying to engage them as they were out of effective range of the SLRs and the orders strictly forbade them taking on targets south of the border. That didn't stop Bomber once again wishing he had more trained snipers. Zika, his best shot, was with six two Alpha.

As Bomber listened, he could tell the firing was getting less from six two alpha's position, with just the odd burst of automatic fire.

"All of six two alpha are okay boss. The SAS boys are reporting several attackers killed or wounded," Dusty reported. Then in a quieter voice he said, "It appears the attackers left their vehicles and started walking straight to six two alpha's position, probably without knowing they were there."

"Okay Dusty, call this in." Bomber handed him his note book containing their own contact report.

"Seems some want to fight and some want to go home. Crazy day," muttered Bomber to himself.

Bomber decided he needed some thinking juice so, turning to Harris he said, "I think we deserve a brew and as you are the best tea maker I know….." The sentence wasn't finished before Harris said "Yes, boss."

Crawling backwards into the depths of the OP he said, "I'm on it, tea for four coming up."

Bomber mulled over the events. *'Their own ambush worked perfectly. Six two alpha situation was different, so did the terrorists know they were there? Or, after the first ambush, were they trying to flush out any OP? Was the Garda patrol checking the coast was clear or trying to suss out Bomber's OP position for the attackers? Strange, the Garda turned up, just took a look and then left just before the gunman turned up. On the other hand they could have been a plain clothes Garda team hunting the terrorists.'*

Bomber's thoughts were broken when he heard Dusty acknowledging a radio message.

"We are being pulled out at first light, boss."

Bomber made a mental note that if they did this again, he wanted the Ferret armoured cars close so that they could bring the Browning machine gun into action should it be needed.

"Here, boss, get your laughing tackle round this while it's still hot." Harris thrust a mug of tea into Bomber's hand. "No biscuits?" Bomber asked, without looking at Harris.

"Fuck me! I should have been a bloody butler, not a soldier." Harris crawled backwards again and returned with a half packet of Jammy Dodgers, everyone's favourites.

Sipping the tea, Bomber felt tired and his mind wandered back to his short leave. *'I wonder what Jenny is doing? Is she wondering what I'm doing? Or has she given up on me as a waste of her time?'*

He recalled how he had seen her to her digs in Cambridge that evening and then the confrontation with the man who had been following them.

After seeing Jenny into her college digs, Bomber had turned and stepped out, heading for the Round Church and back towards the Baron of Beef pub. The shadow tailing him kept pace. At one point he thought the shadow had stopped following him but a quick check and he could see the suited and booted man still on his tail. At the back of the church he stood in the shadows and waited. The man came into sight. Bomber thought he looked a bit tubby. He stopped and looked left then right, seemingly confused that the street was empty. Then he walked to where Bomber was standing, hidden in the shadows. As he drew level Bomber drove his left leg out and into the side of Tubby's right knee. He went half down and

Bomber hit him hard in the ribs. He grunted and turned, then hit Bomber back in the body with a blow that, because of his off balance position, lacked any body weight behind it but the force of it still knocked the stuffing out of Bomber. He realised that the shadow wasn't fat but solid muscle and was now ready for a fight.

'He's bigger and harder than you, sucker, so, now what?' the voice in his head chimed.

Bomber wanted to tell the voice to go to hell but instead he pulled out the Beretta and levelled it at the man's face.